W9-BUX-035

The Brontë Plot

Center Point
Large Print

Also by Katherine Reay and available from
Center Point Large Print:

Lizzy & Jane

**This Large Print Book carries the
Seal of Approval of N.A.V.H.**

The Brontë Plot

Katherine Reay

CENTER POINT LARGE PRINT
THORNDIKE, MAINE

The text of this Large Print edition is unabridged. In other aspects, this book may vary from the original edition. Printed in the United States of America on permanent paper. Set in 16-point Times New Roman type.

ISBN: 978-1-62899-861-0

Library of Congress Cataloging-in-Publication Data

Names: Reay, Katherine, 1970–, author.
Title: The Brontë plot / Katherine Reay.
Description: Center Point Large Print edition. | Thorndike, Maine : Center Point Large Print, 2016. | ©2015
Identifiers: LCCN 2015042515 | ISBN 9781628998610 (hardcover : alk. paper)
Subjects: LCSH: Booksellers and bookselling—Fiction. | Large type books. | GSAFD: Love stories. | Christian fiction.
Classification: LCC PS3618.E23 B76 2016 | DDC 813/.6—dc23
LC record available at http://lccn.loc.gov/2015042515

For all of us,
and the choices we make every day.

"Did you ever know a lover of books that with all his first editions and signed copies had lost the power to read them?"

—C. S. Lewis, *The Great Divorce*

Chapter 1

Wednesday was Book Day. With so many other demands, Lucy felt it important to pick a day, name it, and savor it. By plopping it in the center of the week, she secured a shining moment to anticipate at the week's front end and a delicious one to revisit at the back. And in so doing she could endure the mercurial whims and incessant demands of her clientele any day of the week.

Book Day always began with the twist of the old key in the lock, the street still quiet, despite being located in the center of Chicago's Old Town, and a hip-check through the door that read *Sid McKenna Antiques and Design*. First Lucy would touch base with her favorite online booksellers, monitor the current auctions, and place bids, keeping a keen eye on special requests or tempting offerings clients might find irresistible. After, she'd open the mahogany corner cabinet first, the nineteenth-century breakfront second, and rub Fredelka Formula into her beloved books' soft leather covers, dust their gold-tipped edges with a worn linen rag, and gently separate any pages humidity had fused. And, if there was time, she'd relish a passage or two.

This Wednesday, Lucy silenced the shop's alarm

and leaned against the doorjamb. She let her eyes roam, as it was one of the first mornings in which the sun beat her to work. Sid's gallery always brought a smile of satisfaction, one of complacency—as if the space was her own and not another's. But that thought never took root because she could never imagine possessing Sid's brilliance. Sid McKenna married substance with style—from the deep-red lacquered door mounted on the far wall next to the Louis XIV end table to the black-and-white monographs of unknown artists stacked on its top, and those resting beneath a carelessly laid Montblanc pen. Sid threw down a disparate but symbiotic alchemy of beauty with every flick of his wrist, and this mix of old and new with the something unexpected had firmly established him as Chicago's premier interior designer.

Lucy closed her eyes and absorbed the shop's scents. Underneath the jasmine, she caught the tang of the polish she applied to the furniture every other day, buffing each piece until it felt velvety and gleamed. She also caught the musty scent of ink on paper within the books stacked for sale, on their sides so as not to warp their fragile spines. And dancing beneath it all, she caught a hint of fresh pine from her favorite organic floor cleaner, the one she found at a one-man shop in Vermont.

She glanced to the corner. The books . . . Lucy

opened her bag and pulled out her latest acquisition. While it wasn't a particularly fine find, of no distinction and without provenance, the novel was one of her favorites. And it wouldn't take much to make it something special. A good inscription always helped. A story behind the story, the generational passing from hand to hand, always added interest and a few dollars.

She turned the pages, absorbing snippets— *an unbroken hush; a demoniac laugh—low, suppressed, and deep;* or a man growing *quite savage in his disappointment*—as she carried it to the right front corner of the gallery and opened the cabinet's glass case. *Delicious.*

"Welcome home," she whispered. She held it to her nose and inhaled the leather, dust, ink, and history in a single whiff before placing it on its side atop two others. "All the sisters, together. Again."

Lucy stepped away as a soft "Good morning" drifted across the room.

Sid McKenna leaned on the workroom doorjamb. "I tried to say that gently."

"You're not supposed to be here," Lucy moaned. "What happened to my quiet Book Day?"

Sid chuckled and held up both hands. "I know, 'trespassing on sacred ground' and all that, but I have a meeting this morning and need the Benson drawings. I'll be out of your hair in a moment."

He turned back into the workroom and grabbed

things at random. At six foot two and lithe, Sid exuded an energy that, although twenty years younger, Lucy only dreamed of possessing. His brain and body moved like a kaleidoscope, myriad directions at once, but all congruent and, in the end, masterfully creative.

"What are you doing?"

"Veronica is wavering. She declared yesterday that she's 'not good at big decisions,' so I'm taking things to give her a sense of space and texture. Tactile stuff. She needs to *feel* that her home reflects her family and her wants and is not being imposed on her." He tossed Lucy a smooth leather ball slightly larger than a golf ball. "That ball has the same silky texture of the leather we selected for her study and the same relief stitching, but in cream. And this lamp carries the knobbiness and aesthetic of the small industrial sculpture we chose for her living room." Sid loaded his treasures into a box. "She better not like that more, though; I found it at Goodwill."

Lucy joined in the hunt. "Most of the cuttings have arrived; you can take this bag too."

"Excellent. Those have Seussian textures."

"They're smooth, they're bumpy, they're fancy, not frumpy? Something like that?" Lucy caught Sid's wink and continued to survey the room, looking for more inspiration. "Your sweater!"

Sid looked down. "What about it?"

"It's the exact color of the paint I prepped for

her powder room. The one you're going to stipple with umber? Be sure to point that out."

"So it is. I knew something felt good about this color today." Sid narrowed his eyes at her. "Or you could give me a cutting of your hair."

Lucy grabbed the precisely clipped end of her low ponytail and held it before her nose. "Not funny. And it's auburn. A lovely auburn."

"You keep telling yourself that." Sid chuckled, hoisted the box high, and headed for the alley door. "Enjoy your morning and don't neglect any hapless soul who might invade the shop."

"I'll try."

She heard a faint "*Adios, mi roja belleza pelo*" as the door clicked behind him.

Lucy knew he was gone, but called out anyway, "Again. Not funny. It's auburn!"

Lucy usually savored the quiet. There was so little of it with Sid's clients calling at all hours and Sid himself moving in and out of the gallery like a hurricane. But today was different; eight hours with not a single walk-in or anxious client made Lucy ache for a distraction. Sid's morning meeting with the Bensons and their architect had gone long. None of her friends were free for lunch. And her mom was hosting an open house and couldn't chat.

While the gallery's price points kept most casual strollers away, the scented candles, Battersea boxes, fine pens, linen stationery, and assorted table smalls usually enticed a daily few—at this point, Lucy would settle for a daily one.

The door chimed and Lucy jerked the pen, cringing as an errant drop of ink fell to the page's corner. But eager to talk to another human, she quickly blotted it and placed the opened *Moby Dick* into her desk drawer to let the ink dry. She stood, smoothing both her skirt and her ponytail, and drew her hair over her shoulder as she scrambled to the front of the gallery.

"Hello?" a deep voice called as Lucy crossed from the workroom's concrete floor onto the polished wood. She slipped and caught herself.

"Whoa," he called again and hurried forward.

"All good." Lucy blew her long bangs out of her eyes and took in her visitor. *He came back!* The young man, about her age with dark brown, almost black hair and eyes equally dark, smiled at her. *Chocolate brown—70 percent.* "Must remember not to polish that for a while. Slippery." She followed his gaze to her feet. "Or wear lower heels. One of the two. Maybe both."

"They certainly make you tall." He stood only a few inches from her now, almost eye to eye. Then, as if recognizing their close proximity, he stepped back. "I don't know if you remember me, but I was in here a couple weeks ago—"

"Kidnapped," Lucy blurted, then tucked her lips in.

"You remembered." A crooked smile escaped.

"I always remember the books." Lucy laid her hand on the base of a Chinese bell jar lamp. "Buy this lamp and I'll forget you before you hit the door." She grinned to soften the delivery. "It was for your father. Did he like it?"

"He did. He has a wonderful book collection, and *Kidnapped*'s always been a favorite of mine, so it was a win-win."

"You've read it?" Lucy challenged.

"Is this a test?" He smiled again.

The way his smile tipped up on the left side was so perfectly imperfect that it took all Lucy's willpower not to push up the right side to match it. It had struck her with the same force the first time he'd entered the gallery too. "Perhaps," she replied. "Did you show him the fore-edge drawing?"

"I did, and I fanned the pages just like you showed me. It's remarkable how the picture is just on the tips." He held his index finger and thumb together as if dotting tiny pictures in the air.

"I know!" Lucy exclaimed. She had stepped forward again and found herself too close. She retreated, one step, then two. "So . . . do you need another gift?"

"Something for my grandmother, and she doesn't need a lamp."

I won't forget you. Lucy felt her cheeks heat at the thought and spun away, fully aware her face now matched her hair. Several former boyfriends had told her that it was not a good look. A comparison to "Animal" from the *Muppets* had even been suggested—twice. And she didn't want this man with his adorably quirky smile to see that—to remember her flush—as his first impression of her.

Lucy surveyed the shop to buy time. She knew every item and yet she didn't want to find one too soon, because then he'd leave and might never return. She took in the Henry Moore prints on the south wall. *Too expensive.* Sid's potpourri of modern works. *Too abstract and too expensive.* The mixed media sculptures. *Too industrial.* Various silver pieces, perhaps a pillbox or dish. *Perhaps.*

She returned her gaze to the man and wrinkled her nose. "I'm going to need a little more information. Is she a scented candle kind of lady? Or a pillbox? We have Halcyon Days and Moorcroft."

"What about a book?" His whisper came out low and suggestive with a pinch of adorable uncertainty.

He's flirting? Lucy caught another of the off-kilter smiles and was lost. "I thought of that, but my range is fairly tight and a little pricey."

"They're overpriced?"

"They're valued perfectly," she shot back as she twisted the large brass key and reached for a book. "None of these are first editions, but they're beautiful and limited. And in some, like this one I put out this morning, you'll find beautiful inscriptions in the front."

Lucy opened the small volume to reveal a swirled and loopy *To my darling Betty, 1898* above a more strident and straight-lined *Now to you, dear Laura, 1939.* "This reveals another layer of story behind the one we read within the pages, and this interaction, these inscriptions, add value to the book."

She closed the *Jane Eyre* and fanned the pages' edges to reveal Jane and Rochester standing beneath a tree. "And, like your *Kidnapped*, this copy has a fore-edge painting. The colors are amazing; it's the famous scene when Edward tells Jane that the cord between them will snap when she leaves him for Ireland."

"I like that moment and was very relieved that the tree didn't light up above their heads, but I like it better when she comes back and finds him at Ferndale." He lifted one brow. "What a woman!"

Lucy's lips unfastened. She felt her jaw fall and clamped it shut. "I'm sorry I tested you."

"English literature major." He laughed. "You assumed I couldn't read, didn't you?"

"Not couldn't. Didn't. Clearly my mistake."

"What's your favorite?" He stepped to her and picked up the books one by one.

"Story or edition?" She reached for another. "Right now it's one and the same. I always veer to

Victorian literature: the Brontë sisters, Dickens, Gaskell, Eliot, Thackeray, but this one has my heart." She reached again for the *Jane Eyre* and handed him the soft maroon leather book. "It's one of the first bound in one volume rather than three."

Lucy pulled down *Middlemarch* and *Mary Barton* and three others and placed them on the breakfront's ledge. "These are all a little less and still very nice."

He ran his finger over the books, still holding *Jane Eyre*. "I suspect she'd enjoy this best." He held out the book. "I'll take it."

"Yes, but . . ." Lucy shook her head.

"You love it, don't you?" He held the book out to her but didn't release it when she gripped the other side. Neither pulled. Neither moved. "You're not going to be very successful as a bookseller if you can't part with dear Helen or Jane or Adele or Blanche . . . Never mind, Blanche is easy to part with, isn't she?"

Lucy felt her face redden again. To have those dark eyes looking straight at her, intense and inviting, was too irresistible, too alluring, and then to add all the characters from *Jane Eyre* to the mix . . . Too heady altogether. Lucy's gaze dropped to the book and her mind drifted to the scene discussed—Rochester's description of the *cord of communion* that bound him to Jane.

"I'm James, by the way. James Carmichael."

"Lucy Alling."

"It's very nice to meet you, Lucy Alling." James held her eyes until she gently pulled the book away and headed back to her desk.

Lucy recovered on her walk and James followed. She opened the cover to show him the price, marked lightly in pencil. He afforded it the tiniest glance and returned his gaze to her. He then lifted the same eyebrow he had moments before and reached for his wallet, never breaking eye contact. She was the first to look away.

As she rang up the sale, she couldn't resist quick peeks as James paced the gallery. She almost laughed as he picked up or touched every item on display. Sid knew his job well. *Always keep tactile objects at hand. You want engagement.* James ran his hand down a warm wooden sculpture sitting atop a book on architectural design and lobbed a forged-iron apple in his palm like a baseball. He then stood stymied in front of a display of scented candles.

"Those smell beautiful," Lucy called out.

"My mom loves scented candles. Which is better?"

Lucy reached in front of him, brushing his sleeve with her fingers as she reached for two candles. "They both smell like the actual flowers, not sweet or cloying at all."

James shook his head as she held out one then the other. "I can't tell the difference."

"Hmm . . ." Lucy weighed both in her hands as if that was the determining factor. "The jasmine's been selling better, but I think that's because I've had one lit for a couple days. I prefer the gardenia and switched to that this morning."

"Will you add one?" He tapped the gardenia candle in her hand.

"Sure." She walked to her desk and wrapped both the book and candle in plain brown paper, tying them closed with black grosgrain ribbon. She was so focused, she didn't hear James approach until she felt him near.

"Would you have dinner with me sometime?"

It took Lucy only a heartbeat to reply. "Yes."

"Okay then." He beamed. "I can stop buying books. . . . Tonight?"

Chapter 2

The door chimed and Lucy hastily backed out from beneath the Louis XIV side table, banging her head on the way up.

"Lucy?"

She sat back on her heels and felt her face flare. James stood above her with an ear-to-ear grin. "That was not a sight you needed to see." She rubbed her head.

"Are you okay?" He laid his hand on top of her head.

Lucy rested there a moment until she caught movement in her periphery. She shot up as she noticed an older woman standing beside James.

"Hi. May I help you?" She gestured back to the table. "It had a wobbly leg."

The woman looked to James, who picked up the cue. "Lucy Alling, I'd like you to meet my grandmother, Helen Carmichael, recipient of the beloved *Jane Eyre*."

Lucy reached her hand out and clasped Helen's within hers. It was pale and thin, cool to the touch. "It's so nice to meet you, Mrs. Carmichael." Lucy held her eyes. They were bright blue, but as they held hands Lucy saw Helen's eyes widen, then darken and narrow. Benjamin Moore #810 *Blue Dragon*. Lucy bit her lip and dashed a quick glance to James. He was unaware of anything amiss.

"Please call me Helen. I've heard about nothing but you for the last two weeks."

"Grams," James chided.

"It's true." Helen tilted her head to Lucy. "You have a most unusual eye color."

Lucy smiled. "A gift from my dad. Sid, my boss, calls it #574 *Once Upon a Time* veering to #559 *Paradise Valley* when I wear yellow. We talk a lot in paint colors around here."

"*Once Upon a Time* fits perfectly." Helen looked around the gallery. "I know Sid. He did some work for me about five years ago. He's a rare talent."

"He is. I started here four years ago this spring. I just missed you."

Helen turned back to Lucy. "And your family lives here in Chicago?"

"Yes and no. My maternal grandparents and my paternal grandfather are from here. But my dad moved us around a lot when I was a kid, so I didn't call it home until I was eight—when he left and Mom moved us back here. I can't imagine going anywhere else now. A true Chicagoan."

"Are your grandparents still here?"

"Not anymore. My mother's parents retired to Arizona a few years ago and my father's are both dead."

"Dead," Helen whispered.

"Yes, my grandmother died years ago when my dad was thirteen, and my grandfather died when I was about two."

"Grams is a Chicago lifer too," James added. "You might've known them, Grams."

Helen frowned.

Lucy offered a light laugh to dispel the awkwardness. "You all probably didn't move in the same circles. My grandfather owned a watch shop in the South Loop."

"My generation is disappearing." Helen looked up at James. "Growing smaller with every conversation."

"Grams," James chided again, this time in a different tone.

"I . . ." Helen wobbled.

"Grams?"

"Oh . . . Please sit." Lucy lunged for a high-backed upholstered chair and pulled it over.

James led his grandmother the two steps and seated her.

"Let me get you some water." Lucy ducked to the back room and grabbed a small water bottle from the refrigerator, twisting the cap open as she walked back into the gallery. She knelt before Helen. "Here."

"Thank you." Helen took a few sips and recapped the bottle. "James, I think I'm done for the day." She passed the bottle to James then faced Lucy, who was still squatted next to her. "Extraordinary eyes," she whispered more to herself than to Lucy.

Lucy reached for her hand to help her stand. Helen nodded her thanks and added, "I suspect we'll meet again if James has any say."

James offered an awkward chuckle and an eye roll before he reached for his grandmother and led her toward the door.

As they left, he called back, "I'll text you later. You still here tonight?"

"I am."

"I'll bring the Chinese."

Lucy threw him a bright smile, but as soon as the door shut, it fell. *That did not go well.*

• • •

Lucy's phone beeped with a text.

At the alley door.

She tapped it off and dashed to the work-room door. Pushing it open, she found James standing in the dark but brightly lit by the security light. He hoisted a white plastic bag high. "Dinner!"

"Thank you. And thanks for texting." Lucy swung the door wide.

"I figured if I knocked without warning, it might scare you."

"Opening a solid metal door into an alley at night does feel unwise." Lucy held the door open with her shoulder so he could enter.

James stepped into the workroom. "So this is where all the magic happens."

"Have you not been back here?" She cleared the worktable and brought over two stools as James spread out their meal. "Not that there'd be any reason for you to, but yes, this is Sid's magic kingdom."

"I've got Kung Pao chicken, Shredded Beef and Broccoli, and General Tso's Surprise. Delicious, but not a surprise."

Lucy grabbed a couple paper plates and forks from the top of the refrigerator. She waved a fork at James.

He shook his head and handed her a set of chopsticks.

"A purist, huh?"

"Always." James served up two plates. "So why are we here again?"

"I'm waiting on Sid's delivery from Round Top Antiques Week. It's the biggest antique show in the nation." Lucy rapped her chopsticks together. "Actually, I'm not sure how big it is . . . Anyway, the driver called and said he'd be here between nine and ten o'clock and Sid had a client dinner."

"So what happens?"

"Just like you, he calls and I open the alley door. After they unload, we lock up and go home." Lucy dropped a shrimp into her lap.

"Okay, then." Without looking at her, James handed her a napkin and reached for the Beef and Broccoli. He waved his chopsticks around the room. "What is all this stuff?"

"The behind-the-scenes view of Chicago's top decorator. Fabrics, sketch boards, his 'gems' he finds all over the world, paint decks . . . And you wouldn't believe some of the names that work with Sid, all wealthy, expectant, and *highly particular*." Lucy dropped her voice on the last word á la Cruella de Vil, and then bit her lip, regretting her ill-thought-out impersonation.

"Is my grandmother as hard to please as all that?" James raised an eyebrow, but his smile let Lucy know he was teasing.

"I wouldn't know. She was a client before my time. But I got a call from one yesterday demanding an off-production Scalamandre fabric *immediately*. And that's never fun."

"What'd you tell her?"

"Nothing. I simply found it and finagled six yards to be delivered by Monday." Lucy wrangled some rice onto her chopsticks. "I've become friends with the showroom staff and they had the yardage on hold, between three different designers. So I called each one and bartered, traded, didn't steal, but came close, and, in the end, got every yard. Everyone loves a good story."

"A story?"

"While it was true that I needed the yardage, it wasn't true that I'd secured a certain Fortuny trim one of the designers at the showroom needed. But once he was on board, I got a promise for the trim from Fortuny. I really needed the Scalamandre, and I simply greased the wheels by giving them a story. As I said, everyone loves a good story."

"You'd make such a good lawyer," James quipped.

Lucy scrunched her nose. "I know you're a lawyer, but no one says that as a compliment."

James raised both brows, considering. "Probably not, but it was a joke."

"It's just that . . . as I told the story to you just now, it didn't sound good to me either. I don't know why I do it. I mean it's not really bad, but . . ."

James took a bite and watched her.

"My father told stories, James, and I promised to never be like him and now . . . I suddenly hear myself and I am like him. I can't tell you how often I do stuff like that."

"It's hardly a big deal, Lucy. Wheedling your way into six yards of salamander fabric hardly constitutes a capital crime."

"Scalamandre." Lucy popped a bite of beef in her mouth to save herself further reply, but she remained unconvinced. "Your grandmother didn't like me, by the way."

"I don't know about that. I told her about you when I gave her the book and she's been asking questions ever since. And on the way home today, she asked a million more, especially about your eyes. You'd think the woman had never seen green eyes. She's definitely interested in you." James swiveled toward her. "And she wasn't feeling all that great. Maybe lunch then visiting you was too much."

Lucy's call came just as they were cleaning up and James was wiping down the worktable. Within minutes she was organizing the delivery of three various chests, two Tahitian water jug lamps, two Stickley chairs, and a gorgeous oak dining table—all while James roamed the workroom and gallery.

After the delivery truck pulled away, Lucy checked the gallery and shrugged on her coat. "You ready?"

James stood by her desk, tapping a book. "Is this a book you're selling?"

Lucy followed his gaze and narrowed her eyes, annoyed she hadn't hidden the book, hadn't tossed it. She turned away to search for her keys. "No. My father sent it to me. It arrived in the mail today."

"You rarely mention him, except tonight."

"Not much to say." Lucy heard her tight voice and lightened it. "All my memories of him are wrapped up in reading and stories. He told stories all the time, lived them really. That's what I meant, James, when I said I was acting like him earlier. He made up stories, told lies. He was a grifter."

"A con man? A real one?"

"Not glamorous. Not like TV." Lucy arched a brow. "He was always looking for the 'coming thing,' something really big, but he never worked for it and it never arrived. It usually involved some scam and because he had this beautiful English accent people innately trusted, he was able to pull off the initial steps. Then when the plan flopped or he got scared, we moved—until he left for good."

Lucy leaned against the worktable and gestured toward the book. "I call that my Birthday Book.

Each and every year, I get a book—haven't seen or heard from him in twenty years, but he keeps track of me because there's this year's book."

"When was your birthday?"

"A couple months ago. This one's a little late."

"No communication? There's no note? Nothing?" James opened the book and leafed through the pages.

"Never. But it *is* his first nonfiction selection and it's used. I'm assuming it was his, and maybe there's some meaning in that." Lucy pushed off the table and came to stand beside him. "I looked up John Ruskin. He was the Victorian era's most renowned art critic. That's new and intriguing. Or perhaps it means nothing at all and that's my own bit of fiction."

"Considering he's sent a book every birthday for the last twenty years, I think you can read meaning and significance into that."

"Perhaps." Lucy laid the book on her desk.

"You all set?"

James grabbed his coat and Lucy set the alarm.

As he walked out, she said, "You want to really earn sainthood? A bunch of friends are meeting at the Girl and the Goat tonight and they'd love to meet you."

James winked. "I'm all in."

Chapter 3

Four Book Days passed and Lucy barely noticed. Spring had hit Chicago, trees blossomed, and as the populace emerged from hibernation, clients clamored to "freshen" their homes. Sid ran himself ragged meeting the demand and Lucy struggled to keep only two steps behind.

"I've got two new client meetings today." Sid drummed his fingers on his red leather appointment book.

"Anything I can pull for them?"

"I don't know enough yet. The Ryans saw that magazine shoot of the Cramer home and they've decided taxicab-yellow walls are the way to go."

"Aren't they? Always?" Lucy checked off the last of the samples she was cataloging and placing in bags.

"If you're bold enough, yes. Nothing sets off art so well, but I'll have to see. There's no greater mistake than giving a client what she thinks she wants rather than something reflective of who she is. Do that and you're simply teeing up the next decorator."

Critics and clients believed Sid's genius came effortlessly, but he worked. He listened, he watched, and he strived to understand people at their very core. And in the end, he mixed textures, fabrics, case goods, and smalls in creative ways that delighted and amazed clients, critics, everyone he met. Taxicab-yellow walls, dining room table chairs upholstered in a rainbow of colors set against stark glass, weathered wood, lacquered trim, and doors in shocking colors . . . Lucy particularly liked his scandalous belief that the Europeans had it right, "A little lead in the paint makes the color pop." But it was these quiet moments that Lucy valued, when she observed Sid pondering what made clients tick, who they were, and what brought them joy.

Lucy's desk phone rang. "Sid McKenna Antiques and Design."

"Hey, beautiful."

"Hey, yourself. What's up?" Lucy caught Sid glancing her way and reddened. He knew exactly who was on the other end of the line.

"I scored two tickets to *Pippin* tonight. You free?" James whispered in an *I sit in a cubical surrounded by ears* fashion.

Lucy closed her eyes and pictured his face. She imagined that his dark brown hair, brushed back this morning, had already lopped forward and poked into one eye. "I need to cancel a girls' night out, but I think you're worth it."

"If I'm not, *Pippin* is. The reviews are great, but it's up to you. This is last minute."

"They won't mind. We tend to be very forgiving about dates. What time?"

"Show's at seven thirty. Do you want dinner before or after?"

"After, and I'll get the reservations. I've got just the place." Lucy laid down the phone and noted the absence of movement. She glanced up to find Sid staring at her. "No comment from you."

"You've been seeing him for well over a month. You're going to have to let me comment soon."

"Not yet." She rolled back in her desk chair. "What was the name of that restaurant you took the Corlings to last week? The one that—"

"Domestique?"

"That's it." Lucy rolled back to her computer.

"You're going to have to impress your boy-friend another way, *mon petit*. Domestique books months in advance." Sid chuckled again and resumed his pondering.

James's eyes widened as the waiter set a broad ramekin of crème caramel in front of him. He lifted the lavender sprig from the top and eyed it warily. "This reminds me of Grams. It should not be on a dessert."

Lucy laughed and reached for the sprig. "It's one of my favorite smells." She sat back, holding the lavender beneath her nose. "You know, *Pippin* was really a search for identity . . . That surprised me. I thought it was just a bawdy vaudeville romp—all show, no substance."

"I didn't know even that much. *Les Mis* was the

last show I saw, and that was years ago." James took a bite and scanned the restaurant. "And look at you . . . How'd you swing this?"

"I . . ." Lucy threw up her hands. "Why do I look at you and feel this compulsion to get all honest?" James widened his eyes and put another bite of crème caramel in his mouth. He didn't answer. "I was going to tell you that I've been here, but only Sid has."

"And?"

"And I basically bullied my way into a reservation. I wanted you to see it. It's *the* place right now."

"But, Lucy, I don't need *the* place. Please don't do stuff like that for me, because it only tells me that you're not comfortable with me."

"But look at your family, James. They're pretty perfect. And I noticed you didn't tell your dad about my dad at dinner last week." James's lips parted, but Lucy waved her hand. "I'm not blaming you. When he asked, I was right there with you. You didn't see me offering up family details. But you can see why I'd want to impress you, can't you?"

James leaned over and laid a light kiss on her lips. "No more, okay? It doesn't matter where we eat or what we do. I just like spending time with you, and I'm sorry I waffled when my dad asked, but it wasn't my story to share and I didn't want to put you on the spot."

"I know, and I appreciate that."

James waggled the spoon at her. She leaned over and tasted the offered dessert. It melted in her mouth, slowly, allowing her to sit in silence and watch the room while she digested the conversation. *Why do I look at you and feel this compulsion to get all honest?* It was true and the question poked—had started poking some time ago. At first, it was a niggling feeling, a pebble in her shoe, and one she could easily remove and forget. But that time passed and the pebble had left a blister that wasn't so easily dismissed.

She focused on Domestique's sleek décor: high cream glazed walls, modernist art, and highly polished wooden tables.

"What do you think the designer meant by that?" Lucy asked, titling her head to an alcove. It was an oddity that had bothered her throughout dinner. It featured a ten-top table, knotted wood and weathered, surrounded by vinyl chairs and low faux walls, papered in a 1950s kitschy style with cherry baskets.

James followed her gaze. "That's your field. Maybe it's the chef's childhood kitchen? I got it— it's a rail against the rest of the place's post-modern sterility, a call to family values. Or—"

"Enough!"

"You asked." James grinned.

"It must mean something. I feel like it's taunting me with its secret."

James considered the alcove again. "It kinda reminds me of Gram's kitchen growing up, warm and simple. To me, it feels like the opposite of a secret. It's the heart hidden within all this show."

"I like that." Lucy leaned back in her chair. "I guess I find it hard to differentiate sometimes."

"But speaking of show with no heart . . ." James turned and poked a finger across the dining room.

Lucy trailed his gaze to a four-top near a front window. Bespoke-suited men and resplendent women sat straight yet relaxed; their very posture had the waitstaff snapping. "Who are they?"

"The two partners who define my firm. Talk about blurry lines. Dawkins, the one in the black glasses, practically called me a liar when I mentioned we were coming here after the show. He said it was impossible and that it took him months to get a table. Tonight, too, of all nights." James took a scoop of his crème caramel, chewing more intentionally than the custard warranted.

"See, and if I hadn't—"

"I wasn't saying that." James covered his mouth with his hand as he spoke. He swallowed and continued, looking back to the table. "He runs the case I'm on and he flirts with that line . . . Always legal, but sooooo close." James rubbed his thumb against his forefinger, denoting a minute distance, before twisting his wrist and changing the gesture to mimic rubbing dollar bills between his fingers. "Associates usually work two cases at a time, but he's got me exclusively on his because a senior one allows him to charge double. So I get everything, down to the filing and coffee."

"That's terrible."

"But I've got a way out," James chirped.

"How?"

"I'm going to win that trip to Hawaii." James waved his spoon.

"How does a trip to Hawaii give you a way out?"

"The trip's the icing on the cake. Top associate goes with all the partners to Hawaii for vacation and he picks his own cases once he gets back."

"He?" Lucy arched her voice.

"This time. Hendricks and I are the only ones in the running and there are only two weeks left until the partners meet to decide. So yes, 'he.'" James tapped her nose with the final threewords. "And this 'he'"—he flattened his palm on his chest—"will pick a pro bono case without having to leave the partner track. Problem solved."

"And if you don't win it?"

James looked back to the table. "Then it gets a bit more complicated. I want to do pro bono work, Lucy, but leaving the partner track is a big deal. There are . . . expectations in my family. You've met my dad. This is what I've been trained to do. Told to do." He furrowed his brow. "Forget it. I'll win the trip, and that'll fix all of it."

"No more shows or dinners for two weeks then.

All guns point to Hawaii. Got it." Lucy snagged James's spoon and licked the custard from its bowl.

James recovered his spoon and quietly attacked his dessert.

The remainder of the meal and the car ride to Lucy's apartment passed quietly. Lucy assumed James was lost in Hawaii.

"Here you are, Sleeping Beauty." James pulled his car into a vacant parking spot near her brownstone.

Lucy stifled another yawn. "I'm so sorry. This week has caught up with me." She rolled her head on the headrest to face him. "This spring has been too packed."

"Will it let up?"

"It naturally turns in summer when clients go on vacation. We'll be there soon."

James looked around. "This is a sign, by the way." He quirked an eyebrow. "I don't think I've ever found a parking spot so fast. Can I come up?"

"Tonight?" Lucy gulped.

"I want to see your home, Lucy. You've been to my place plenty of times." James twisted; the seat belt pulled at his shoulder. "Don't you want me to see it? Again, you don't need to impress me."

"It's not that . . ."

"I won't stay long." His tone made it clear that he was clarifying his intentions.

"I wasn't thinking that." She smiled.

"I am . . . Why aren't you?" he lightly teased

before his eyes flickered concern. "Then, what?"

Lucy weighed her options and her reply. She came to a conclusion and gave a slow nod. "All right, you asked. Come on."

Lucy got out of the car and when she looked back at him, she almost cringed at the hope and gentle excitement that danced in his eyes.

She unlocked the door and James held it for her. She then crossed the lobby and led him up two more flights. He remained silent as she unlocked her front door and pushed it hard, past its sticking point. "The humidity swells it each spring. Now . . . It isn't much . . . I haven't done much decorating."

"I'm sure your place is perfect." He kissed her cheek and pressed his palm against the door, holding it open for her to enter first. Her thoughts flew to James's apartment, which though masculine in aesthetic, was still lively with its framed concert posters and signed baseball jerseys; its wool rug, thrown down by his mother; and its cacophony of comfortable furniture. Images of a much starker nature arose when she imagined what he'd see in hers—an *inhospitable hearth* more fitting for Heathcliff than the young Mr. Lockwood, who kept calling at Wuthering Heights. Would James, too, remember that *only four miles distant lay* his *delightful home* and want to run straight back?

James passed into her two-step hallway and stopped.

Lucy dropped her bag by the door and laid her keys on the American chest Sid had given her as a Christmas bonus the year before. She ran her fingers over its parched rough top as she watched James take a slow survey of her one-bedroom apartment. She followed the trail, trying to discern the thoughts chasing each other round and round in his mind. His expression revealed nothing.

He turned his head from her living room, past her single armchair and solitary table, to the naked front bay window. He continued to the left and took in the small kitchen with its single stool at the counter. He then gazed across to her bedroom door. From this vantage point, she knew he could see her queen-size bed resting on its metal frame, and one corner of a mid-nineteenth-century French dresser. What had once felt like an evolving creation was, in its bald reality, an empty apartment.

"Not what you expected?"

He stepped into the living room, loafers tapping on the bare wood floor. Something caught his eye and his hand darted to the mantel. "You framed it?" He picked up the lone picture frame featuring an index card written in a precise hand.

Roses are Red.
Violets are Blue.
You've stolen my heart.
I'm in love with you.

"I liked it." Lucy lifted a shoulder.

"I'm pleased my little note warrants such a place of honor."

She waited and he said nothing more, so she repeated her question in the form of a statement. "It's not what you expected."

James didn't answer. Instead he asked a question of his own. "Where are the curtains you always talk about?"

"I don't always . . . Here." Lucy crossed to the bay window. Her high heels clicked like bullet fire echoing off the empty surfaces. She tiptoed to stop the sound and picked up one of the two panels lying on the floor. She whipped it out like a blanket, spreading it broad and smooth across the floor. "This one's finished. It's amazingly heavy." She grabbed the other one and spread it out next to its twin and knelt down to flatten its edges. "This is the second one, and I need only a few more remnant squares to complete it."

She studied the intricate pattern created by hundreds of five-inch squares of fabric—deep, bold colors moving across the panel to soft pastels with threads of gold and silver squares stitched in the center as if pouring down like a waterfall. "When pulled, they'll be large enough to cover the entire window."

"They're beautiful, Lucy." James squatted beside her and ran his hand over a square of royal velvet, basted between a silk brocade and heavy jade linen. "There's a design in here."

Lucy ran her hand across the first. "It starts here with the dark tones of winter then travels through spring to the high summer and closes in the bottom corner in fall. It's not linear. I tried to capture the movement of the seasons and where they cross through texture more than through color." She pulled the second panel toward her. "This one is a life. You start innocent and young and fresh and then the colors change—"

"They get pretty dark here. What's this?"

"I'm not sure. I made that section last year, but I think I was envisioning that questioning time, kinda like Jane Eyre's time on the moors or Helen Graham's months back with her abusive husband or Molly's time when Roger is engaged to Cynthia. All the books have it . . . That time when you don't know where you'll be, but you can't stay as you are. In life or in literature, that time rarely feels good." She peeked at James, thinking perhaps sharing her panels was not her best idea. "It gets lighter here with more texture as one comes to truly understand oneself and can answer those big questions with some certainty. I have this vision of completeness and that's this gold through the orange." She ran her hand along the curving gold path.

"And that leaves what? Death?"

"I haven't found the right fabrics yet." She sat

back on her heels. "I hope you don't think it's morbid. It's more of a journey than a real life. Think of it as a book, not as me. I'm not trying to find the right fabrics for my own death."

"I didn't think that." James stood. "I think it's spectacular, beyond brilliant." He reached down and pulled her to stand beside him. "When you talked about them, I couldn't envision them and certainly never got close to this."

"Sid's clients have good taste. It wouldn't be so pretty with felts and cotton twill. But beyond that, I choose each because of a memory or a texture that speaks to me. Some are simply my favorite colors. Like that orange with the gold fiber? The midlife? That's a sunset to me." She pulled, first at one panel then the other, and folded them under the window. "It's probably taken too long to finish it, though. Four years borders on strange."

"How much is left?"

"Fourteen squares. Some of the fabrics Sid's clients have chosen this spring are extraordinary; I expect I'll find the perfect pieces and have it ready for the finisher by summer."

James raised his eyes and looked back across the apartment. "And your table? It's not what I imagined either."

"I thought I described that pretty well—books stacked for the legs and glass on top."

James walked to it and squatted again. "It's a little more than that. You've got an order down here, don't you? Americans in this leg . . ." He twisted to the right. "And English here. Victorian mostly." He leaned farther. "But also here. What's the difference between these two legs?"

"Both English. These are the love stories, though not all romantic. Austen, Brontës, a couple Dickens, Hardy, Gaskell, and these . . ."

"Mystery, deception . . . That's why Shakespeare's in both." He walked around to the fourth leg. "Whoa . . . Childhood." He crouched again. "*The Velveteen Rabbit.* I loved that book. And Beatrix Potter. And *Frog and Toad*. These are fantastic. Do you read any of these?"

Lucy picked up the inch-thick glass top. "I just pull off the top, and *voila*. But I have to put them back before I can replace the glass or it's not even—so, no, I don't read any of them very often. They're best under here. Maybe someday I'll get some bookshelves—and a real table."

"Don't you miss reading them? You of all people."

Lucy stared at the table, pondering it. "Yes, some are my favorite stories, but they aren't particularly my favorite books." James shot her a questioning glance. "Many of those are Birthday Books and, while I love them, I don't mind seeing them squished a little."

James turned away, scanning the apartment again.

"You expected more . . . Stuff that reflects me,

who I am, collections, something . . ." Lucy slowly spun around in the empty room as well. "But I wanted to bring in things that have meaning, objects that I truly love, and it's so hard to find—"

"Hey, hey." James caught and tugged her arm until she was folded into his embrace. "Stop. What you have here is gorgeous, creative, and thoughtful." He whispered into her hair and pulled her closer until her entire body pressed against his. "So you put too much pressure on case goods. There's no shame in that. Home doesn't always come easily."

She laughed into his shoulder. "Case goods?"

She could feel his lips pressing against her hair. They moved from her crown, to her forehead, to her cheek. "And you thought I don't listen."

"I never said that," she whispered.

"I can tell." He pushed her hair back from the sides of her face and kissed her. Firmly. Completely. Lucy ran her hands up his back and held tight. After a few silent delicious moments, he whispered softly, not breaking contact. "And you've won. I'll lend you that leather armchair you love so much and maybe a bookcase or two—not all of those are Birthday Books. Some need a breather."

"Ah . . . My master plan." She kissed him. Once. Twice. "You're so easy."

"Always." James quit talking.

Chapter 4

The next morning found Lucy dwelling on the evening's more exquisite moments and dreaming up ways to congratulate James once he won his trip. *A book? A pen? A print?* Nothing felt right. She had poured her second cup of coffee and curled into her armchair when her phone rang.

"Look outside," James ordered.

"No 'Good morning'?"

"Good morning. Look outside."

Lucy uncurled and walked to the window. It took a moment to drop her eyes to street level and comprehend the sight below her. James stood next to a small U-Haul truck and waved up at her. "You did not!" she squealed.

"I did. Brad helped me load them, but it's you and me now."

"I'll be right down. Stay there." Lucy ran to her room. Throwing on jeans, sneakers, and a sweatshirt—pausing only for a quick swipe with her toothbrush—she hit the front stoop in under three minutes and launched herself into James's arms. "You brought me furniture!"

"Do they have enough meaning to make the cut?"

"They're from you. That's all the meaning they need." She climbed into the back of the truck.

"And I love this chair. You can tell how good it is . . ." She ran her fingernail across the armrest, making a scratch.

James launched in after her. "What are you doing? That's still *my* chair."

"Watch." She rubbed at the spot and it disappeared. "Good leather does that. It can absorb a little abuse. Cheap, thin leather holds the scratches. It's very sad."

"You're lucky I own a happy chair."

"I knew it the first moment I laid eyes on it." Lucy turned to the bookcases. "And both? You only have these two." She traced a finger along the scalloped trim at the top. "These had to have come from your mother."

"Grandmother. She had them in storage for half a century."

"Helen? They're lovely." Lucy ran her hand along one broad shelf. "What about all your books? You can't stack them around your apartment. That'll drive you nuts."

"I already ordered two new ones from Crate and Barrel." At her shocked expression, he continued, "My standards aren't as high as yours. I require shelves for my books; they don't have to have decades of experience to prove they're qualified for the job."

"My books are fine, though. Don't bring these in." Lucy hopped out of the truck. "They're your grandmother's. That's special."

"They're mine and you're special. Besides, smashed books are hardly books at all."

"Okay. I've done my best." Lucy clapped her hands together. "I accept."

"That's my girl. Hop back up and take this end and I'll step down first. It'll be easier for you." James stepped off the back of the truck and shouldered a majority of the chair's weight.

In the end, Lucy provided minimal load but maximum navigational support. Three trips, one scuffed doorjamb, and two hours later, they flopped into her two armchairs and faced her bookcases. One entire shelf remained empty.

"I need more books."

"Not today." James groaned.

"Not today, but soon. I'm going to visit that secondhand bookstore in Hyde Park, the one where you found that old *Catcher in the Rye*."

"I'll go with you . . . Next weekend."

"Fine." She drew the word out with as much drama as her sore muscles allowed.

"Borrow some from your gallery. Or get them at auctions. You always say you know how to get the best prices."

Lucy considered a moment. "No . . . Not those. Not here." She recognized the oddity of her comment. "Besides, I'm not trying to collect books, per se. I like copies I can read and fold and wrestle around with. The ones at the shop are too delicate to really dig into."

James stared at her. "I've never heard anyone talk about books like you do. It's like they're your friends."

"Aren't they yours?"

James raised his eyebrow.

Lucy laughed. "Don't even. They're as much your friends as they are mine. I don't mean it in some strange or creepy antisocial way. I mean that reading forms your opinions, your worldview, especially childhood reading, and anything that does that has an impact. So call them friends, call some stories enemies if you want, but don't deny their influence." She popped up straight. "You learn drama from the Brontës; sense from Austen; social justice from Dickens; beauty from Wordsworth, Keats, and Byron; patience and perseverance from Gaskell; and don't even get me started on exercising your imagination with Carroll, Doyle, Wells, Wilde, Stoker—"

"Fine," James cut in, mimicking her tone.

"But you've got a point . . ." Lucy slouched back into the chair and studied the cases as if they held the answer to a long-held secret. "For me, they're also a connection to my dad, my only connection, and I have taken that, I suspect, a little too seriously."

"Have you ever thought of searching for him?"

Lucy sat still for such a long time that James reached over and squeezed her arm. "Sorry I asked."

"Don't be . . . My friends were bugging me about that the other night. And every year the postmark on the Birthday Book gives me a clue. So every year, yes, I know the town in which he lives and I could probably find him. You can find anything on the Internet. But I haven't. That's what I was thinking about, and that's what I can't answer. Why haven't I?"

"Don't know, but don't blame yourself either. One, you're the kid and, as the parent, I kinda think the ball's in his court. And two, he clearly knows where you are because you get the books every year. It's like a string he tugs annually, and something about that makes me suspicious. You get all twitchy when I say it, but people don't change."

"While I disagree—again—those points do smack me every year, but still . . . I've been thinking about it a lot lately and it'd be good, don't you think? Answer some questions . . ."

"I suppose it would. Do you have any?"

"Wouldn't you?" Lucy peered over. "Well, not you. You don't have questions because your family is all there, all whole and transparent. No mixed messages, bad examples, and crooked roads."

"Ha! Shows what you know. My family is completely opaque with massive expectations and very little true conversation. We raise passive aggressive to an art form."

"Still . . . It feels like a wave is building. I need to find him."

"Come on." James stood and reached for her hand. "Enough of this. You're going down your rabbit hole and that means it's time to eat." He pulled her up and pushed her to the door. "Let's grab sandwiches at Snarf's and go for a walk."

"Do I get you for the whole day?" Lucy let herself be pushed.

"I'm all yours."

Monday morning found Lucy's thoughts dwelling once more—this time on the entire weekend. Saturday's lunch had turned into a walk; the walk into a romp around the zoo; the zoo into dinner at a tiny Thai restaurant; and the day ended with a movie back at James's place because, despite the loss of an armchair and two bookcases, he still owned more furniture—specifically, a couch and a television. And Saturday wasn't the end. Sunday involved brunch with his parents and a flurry of texts and phone calls all afternoon while he worked and she sat reading in her new leather chair. Altogether . . . a perfect weekend.

Not quite. Lucy's thoughts shifted to the tidal white noise. Thoughts of her father continued to churn in the background—and refused to retreat.

"I'm thinking *not* a good daydream. You're scrunching your nose."

Lucy glanced up to find Sid standing with one hand held high as if he'd snapped his fingers.

He chuckled and strode toward the back room, calling over his shoulder, "You're going to need to share that one."

Lucy stood and followed him. "I need a surprise for James. He's in the running for top associate and, after a year of hard work, a book or a dinner out doesn't seem fitting. And he's done a lot for me lately."

"Explain." Sid laid down the fabric books and leaned against his worktable, ready to dive into her problem.

"He gave me furniture, Sid. It was incredible. He just showed up at my apartment Saturday morning with his favorite armchair and two bookshelves."

Sid's eyes widened. "Most guys don't think beyond flowers. You might want to keep that one."

"Hence the need to come up with a fantastic surprise. Come on, you're creative. Help me."

Sid thrummed his fingers together. "What about something from you? Not something you buy but something equally sacrificial? Make him dinner. Write him a nice letter. Start a panel project for his windows."

"There's no time for drapery, but a letter?" Lucy added a touch of sarcasm to her voice. She needed better ideas, grander ideas.

51

"Doesn't everyone enjoy a heartfelt note?"

"Your generation might." Lucy caught herself. "That's not true. James wrote me one and I love it."

"See?" Sid stabbed a finger in the air. "A good idea. Now to business. You texted *me* about a surprise?"

Lucy grinned. "A big one."

Sid, as expected, started tapping his foot. He hated surprises and he hated to be kept waiting. She knew the text would drive him nuts, but now she let the moment linger.

"You know I love you, but you're being mean today."

"You'll be sorry you said that." Lucy pointed to a large crate in the workroom's corner.

"Noooooo." Sid drew the word out like taffy and covered the distance in three strides. "You haven't opened it?"

"It's for you. Here." She handed him the heavy yellow DeWalt drill and watched him expertly pop at least forty screws from the top of the wooden crate in under a minute, knocking each off the drill's magnetic hold with a flick against the crate's top.

"How is this possible? They were backlogged two years and I only got on the list six months ago." Sid extracted the final screws.

"Maybe people got fed up and backed out?" Lucy bit her lip.

"Impossible. This shooting star has substance; it's not going to fall."

Lucy helped Sid lift the crate's lid. He dove his lean frame over the four-foot-high lip—one hunter-green-driving-loafer-clad foot flying up to maintain balance. Lucy resisted the urge to yank him steady by his belt.

Sid shot himself upright, packing popcorn flying with him, and hoisted a large, brown-paper-wrapped object high into the air. Then, tucking it close like an infant, he stood a moment and gazed at his new baby. Lucy rushed to the work-table to clear fabric and tile samples.

He followed in careful, measured steps. "This isn't mere art, Lucy. This is history. A reclamation of art for the home. Artists naturally reach for the stars and all that comes with it. But MacMillan? He's keeping his prices purposely low to keep these treasures in homes. A liberation from museums. I haven't seen an expression like this in home arts . . . and I don't mean big names made available, a napkin signed by Warhol or a Rembrandt sketch. I'm talking about artists purposefully honoring the home arts . . ."

Lucy smiled. Sid had lost his train of thought and she expected him to soon shed a tear.

The pricking in her own eyes surprised her as Sid tore away the brown paper. The vase stood about twenty-two inches high and fifteen inches wide at its apex and it danced, danced with light and color.

"It's breathtaking. I've only ever seen one in person, in London, a couple years ago. His work is very similar to some of Chagall's vase work, but he also infuses glass into them and I enjoy these colors and the movement more. I've heard he uses a ground diamond powder in some of his blues and organic pigments that no one even remembers anymore. That's how he gets this yellow. You want to lick it, it's so rich." Sid held the vase above his head, turning it in his hands to view all sides in the light.

"It's exquisite," Lucy rasped, stunned by the realization that the vase mirrored the complexity and beauty she'd sought when forming her drapery panels. It evoked the same emotion—that feeling when her heart moved just high enough in her chest to catch her breath.

She looked toward the door to the gallery with a new understanding: this was what people sought when they hired Sid, spent money, decorated lavishly, and invested deeply—they hoped to own this feeling, this serenity, forever.

Sid rested the vase on the worktable. He stepped back, never taking his eyes off his prize. "He's purposely keeping prices low and not outsourcing anything. No minions . . . I love it, but I don't understand it. It's either foolish or the greatest marketing technique ever developed." He turned back to the crate. "How many are in there? I ordered three."

"All three."

Sid's eyes watered anew.

Lucy moved aside as Sid circled back to the crate, watching in silence as he dug out the remaining two vases. He cuddled them, unwrapped them, and adored them. Lucy found herself watching Sid more than the vases. His delight was contagious and she enjoyed making him happy. He'd trained her, coached her, and guided her with patience. He'd given her more care and stability than she'd ever experienced and more than she knew she deserved. He did the same for every client, every volunteer project. To bring him joy mattered. Perhaps he wouldn't care how she accomplished it.

Sid stood absorbing the vases, then paced around them, doubled back, and looped the table again.

"Who are your lucky buyers?" Lucy asked.

"Only the most beloved. Torrance Bergen would adore this one. She understands color—she's such a delight. And can't you see this one"—he touched the center vase, which boasted shots of gold through bright red—"in the Palmers' entry? It will ignite the black lacquered walls. But this one, we keep, at least for now. Go ahead and put it atop the George III chest. There's plenty of time to sell it, and we deserve some fun too."

"Perfect. It's my favorite." Lucy reached for the third vase and clutched it against her chest, fearing Sid's love could evaporate if she broke it.

He followed close on her heels. "I want to stay," he whined. "I want to stay and bask in its beauty, but I have an appointment with Monica Dickerson. I'll need the swatches you pulled."

Lucy set down the vase and positioned it so her preferred side faced out—a swirling scene of midnight blues with a hint of yellow, of hope, blurring to gold as it broke over the rim and cascaded down the side through layers of green and orange. "They're propped against my desk."

She heard Sid sigh and step away, the knobbed soles of his shoes squeaking across the wood floor then squealing when they hit the cement. He returned seconds later with two sample bags and an iPad. "You'll have to show me how to use this again." He rested the bags at her feet.

"First"—Lucy picked up one bag—"this blue bag has all the samples from tile and flooring to fabrics and lighting for the main level. It's everything for that entire floor. And I've stapled a price sheet together too." She dropped it beside the red and lifted that one. "Then go to this bag for the bedrooms. I clipped each room together, rather than show continuity by organizing it color-wise, as we did for the Benson home."

Lucy reached for the iPad. "And here . . ." She stood next to him, almost eye to eye in her four-inch heels. She tapped the screen and held it facing him. "The entire home is set up just like before."

"Are my sketches there too?"

"Yes. And scroll your finger across and you can tour the rooms."

"Brilliant."

"Computers are easy." She winked. "They're my damasks, silks, and toiles."

"Books are your damask, silks, and toiles. But you're good at this stuff too, I'll give you that."

"Thank Advanced Programming C-10, best college class you can take."

"I'll trust you on that one." Sid walked to the door and leaned against it. "I meant to mention it when I first walked in, but I got distracted by those." He flicked a finger at the two vases sitting atop the worktable. "I scanned those specs and sketches you found. The sources aren't reputable enough for us to consider purchasing."

"But two are Miro? And the Warhol? Didn't Darlene Graber request a Warhol? The prices are excellent."

"Both sellers have questionable integrity. It makes me uncomfortable."

"But—"

"It takes a long time to build a reputation, Lucy, and only one faulty sale to topple it. Buying from a questionable source can ruin every-thing. Darlene Graber can cool her jets."

Lucy nodded.

"With these MacMillans, why do we need a couple suspect Miros anyway? And Warhols are getting ubiquitous; Darlene needs more originality. We'll kick back and warm our toes by the fire and watch the light play on those gorgeous vases, shall we?"

Lucy raised a brow. "You warm your toes by the fire?" At Sid's chuckle, she said, "I'll withdraw my queries, then."

As Sid pushed his way out the door, arms laden, Lucy sank into her chair and opened her computer. She'd always meant to do it right. Sid deserved that. When she'd started working for him, right out of college, she'd sought reliable sources, learned the protocol, and tried to make true connections with buyers, sellers, and collectors. But it all took so long. Nothing moved as fast or as efficiently as it might, as it should, and computers brought the world to her doorstep.

Although it wasn't Sid's style, she learned if she could contact a dealer in Atlanta, another in San Francisco, and yet another in Dallas, all selling the same case good or holding certain bolts of fabric on reserve, then she was fairly certain that she could convince at least one of them to drop the price, ship it for free, or pay Sid McKenna Antiques and Design a finder's fee for bringing a client directly to them—especially if she told them a good story. Then everyone won, or so she had thought.

As Lucy withdrew the gallery's interest with the two dealers, her conscience pricked her again with regard to her latest literary acquisitions. The books weren't rare or exceptional and she knew some of her own sellers were questionable. They dumped volumes on the market at irregular times and with a veil of "no questions asked." *It takes a long time to build a reputation, Lucy, and only one faulty sale to topple it.* But it wasn't her reputation at risk with each manipulation, book purchase, or fabricated inscription. It was Sid's.

Lucy closed her laptop and peered into the gallery—a straight line of sight to the George III chest and the MacMillan vase standing proud with its gold and yellow cascading over the side. As she stared, the hope that had glowed within the colors moments before faded into shadow.

Chapter 5

Spring was still moving too quickly. Lucy found herself behind on ordering, billing, designing, filing . . . Clients wanted items yesterday, her go-to installer was overbooked, Sid's favorite fine arts painters were out with a spring flu, and several pages of her beloved books were sticking. She was gently pulling apart *Wives and Daughters* with her last whisper of patience when a knock startled her. Helen Carmichael pressed her hands against the glass door, her light blonde wool coat creating a monotone beige blob from top to toe.

Lucy laid down the book and approached the door, smoothing her skirt with the first few steps. She gestured the older woman inside. "Mrs. Carmichael? How are you?"

"Helen, please, and I'm fine. I simply couldn't push the door open."

Lucy reached to the top hinge. "This probably needs oiling again." She shut the door. "What can I do for you?"

"I wanted to see the shop again. I wasn't able to last time and I barely got to talk with you at dinner the other night."

"That was nice of James's parents to invite me."

"Leslie is a wonderful hostess." Helen looked around and raised her hand to her forehead.

"Are you feeling well?"

"I am, but it's warm in here." She started to shrug off her coat. Lucy reached over to help, catching a whiff of a delicate floral, and most likely French, scent.

Lucy pulled the heavy coat from the older woman's shoulders to find her dressed in a pale blue cashmere sweater set and a thick wool blazer. "You have on a few layers. Do you want me to help you out of your blazer as well?"

"I'm much better now. I've been so cold. Spring is late this year."

"April's not for another week so there's probably a little more winter ahead of us."

"Are you busy?" Helen sat in a chair as if settling in for a long chat.

Lucy dropped into the chair beside her. "Not at all. Sid volunteers on Wednesday mornings so he's never here and the shop doesn't open for another half hour. I call it Book Day because it's the morning I take care of the books and catch up on everything for that part of the business." She spread her hands across her lap. "So you've caught me at my very favorite time of the week." Helen didn't reply so she searched for a new topic. "How do you like your *Jane Eyre*?"

"Such a beauty, but I'm not pleased James spent so much on me."

"I did try to dissuade him. He was determined."

"Once we met, I better understood." Helen reached into her bag. "I brought it with me."

"You did?"

Helen handed the book to Lucy. "When James gave it to me he showed me a picture, but I don't know where it's gone."

Lucy held it between her palms. "This is a favorite of mine. An early edition bought at auction by a collector in London." She gently laid it in her lap. "I believe it came originally from an estate sale in Yorkshire and I don't think he would've let it go, but he was forced to liquidate his library . . . Just think, a copy that hasn't traveled far from its home since written and published over one hundred and fifty years ago." She opened the cover and fanned the pages on their edges, sliding them minutely apart. The picture of Jane and Rochester reappeared. "Here is what you're after . . ."

"There it is. It's absolutely lovely."

"It is, isn't it?" Lucy handed the book back. "Some say they're tacky because they weren't originally printed with the book, but I love them. They're special, like secret treasures, and always make me smile."

"I agree with you." Helen glanced past Lucy's shoulder to the bookshelves. "You have quite a focused selection here."

"Victorian. I try to buy for value, but it happens to align with my interests at present so I've probably gone overboard. My budget won't let me near Austen and Regency or even twentieth century right now, except for a few Russian novels, and they leave me vaguely uncomfortable."

"Good fiction can do that. Dostoyevsky's *Crime and Punishment* is a favorite of mine." Helen stood and moved to examine a small sculpture sitting on a nearby chest. "Tell me more about your family. I find your accent fascinating."

"Ah . . . my South Side meets the West End?" Lucy joined her. The bronze sculpture was about the width of a hand and twice as tall, an abstract interpretation of an elephant. "It's from my father. I don't think of myself as having an accent, but some words come out a little more rounded and my intonation sweeps up at times. And I've never even been to England."

"At dinner you said your grandmother was from London."

"My grandfather moved over there in '57, I gather, and met and married her. She died in '75 and my grandfather brought my dad, their only child, back to his home. He was something like third generation Chicago and missed it a lot." Lucy shrugged. "But my dad never thought like that. He tenaciously held on to his accent and moved us everywhere when I was a kid. Then when he left us, Mom came back home to Chicago too. She grew up on the north side—though she moved out to Rockford when I went to college, almost a decade ago."

"Well, it's a lovely accent."

"Thank you. I got my love for books from my dad too." Lucy pointed across to the shelves. "He used to read to me all the time and his accent was strongest when he read English authors or children's books. I think that was because he always chose his favorites, books his mum read to him."

"'57? I imagine things were still quite unsettled over there after the war."

"Dad didn't talk about his childhood much. But, working in arts and antiques, I've learned you're right."

Helen stayed a few more minutes, falling into a fairly easy conversation on books, antiques, and life. As she left and Lucy locked the door behind her, Lucy felt a soft questioning as to whether the visit had been a social call or an interview.

Chapter 6

Sid pushed through the door long after the gallery closed. Well beyond when Lucy should've shut off the lights, locked the door, and headed home.

"Why are you here? It's too late." He moaned and dropped three fabric books and two bags onto his desk.

"I'm still behind, Sid. We've been busy, too busy. I don't know how you do it."

"I've been thinking about that and it's only April. We may need more help when fall ramps up again."

"I agree. Walk-ins are up and that's telling, right there. I sold the Louis XV wedding armoire today. Fifteen minutes and . . ." Lucy briefly searched her screen. "A Lila Jenson plopped down twenty-two grand. The guys will deliver it tomorrow."

She watched Sid rub his eyes, noting the circles beneath.

"I'm glad that piece found a home. Good job." Sid stretched his back. "Spring is always like this. I love it, but I'm getting older too. And you? Go home, call your friends. You should be out. Antiques, by definition, cannot be urgent. The air is soft tonight, highly unusual, and it won't last. Go have fun." He waved his hands toward the door. "Go. Go. Call James."

"It's the last week before the partners meet. I wouldn't be surprised if he hasn't been home all week. I've barely heard from him."

"You're no better. Are you sharing in the crazy?"

"I'm catching up. We've got our own crazy."

"Well, I give up." Sid palmed his car keys and waved. "See you tomorrow, *mon coeur*."

Lucy finished the billing then strolled through the gallery, making sure everything was in place for the next day. A few items had to be tilted this way or that and the work was done within minutes. She ran her finger over the chests and tables and recalled her parched nineteenth-century American one at home. *Must remember the furniture oil.*

She lit a gardenia candle and it reminded her of the day James first asked her out. She breathed deep, waiting for the scent to give her a lift before she grasped the linen cloth from her desk drawer and headed to the books.

Sid's warning about *one faulty sale* had stung for two weeks. And like a child, fearful of fire, she'd stayed away from the sellers she knew posed a risk. The books she'd already purchased from them gently condemned her and pricked her conscience every time she dusted, sold, or even touched one. Sid trusted her judgment and had even handed over the gallery's small but growing antique book business completely to her care. She knew she had violated that trust, but was unsure how to fix it.

Lucy reached up and pulled down an early edition of *Wuthering Heights* and carefully spanned the pages to see the portrait of Cathy emerge from the edge, with Heathcliff standing guard behind her. She sighed and let the pages rustle into place as she settled behind a small writing desk. "Just a moment, then home." She gently opened the book and started to read. *A perfect misanthropist's Heaven—and Mr. Heathcliff and I are such a suit-able pair to divide the desolation between us . . .*

The door grated as someone pushed it open. Lucy jumped up, realizing she'd forgotten to lock it.

James walked in.

"I didn't think I'd see you tonight." She laid the book down and reached out her arms. She pulled away as she absorbed his expression. "What's wrong?"

James approached her, pulling his bag strap from his shoulder. "Remember how you told me inscriptions, the provenance, increase the value of a book? Tell the story behind the story?"

"Yes . . ."

"I was at Grams's last night and she thanked me again for that *Jane Eyre*." James reached into his bag and pulled it out. "This *Jane Eyre*. And I looked at it, really looked at it, and I noticed something. Then I went and got *Kidnapped*." He reached back in and pulled out *Kidnapped*. He laid both books on her desk and crossed to her bookshelves. He pulled out several volumes and slapped them down on the ledge.

"James, I . . ." Lucy's voice died as he opened one, two, three . . .

"All different names, I'll give you that. But the same handwriting. Lucy? Why?" He turned back to her.

"I . . . I wanted them to be valued."

"They're stories, Lucy. They aren't people. They aren't real. They are valued for what they are, nothing more. And this—what you've done—*devalues* them. And you." Lucy opened her mouth, but he went on. "I trusted you. I thought you trusted me enough to be honest with me."

"This was different . . . It was meant to create a sense of connection—to tell a good story."

"I had to tell Grams and my dad."

"What did you say?" Lucy stilled.

"I took their books, Lucy. I had to explain. Everything."

"What exactly does that mean, everything?" Lucy held her gaze steady. "You told them about my father?" Her voice ended in a whisper.

James didn't reply.

"I see . . . We're lumped together now, aren't we?"

"That's not fair. I—"

"No. I get it." Lucy felt tears prick her eyes as she cut him off. "I wasn't criticizing; I wouldn't want to disappoint them either." She held both hands in front of her. "You say they're tough and have expectations, but they're good people and . . ."

"Just tell me you didn't do it. That it was a mistake."

"You want me to lie to you?"

"*Now* you stop lying?" James snapped back.

"James—"

"I have to go." He rapped the desk with his knuckles. "We can't keep those. I'll e-mail you after I sort out what to do."

Lucy heard the "we" and knew lines had been drawn and doors shut. "I'll refund your money."

"I don't care about the money right now!"

"I know." Lucy nodded.

He grabbed his bag and slung the strap over his shoulder. "I've got to get back to work."

"This late?"

His shoulders slumped. "I've got only a few hours left and it's too hard, Lucy. This is too hard. Last week, I worked one hundred and twenty hours. This week will top it. And Dawkins, that partner I pointed out at the restaurant, gets this gleam in his eye every time he sees me, because he knows he owns me. I'm so tired of being used. Maybe if I wasn't in this place, I'd have a better sense of humor about this, I could fight for . . . I don't even know what. But I can't." He pulled open the door and walked out without another word or look back.

Lucy followed him and locked the door. Through the glass, she watched him cross the street and turn at the corner. Part of her wanted to run after him, but most of her knew to stay. James was tired, strung-out, and he was right. What could she say to change that?

She stepped back to her desk and picked up the books. *Kidnapped* and *Jane Eyre*. They were there when she met James and now they'd witnessed the end. She carried them to the bookcase and carefully restacked each of the books James had slapped down—*Oliver Twist*, *North and South*, *The Tenet of Wildfell Hall*, Dickens's *Christmas Books*, and a copy of Charles Lamb's *Adventures of Ulysses* signed by Mary Shelley. Genuinely signed by Mary Shelley.

Lucy gripped the last one tight. *What were you thinking? What more did this or any of them need?* She placed it on the shelf, running her finger across the stack of spines. All the books, with their worn warm covers, were special, in and of themselves, and James was right; they needed nothing from her. Lucy slowly shook her head as she finally tucked *Kidnapped* and *Jane Eyre* beside them.

Locking the glass door, she took in the gallery. It looked exactly as it had fifteen minutes earlier. Yet now every book felt tainted, the antiques clouded and cold. The spectacular MacMillan vase mocked her, and the oversweet scent of the gardenia candle cloyed in her nose. Lucy clamped her fingers over its wick. It burned her and sputtered out.

Chapter 7

Lucy straightened from filing as the front door-bell chimed. She smoothed her long ponytail and rushed to the front, hoping to find James. Three days and he hadn't answered her texts or calls.

Her smile faltered. "Helen, how are you? James mentioned you'd caught a cold."

"The cough is still there. Doctors say it could take several more weeks to clear. I'm on more antibiotics than I can count." Helen huffed and laid her handbag on a small Queen Anne chest, leaning over the upright handles. "This getting old is not for the old."

"I'm so sorry."

"My grandson tells me you have my *Jane Eyre*. I'd like it back."

"I have his father's *Kidnapped* too." Lucy pulled them down. "Here they are. Did he tell you why I have them?"

"He did, but it's still mine and I love it. He had no right to take *Jane Eyre* without my permission."

"I'm sorry . . . I can reprice them. There are algorithms for calculating valuations. Or I can refund his money." Lucy dropped her hands to her sides. "I don't have any excuse to give you, Helen. Sid doesn't know, so please don't think he—"

"Hush." Helen held up a hand. "A little ink on the title page didn't affect my enjoyment of the book before I knew you were the author of that ink. Why should it bother me now?"

"It should," Lucy declared.

"Perhaps, but it doesn't. You and I aren't going to discuss this anymore." Helen waved the two books in her hands and gently placed them in her bag. With the same motion, she retrieved a slim silver case. "I have something else I want to discuss, but not now either." She took a deep breath. It rattled in her lungs and emerged on a soft cough.

Lucy watched as she slowly worked the case's small latch.

Helen's fingers fumbled a few times before the case popped open on a tiny spring. She handed Lucy a stiff white calling card. "My address is on the back. Will you come to my apartment tomorrow?"

"Of course." Lucy wondered if Helen was waiting to canvas the issue with Sid then.

"Don't look as if I'm going to eat you."

"Do you want me to bring Sid?" Lucy ventured.

"I want to talk to you and there's nothing you need to bring. Well, your laptop might help. Let's say ten o'clock?"

"Okay." Lucy fingered the embossed card. "Did James say anything . . ."

"This has nothing to do with James."

"Is he okay?" Lucy asked the question softly.

Helen's eyes softened. "He seems to be doing about as well as you are. But James doesn't bend easily, dear."

"I wouldn't want him to, really . . . Except in this case." Lucy rubbed her nose with the back of her hand. "Why do you want me to come tomorrow?"

"I have a favor to ask." Helen lifted the black Hermes bag and draped it over her arm. "And tomorrow is Wednesday. You said it was your favorite day, so it's the perfect day to discuss things."

Sid was twenty minutes late. But what an entrance! Lucy recognized him from his highly buffed cap-toed oxfords and his rich brown wool pant legs. And if his clothes hadn't provided enough clues, the bag of fabric remnants hanging from his wrist gave him away. The rest of him, however, was lost somewhere behind the largest bouquet of flowers she'd ever seen. She hurried across the floor to help.

"I'm simply speechless," Lucy simpered. "You shouldn't have."

"Cute. They're for Bitsy Milner. A final flourish to finish the house."

"You're late."

"I called her and told her to expect me at three o'clock. Gerald took longer to build this than he anticipated." He rested the broad crystal vase on the worktable. It was filled over two feet high with layers of tight roses, peonies, tulips, and other bright, strong flowers, artfully cloistered between and around paler, softer buds, dense and precise.

"There are over a hundred flowers in here and the vase is stunning. This must've cost a fortune."

"It's heavy enough."

"Thank goodness I didn't handle the order. I wouldn't have imagined anything like this."

Sid dropped into his desk chair and rolled back a few feet to see the flowers from a distance. "What would you have chosen?"

"I guess looser, wilder ones in softer tones. Like a garden all mixed together with greens and grasses, maybe in a silver vase."

"It sounds beautiful and just like you. That's the secret of design, you know, to listen and to look. You have to find what excites a person, brings her alive, and lets her feel safe and yet . . . exotic. It's easy to build a showpiece. Harder to create a home." He rolled himself toward her, dangling the bag from his fingers. "And here you go for your own home, the remnants from the Saltner job. There are some gorgeous ones in there. You'll need to show me your project soon."

"I will." Lucy smiled warmly. She knew Sid would appreciate her panels and understand them. "When it's finished, you'll be the first."

Sid studied her. "I've got another surprise for you too."

Lucy looked down at herself, following his line of sight. She was wearing black heels, buffed and polished. Black tights. Pale lavender velvet skirt, circa 1960s, but perfectly tailored and ending precisely midknee. Thin, black cashmere sweater, sleek and tucked in. The straightened blunt ends of her ever-present low ponytail lying over her shoulder. "What?"

"It's like the flowers. You've found what suits you. Four years ago, you interviewed in jeans, gray wool Converse, and a sweatshirt. Now I find a poised woman before me, dressed with the quality and understated elegance of an antique, and I know she's ready for this surprise. Ready for her first consulting trip."

"A trip?"

"Helen Carmichael called my cell about half an hour ago. She's planning a shopping excursion to London and needs a consultant." Sid squeezed her hand. "You're up."

"London? She was here this morning; I'm meeting her at her apartment tomorrow. She said nothing about a trip."

"She mentioned that. She wanted to clear it with me, as your boss, first."

"I don't know, Sid." Lucy took a step back and felt her hand reach up and circle her neck. "She's James's grandmother."

"What?" Sid's eyebrows shot up toward his forehead. "How could you not tell me this? Really, Lucy, you've been holding out on me."

"I did tell you; you've forgotten."

"Good thing, too, because now I get to enjoy it all over again." Sid rubbed his hands together. "This *is* getting interesting. Better than one of your novels, I think."

"Call her and tell her you can't spare me."

"Why? You and James are adorable."

"And he's not speaking to me. We broke up." Sid opened his mouth, but Lucy cut him off. "Please don't make me talk about it."

Sid watched her for a moment before replying. "What happened?"

Lucy gripped her shoulders tight. "Will you call her?"

Sid rolled away again and crossed his arms over his chest as well. Lucy knew he was considering the situation, considering her.

"Sid?"

"I wondered what was different. You've been

so happy and open. So very creative lately. Haven't you felt it?" He circled a finger as if drawing on her face. He rolled a few feet closer. "Is it more than James?"

"Why would you ask that?"

Sid flicked his head like he was trying to catch a fleeting thought or a burst of light. "I don't know . . . but this feels like mooore." He drew out the last word, dragging the *o* across forever.

"It's not just about James, it's a lot of stuff . . . It's me too." Lucy felt her eyes sting. She willed them to stay dry. "And I'm sorry."

"For what?"

Lucy wanted to tell Sid everything—about the vases and the books—but she knew she couldn't say another word. Not now. She didn't know where or how she could possibly begin, or what to say if she did. A small voice inside asked, *If Helen hasn't told Sid about the books, should I?* She simply lifted a shoulder and let it fall, hoping the defeated gesture would end Sid's questions.

Sid stood. "I won't make the call."

"But—"

"As strange a scenario as this is, it's here and it's yours. Time to step up, *mia cara ragazza*." At her frown, he raised a hand and continued. "You're a good worker, Lucy, and I love you, but you"—he spread his arms around the room— "need more than this right now. You need an adventure. Your father's family is British. Go visit the family manor. Experience something new."

"I don't need new. And my family—"

"Lucy, if anyone needs new, you need new." Sid hoisted the vase of flowers. "And that's the end of our discussion, because I'm officially running late. Will you please grab some packing material to help secure this in my car?"

Lucy grabbed a box and a handful of raffia stuffing and opened the alley door for Sid. "You'll never survive without me," she mumbled. "You should make the call."

He only chuckled.

Chapter 8

The crisp spring weather carried a strong wind that cut into Lucy's thin coat and smacked her hair across her face. She craned her neck to watch the clouds' shadows dance across the upward stretch of The Four Seasons Hotel and Residences. She could feel Sid's *You're up* as she pushed through the revolving door.

Standing in the lobby, she assessed the damage. She no longer embodied Sid's sense of "antique chic," as he'd dubbed it yesterday, but instead evoked comparisons to another Muppet. Dressed in a cream-colored shift dress and matching coat, Lucy deemed the red-mopped Beaker the most accurate. Her hair, smoothed by a straightening iron only hours before, puffed and curled around her at least three times its usual volume. She flattened it as best she could and pulled it into a ponytail as the elevator zoomed her upward.

Seconds later she stood on the thirty-sixth floor in a small hallway with few doors—denoting the sheer size of the units. The elevator closing behind her compelled her to step forward, shake out her coat once more, and ring the bell for number 3400.

James's grandmother, dressed in soft cream slacks and a periwinkle-blue cardigan, answered immediately.

"You're here." She stepped back, inviting Lucy inside. "Come in."

From the entry Lucy could see a full window overlooking Lake Michigan blocks away. "Your view is exquisite." Lucy felt her breath release. She glanced to a table on her left. "These flowers . . . I was describing something very similar to Sid yesterday." She reached out to touch a fully bloomed peony amid a loose arrangement of grasses and irises. "Who arranges your flowers?"

"I do. I find it relaxing." Helen held up her right hand. A Band-Aid wrapped her pointer finger. "One of the roses bit me yesterday." Her hand dipped toward the living room. "Come sit. Your dress and coat are lovely, by the way. I used to own something like them. Escada? Early 1980s?"

"I bought them at Kate's Closet on Ontario. Who knows, they might have been yours?"

"If they were, I never carried them so well."

Lucy followed Helen in where the view spread farther east and south, encompassing Chicago's Magnificent Mile. Art covered the room's interior walls, salon style, and reached two floors high.

"The frames. The paintings. They're from so many periods. They don't even blend, but they work." Lucy heard her thoughts drift aloud.

Helen laughed lightly. "There's something I find exciting about the incongruence." Her eyes swept the wall. "I chose them all and I've never regretted it, even that blood-red frame high on your left."

"Is that a Picasso?"

"My husband, Charles, gave me that to celebrate our thirtieth wedding anniversary. It's a favorite of mine. Would you like to see them with the shades raised?"

"Please."

Helen pushed a button and light amber shades drew up simultaneously. Sunlight flooded the room, electrifying the impressionist paintings, deepening the modernist, and warming the metal statuary. She gestured to the sofa. "Please sit."

"Sid told me this was a trip to London."

"It is." Helen tilted her head. "And I thought you'd be more excited about it. Your father is British, and then there are also your reading interests."

"All that is true." Lucy spoke the words slowly as she laid a few of Sid's antiques and silver books on the coffee table. "But I can't imagine James will find this comfortable and I—"

"It's a buying trip, Lucy, if that clarifies things, which is why I didn't mention it yesterday. It was proper to talk to Sid first. He assures me you are amply capable and qualified to assist me."

"I see." Lucy let the words drift up, begging for the rest of the story.

Helen complied with a quick smile. "While all that is true, there's more . . ." Her eyes lit with secret excitement. "I don't have many, if any, adventures left within me and I want this one. It feels right, and you need to be there." She sat back on the small sofa and crossed her ankles. "Meeting you has stirred up so many memories, some wonderful, some I'd rather have left buried, but they're out now and they need to be dealt with. They've reminded me of someone I once was and I'd like to meet her again before I die. She's worth finding again, Lucy, and I can't do that here and I can't do that with my family, not yet."

"I don't understand."

Helen pulled a gold pocket watch from the side table and held it out to Lucy. "Let's start with this."

Lucy reached across and took the watch. She was surprised by its weight. The watch filled her entire palm and dropped her hand. Its outside case was scrolled with delicate filigree, the name *Parrish* laced in the lattice lines across the case. She opened it. The catch was firm and solid. Inside there was a clean face, a minute repeater dial, and the initials *AGP, EDP,* and *TMP* engraved on the case's interior.

"This is a Patek Philippe. Probably early 1900s. Sid had me do some research on these for a client's study last year . . . This must be worth a fortune."

"It's from the 1880s, and it is. But it's not mine and it's time I returned it." Helen nodded to the watch. "I found out a few days ago that it belongs to the Parrish family in London. I have the address and they are expecting me a week from Saturday."

"When were you planning to fly over?"

"*We* are flying over a week from Friday. Can you make all the arrangements so quickly?"

Lucy opened her mouth to ask another question but stopped at the sound of soft footsteps.

It took only a moment before they became louder across the parquet floor and Helen noticed them as well. She whispered to Lucy, "Hold that in your lap, dear."

Lucy folded the watch in her dress's skirt, clasping her hands above it, as James's father entered the room. She slid the watch onto the love seat, covering it with her handbag as she stood.

"Lucy?" James's father, Charlie, was a man of

medium height, medium build, and medium gray. Lucy found his stable sameness very comforting. He was also kind. Though at that moment, he stared at his mother with a single brow raised in annoyance.

"I didn't know you were coming by today." Helen's voice drifted up in question as she turned her cheek for a kiss.

"I wasn't planning to, but you mentioned 'a trip' to Leslie last night. And Lucy's here?" He flickered her a glance, cooler than usual, but considering all James had told him, not as icy as Lucy anticipated. "Are you well?"

"I'm fine. Thank you." Lucy sat again.

"I've hired Lucy for some silver and antiques consulting. We're headed to London next week." Helen pointed to Sid's books, stacked in proof.

"London? That's a long way to shop. What can't Lucy procure from here?" Charlie flicked his head back and forth between them.

"The experience."

"Mother."

"I need this." Helen dipped her hand to the chair next to her. Charlie sat on its edge as if eager to leave or argue. "And I'm very excited about it. I thought I might get your girls each silver flat-ware for wedding gifts."

"They aren't engaged."

"They will be and we both know I won't be around," Helen countered.

"Mother."

Lucy stifled a laugh. James had sounded just like his father when he said "Grams." Each time the intonation had changed—one word embodying reprimand, love, fear, exasperation, and adoration.

"Then be comforted that I'm crossing the ocean by plane and not by funeral pyre." Helen's voice shot out staccato.

"That's not remotely humorous." Charlie shifted in the deep-purple velvet chair. "Has Dr. Klein said you're well enough? You still have your cough and your count isn't high enough. You're vulnerable to infections and you'll be back in treatment soon."

Charlie leaned forward and continued. "I get the distinct impression you're keeping something from me." He studied his mother's inscrutable expression. "No?" He turned to Lucy, who, with one hand resting atop her handbag, minutely widened her eyes. "You're in the dark too?" he asked before turning back to Helen. "Mother?"

"I need this, Charlie. Please. Dr. Klein has assured me there is nothing I can do to harm myself."

"But why so hasty? Get stronger. Leslie and I can take you this summer."

"I can't wait."

"You can't . . ." Charlie let the words linger. Helen sat mute so he addressed Lucy. "This may not be as simple as she's perhaps implied, Lucy.

Has she briefed you on her medications? Do you have medical experience should something happen? Do you understand how vulnerable she is?"

Lucy felt her eyes widen farther.

"That's not fair. Lucy isn't responsible for any of that." Helen's voice arched high. "You're overreacting."

Charlie rested his hands on his knees, palms up. "I don't think I am. If you're traveling with her, she's responsible. What do you want me to do? You're acting strangely, you make cryptic statements, and you're tired, worn-out tired. You're sick and we both know it. Something else is driving this."

"Charles." Helen's tone dropped and darkened.

Charlie flipped his hands from palms up to palms down and slapped his knees. "This is getting us nowhere. I'll stop pushing. For now."

"Thank you." Helen reached out and laid her hand on top of one of his. "We'll leave next Thursday and be gone only two weeks. Then I'll go back to being just what I always was."

"Hmm . . ." Charlie swung his head as if debating whether to engage further or give up. He gave his mother's hand a squeeze and stood to face Lucy. "Be sure to forward me the itinerary. This one won't think of it."

Helen grabbed at his hand and Lucy caught a flash of raw vulnerability cloud her eyes. "We'll talk as soon as I get back."

Charlie held both her hands. "I'd like that." He turned back to Lucy. "If I don't see you again, Lucy, good-bye."

Completely flustered, Lucy managed a nod.

Charlie leaned down and kissed his mother's cheek. "Call if you're coming to brunch on Sunday." He straightened and walked to the door. "Good-bye, Mother."

"Tell Leslie I'll be there," Helen called after him. At the front door's click, she huffed. "He's going to press at brunch." Her attempt at a sharp tone faltered within a tremulous smile.

"Is everything okay?"

"No . . . It's not." Helen shimmied her shoulders as if redirecting her course. "We have planning to do. Lucy?"

Lucy's mind spun within the currents. She grabbed for the most stable ground she could find. "We are leaving next Thursday and returning this." Lucy held up the watch, swinging it on its thin gold chain.

"Ah . . . To a Mr. Edward Parrish. On Peel Street. What else shall we see?"

Lucy peeked at the watch, quickly wondering if she could or should ask more questions. She laid it down. There would be time. "Let's start with flights and where you'd like to stay. Then, I guess, what you hope to purchase. Silver for Molly and Sophie?"

"You arrange the flights. Dukes Hotel. And yes,

two sets of flatware are now on our shopping list. What do you suggest?"

Lucy tapped the books. "I did some research last night and think the best place will be the London Silver Vaults."

"I also remember stores at the top of Portobello Road. Are those any good? I'd love to see Portobello Market on a Saturday again."

"I'll mark it down." Lucy pulled out her laptop and started tapping out notes.

"We'll need to find a few more gifts too. I want Sid pleased with his commission, so look into some of the antiques dealers in Notting Hill. I seem to remember a few I enjoyed there."

"I will, but don't feel any pressure to buy on Sid's account. He's not like that."

"True, but he's a businessman and he's giving you, and me, this time. I want to make it worth his while." Helen nestled back in the love seat. "Lucy, I was serious about what I said to Charlie; I want us to have an experience. Capital *E*. This is your trip too; let's have some fun. What do you want to see?"

"Anything you select will be fine . . . Why me, if this isn't exclusively for shopping?"

"We'll get to that." Helen drew out the words as if savoring her secret. "Let's simply plan right now. We have our purchases covered; the rocks are in place. Let's fill the rest of our jar with the gems."

Lucy decided to join in the fun. "I vote Charing Cross Road and anything that involves Dickens."

"And Bloomsbury."

"A literary tour?" Lucy laughed. "Is the British Library too touristy and mundane for you?"

"Seeing the largest library in the world is never mundane and the original *Jane Eyre* is there, with her notes. I saw it once and it's special. You'll enjoy that."

Lucy's fingers flew across the keys. "Here's a Dickens Museum that could be fun, and the George Inn. It says here that Dickens and Shakespeare frequented it, though I'm guessing not together . . . But, again, all this may be too basic for what you're thinking."

"This trip is for both of us. Nothing is too basic."

Lucy worked the keys for the next few moments. "There's a museum and tour for Sherlock Holmes, and a real 221b Baker Street. Well, not true, it says the museum is located between 237 and 241 Baker Street. But still . . ."

"I don't know how many walking tours I'll manage, but you may walk them all if you wish."

Lucy's hands stilled. "I'm sorry. This is your trip."

"Our trip. And I want to go to Haworth for a few days too."

"Now you're just playing with me."

Helen laughed. "No, I want to go to Haworth.

Charles and I spent some wonderful vacations in the countryside, Bath, the Cotswolds . . . I've never been to Haworth and after enjoying *Jane Eyre* so much, I'd like that. It isn't too far."

Lucy felt her heart leap and then, just as rapidly, it constricted. James's father was right. Something felt amiss and Lucy needed answers. "Helen?"

Helen's eyes found hers and they seemed to sharpen from sky to steel.

Lucy pressed forward. "I need to know why. I'm sorry to press, but you have James and two grand-daughters, a son, and probably lots more family. And James did break up with me. He's hurt. And this trip . . ."

"It has to be you, Lucy, for many reasons." Helen pointed to the pocket watch. "For starters, you're now the only other person in almost sixty-five years to see that watch, and I can't yet explain it to anybody else."

"But you can to me?"

"Yes. And I suppose I should begin . . ."

Chapter 9

Helen reached for the watch, holding it tightly in her hands. "This watch and the time it signifies have been buried for so long . . . I stole it from a young man I desperately loved." Helen lifted her shoulders, dropped them again. "I wanted to force his hand and make him chase after me, but he didn't. Now it's time to let go. Of all of it."

Lucy opened her mouth to ask a question. Then closed it.

"He wasn't my husband. This was before I met Charles, and I should say that I dearly loved Charles. That's not what this is about. I didn't make a wrong choice."

"Of course."

"It doesn't feel that clear . . . I can't say I was so sure myself until I met you." Helen's gaze trailed across the paintings. "I'm not doing this well." Lucy watched her thread the chain through her fingers as the seconds ticked by. She finally turned back to Lucy with a blue steel focus. "I stole this from Oliver Alling."

"That's . . . That was my grandfather."

"I met your grandfather the summer after I graduated college right here on Michigan Avenue."

"How? He . . . He lived in London. With my grandmother."

Helen nodded. "I'm sure that's true, but I met him in '51. You said he moved to London in '57, and met and married your grandmother then."

"He did. He went over with some friends, but I know all the stories and . . ." Lucy stopped and glanced down to her computer, now unsure of all her dad had told her. His stories had glided through the years with the glow of a fairy tale.

The hint that they were, in fact, untrue made sense. But the truth hurt. She flexed her fingers across her keyboard then slowly shut the laptop. She waited.

"I'm not stealing your history from you, Lucy. I'm sharing a little of my own . . . As I said, I met Oliver the summer after college. I took a job at a small jewelry store down in the five hundred block here. I wanted something different, exciting, and that's about as adventurous as I got. A few of my more daring friends went to New York, but Daddy wanted me married and on the North Shore. He gave in, a little, but only if I stayed in Chicago. So I got a studio apartment, a few pots and pans, and I was free. Well, the jeweler was—"

"My grandfather?" Lucy interjected.

"No. He was a friend of my father's so it wasn't quite as daring as I'd hoped. I suspect there were daily reports concerning my comings and goings. But one day, yes, your grandfather walked in the door. He was only a few years older than I was and had so much presence. He seemed to know what he was about and he had the most striking green eyes. Your eyes." She waggled a finger at Lucy. "He sold jewelry to the shops—not jewelry so much as antique watches, lockets, estate pieces. He specialized in English, but sold a few European pieces as well. Sometimes he'd bring in table pieces like silver snuffboxes and service sets. Beautiful stuff. Mr. Jones started purchasing from him after that visit."

Lucy felt the blood drain from her face. "We're not . . . We're not related, are we?"

"Not at all. No. Oh . . ." Helen's eyes widened. "We are not related in any way." She quirked a half-smile. "And as I said, I'm messing up the entire story. This is the first time I've talked about Ollie in over sixty years. It doesn't follow a structure in my head."

"He sold jewelry to Mr. Jones."

"Yes, and he was so handsome and had an energy about him, kind of a James Dean meets that young man today, you know the one . . . Oh . . . It doesn't matter. I flirted with him the second he stepped in the store and he was no better. We were inseparable from that day . . . until we weren't. He took me to nightclubs, dancing, on picnics and motorcycle rides. We even stayed on Oak Street Beach one night so we could catch the sunrise, and he had a Ducati 60 . . . I loved that . . ."

Helen's voice drifted off and then returned abruptly. "I digress. Then fall came. I remember that smell in the air. It's an ending smell to me, maybe has been since that night. You see, I wanted to surprise Ollie at his workshop. I hadn't done that before, but I wanted to be a part of his world, his whole world. He worked out of a garage due west of here. Anyway, as I walked in, I heard him negotiating prices with another man and I learned that everything was stolen. Everything he sold was stolen and there was no mistake."

"Did he know that?"

"He did. That was how he ran things. He bought inventory cheap and without questions, fixed it all up, and sold it to high-end stores all over Chicago. For some things, he could even provide paperwork. Paperwork he'd constructed. And everything worked and was beautifully refurbished. He had the most amazing hands and could fix anything."

"Where'd he get it all?" Lucy's voice came out tight.

"England, the Continent—after World War II, there was stuff around, unclaimed, lost, stolen. Life was more chaotic over there. Jewelry, books, art, you name it and you could buy it, with little care or concern about the original owners. But as wild as I thought I was, I was still . . . It turned my stomach and we fought. I threatened to tell Mr. Jones. Later I realized I only wanted a reaction from him. I wanted him to choose me." Helen pressed a hand into her chest. "You see, I had chosen him."

"What happened?"

"He threw me out." Helen tapped the watch. "I stole this on my way out the door. I wanted to hurt him and knew it had value. I also thought he'd come after it—and that meant he'd come after me."

"But he didn't." Lucy's tone was varnished in relief.

"No, and my father got wind of my goings-on and sent me to graduate school. I took a course in teaching and when I came home for Christmas break, I took the watch to Ollie's workshop. He wasn't there. It wasn't there . . . Perhaps he believed my threat and left Chicago, eventually finding his way to England. I don't know, because I didn't search any further. I hid the watch and met Charles at a family party that same Christmas. We married six months later."

Helen pressed her hand over her mouth then lowered it. "I loved my husband very much, Lucy, but fear the rest of my family might doubt that if they knew."

"That's silly. You were married, what, almost sixty years? How could they?"

"I was in love with another for a very long time. And yet, in the end, our marriage was good." Helen straightened. "But it's a horrid revelation, Lucy, to know you've withheld love—something so elemental, so vital, from someone. I did to Charles what Ollie did to me. He kept enough back to walk away, and for years I approached my marriage the same way. When I saw you, everything turned full circle. That's when I dug out the watch, hired an investigator, and found the Parrish family. Now I need to go back, all the way back, to go forward. I need that now . . ." Helen's voice drifted away.

Lucy swiped at her long bangs. She kept her eyes trained on her lap.

After a long moment she looked up at Helen. "You're sure it was my grandfather?"

"Your last name. And with your eyes, my dear, there's no question."

Lucy conceded the point with a wry smile. "Okay, but . . ." She dropped her hands to her sides. "I don't even know what to ask."

"I'm not going anywhere. Well, to London, and you're going with me. There will be time and I'll answer all your questions." Helen stood and pulled her shoulders back, stretching. "Why don't we take a break? Memories can be exhausting."

Lucy only nodded.

"Would you like to see the rest of the apartment? I also made sandwiches." Without waiting, Helen stood and crossed through the hallway. She pushed a swinging door into a small kitchen with a porcelain farmer's sink, white marble counters, and a countertop eating area. "I eat here mostly, watching *Jeopardy!* Sid updated it; I think he knew I needed a smaller space for meals."

"I sit at my counter watching *Jeopardy!* too," Lucy replied, not pleased with the likeness.

Helen proceeded down another short hallway,

featuring black-and-white landscape photo-graphs, to her bedroom.

Lucy stopped in the doorway. "This is Sid."

"You know his work well." Helen walked deeper into the room. "It's the textures I love and it's not a silly room. Right after Charles died, I needed something new, different, and Sid understood that. But if he'd gone too far . . . Well, I think it would have felt like I was kicking Charles out. These purples and greens, they're different from what we enjoyed together, but not too much so."

Lucy ran her fingers over the velvet-relief fabric on the armchair. Tufts of velvet set in a mesh that blended rough with smooth. "He's used six different fabrics in here, but you don't notice how many unless you count. They're seamless."

"There's another room you must see."

When they entered the next room, light danced across a bedroom with walls covered in pale pink silk, shot through with threads of gold and white. Twin beds with high headboards of the same fabric, with pale-gold trim scalloped along the wooden edge, stood side by side. Deep yellows covered small chairs, moss green and gold covered a tiny bench, and on the far wall hung a delicate but large antique curio cabinet filled with at least a hundred small figurines.

"Hey—Beatrix Potter," Lucy whispered, striding across the room.

"Those figurines were mine as a girl. My granddaughters loved them as children and I can't seem to part with them. Do you know the stories?"

"My father used to read them to me. I think he understood these animals more than people. That's Peter Rabbit and Benjamin Bunny with the bag over his head . . . and there's Jemima Puddle Duck and Squirrel Nutkin. Oh . . . Miss Tiggy-Winkle. She was my favorite." Lucy spun around. "Bowness-on-Windermere."

"What?"

"Bowness-on-Windermere!" Lucy shouted the name. She checked herself and continued more calmly. "I looked it up a few weeks ago, for something else, but it has a Beatrix Potter museum. It's in the Lake District, due west of Yorkshire, so we'll be almost there. I wondered . . ." She dropped her voice to a whisper. "This is a sign."

She addressed Helen again. "You said you wanted to go back to go forward. These are from your childhood . . . Would you like to visit there? Add it to our trip after Haworth? We could steal a day from London and one from Haworth and have two up there without feeling rushed. It's not only Beatrix Potter—it's Wordsworth and Austen and . . . What?"

Helen raised her hands. "You're sweet, but I don't think I need to go back that far." She flipped off the light and stepped into the hallway, calling over her shoulder, "London will do for me, and then let's add that little romp in Haworth. I have a feeling I'll need to get back after that. There will be much to do here."

Chapter 10

Sid called once that afternoon to check in, but didn't relent. Instead he listed several more books for Lucy to take home and cited numerous websites for her to peruse. "You can't go to London unprepared. Get cracking, *mio piccolo viaggiatore*."

"I can't even guess that one," she replied through clenched teeth.

"My little traveler."

Still grumbling over the Italian, Lucy unlocked the door to her apartment and shouldered her way in, balancing Sid's books on English antiques and silver, her satchel, and yet another remnant bag. She pulled off her boots, curled her toes against the cold wood floor, and opened her computer to fill the apartment with an appropriate rich and mournful melody.

"Of course you're dead." She yanked wilted flowers from a tomato sauce jar and shoved them in the trash. She then walked to the window and sank in front of her remnants bin, glancing at the leather armchair. "What do I do with you?" she whispered. She reached into the bin—so many gorgeous fabrics: Fortuny silks with reds, blues, and golds, embroidered and rich in texture; velvets that crushed under her fingers; chintzes with bright English flowers and that almost waxy finish that made them look alive; toiles with pastoral scenes that evoked the serenity of picnics in France, perhaps à la *Scarlet Pimpernel*; and plaids, stripes, polka dots, and countless other basics that added variety and provided the backdrops for so many of Sid's spectacular creations. None of them quite right, not yet.

She searched for a gold and yellow Scalamandre that she'd saved and put it beside a new emerald silk-wool blend peeking from inside the bag. *Perfect.* Side by side they reminded her of the MacMillan vase, sitting atop the George III chest. *Hope.* She added the pair to her second drapery panel.

Her phone rang.

"You're going on a trip with Grams?"

No hello? "James?"

"You have to ask?"

Lucy pushed the fabrics away. "No. I mean yes; I guess I am."

"How? How is that possible?"

"I don't know. She called Sid and no one is giving me a choice." Lucy thought of Helen's story, her grandfather . . . "What did she tell you?"

"That this trip is important to her, that I'm not

to cause problems, and that I'm not to question you." He rattled off his list.

Lucy smiled. "So you're calling me, why?"

"Lucy."

There it was again. One word, one name, filled with a world of emotions. This time she read pain, reluctance, annoyance, and disillusionment—a full paint deck of sad colors. Lucy released a slow, measured breath. "She obviously knows we broke up, that this is beyond awkward, and still she insists I join her. Sid's on board and . . . What do you want me to do?"

"Refuse to go."

Lucy leaned back against the wall and studied her apartment. The light over the mantel pointed right at her new bookshelves, James's bookshelves. Other than that, it was dark. It was an empty, dark apartment, and somehow it now struck her as piteous.

Her eyes trailed the shelves, catching on book titles: *Jane Eyre*, *Bleak House*, *Tess of the d'Urbervilles*, *Moll Flanders*, *Frog and Toad* . . . What had Helen said? *I need to go back, all the way back, to go forward.* And what had Sid said? Lucy reached for the moment, in the gallery, when she'd pleaded for him to make the call and he had refused. *It's the next step.*

She turned back to the books . . . *Swallows and Amazons* . . . Beatrix Potter . . . She inhaled deep and pursed her lips to release it slow, like an athlete preparing for a race. *Bowness-on-Windermere.* She could do it too . . . *Go back to go forward.*

"Lucy?"

"I won't refuse, James. She hired me and it's my job."

"This isn't what's best for her, Lucy. She's sick. She has cancer."

Lucy felt her voice come out calm. "I'm sorry. I know that and I know you're worried about her. You all are. But I also know this, James—with or without me, she's going to London."

"And Haworth?"

"She wants a visit to the countryside like many trips she took with your grandfather."

"She mentioned that you suggested the Lake District."

"I did." Lucy narrowed her eyes. "We're right near there in Yorkshire and I think she'd love it. She's revisiting favorites, and you've seen her curio cabinet. Beatrix Potter has been important in her life."

"She shouldn't be going on this trip at all. You shouldn't be going."

"I agree, and yet here we are." Lucy closed her eyes. "James? What do you want from me?"

"Nothing." He paused and she wondered what he was thinking, what he'd say next. He simply added, "I'll take it up with Grams again. Good-bye, Lucy."

"Hey—" The line went dead.

Lucy dropped to the floor. After a few minutes of watching car headlights bounce off the windowpanes, she reached for another fabric—a black chenille. Placed against the gold and yellow, it tempered it, transformed it, and almost overpowered it. It worked perfectly.

Saturday yawned before Lucy. She had gotten so used to spending them with James that she couldn't think of anything to do. There were friends she could call, errands she could run, movies she could see, but nothing tempted her. Nothing. She held her coffee in both hands and stared at her glass coffee table top, resting back again on her books.

After her call with James and the "good-bye" that was too final to misinterpret, she'd removed the books from the shelves and reconstructed her book table. She had a feeling that the bookcases needed to be ready to go whenever he demanded their return. Or maybe that was her responsibility. But returning the shelves and chair rang their relationship's death knell and she couldn't do it. The shelves sat stark and bare. Lucy looked around. *Just like everything else.*

She tilted her head to examine the books that formed the table legs. She'd constructed them perfectly. One leg, childhood favorites. Those her dad had read aloud: *Alice's Adventures in*

Wonderland, a compilation of Beatrix Potter's best, *Little Women*, *The Wonderful Wizard of Oz*, *Anne of Green Gables*, *The Complete Grimm's Fairy Tales*. Her eyes roamed to another leg, this one more grounded in reality, but not quite touching it: *The Count of Monte Cristo*, Shakespeare's plays, *Great Expectations*. Hidden identities. Reversals of fortune. James had recognized that. And the third leg . . . the Brontë sisters, five Austen novels, *Tess of the d'Urbervilles*, *North and South*, plus a few Hardy and Eliot, and a small, squished copy of *Wives and Daughters*, wedged in last to make it level. Books her father had sent for birthdays or others she'd selected on her own. How much of *her* was stacked in that table and squished under the glass?

Lucy tapped her phone to make a call and again to disconnect it. She curled up in her armchair and tucked her legs under her, small and tight, and tapped it once more.

"Did you just call here?" Her mother's voice sounded far away. She was talking through her earpiece.

"I did. Are you working?"

"Cleaning the kitchen. One person and I'm always cleaning the kitchen." She laughed and Lucy heard dishes clink. "How are you?"

"I'm going to England, Mom." Lucy waited. No dishes. No water. Silence.

"Not to find him?" A question, not a statement.

Lucy sighed. "For work, to London, but he's there. How can I get so close and not see him? That'd be ridiculous."

"I love your logic, but it's flawed. He was hours away when you found the Joliet, Illinois, stamp."

"Mom."

"It's a good reminder, Lucy. Statesville Correctional Facility was fairly close and you didn't seek him out then." The silence stretched before she continued. "He ran cons for a living, Lucy. That's not a good profession. What makes you think he's changed?"

"I'm not saying he has."

"But that's what you're hoping, isn't it? And somehow I doubt Sid has antique dealers or fabric sources in the Lake District."

"No . . . The trip is a literary tour too—I'm in charge of that part, and that area is hugely significant for the client."

No reply.

"It is." Lucy pressed her lips together, annoyed with how high and pitchy her voice had emerged.

"And you made sure it was one of the stops." A statement, not a question.

"What do you want me to say? I almost didn't tell you."

"Don't get upset with me, Lucy." Her mom's words were soft and coaxing. "I don't want to see you disappointed or hurt, and I'm sad that it sounds like you're manipulating things to bring this about. You are so like him at times . . ."

"You say that and it's never good. I haven't manipulated anything. It's not even on the itinerary."

"Yet."

"That's not . . . I just want to see him. How can that be so wrong?"

"I get that, sweetheart, and it's not wrong. But how you go about it might be and, besides, you can't let him affect you like that—not anymore. Make your own choices. Good or bad, they matter. They affect others."

"Believe me, I know." Lucy bit her lip, unwilling to discuss James. She reached for a distraction. "How much do you know about Dad's family? Dad's dad?"

"Very little. He died when you were a baby and we only met once. I know nothing about his mother. She was the one who was English. Why?"

Lucy debated telling the story. It might help in sorting it out. On the flip side, she knew her mom's clear, logical brain would refuse to drop down the rabbit hole with her. She would instead strongly suggest Lucy plug it. "No reason. I just wondered."

"Are you going to tell me what's really going on here?"

"I wish I knew." Lucy took a sip of coffee and

let the moment linger. When her mom stayed silent, she ventured further. "I'm stuck, Mom. I can't explain how or why, but I feel it. And if I could meet him, it'd answer so many questions and I could push through. I know I could. And this trip . . . What if it's a sign? I can't pass this up. Can't you understand that?"

"I understand what you're saying, but I'm not sure it works like that. But maybe . . ." Her mom's voice became clearer. She'd removed her earpiece. "Maybe I've done this wrong too and it works just as you hope. After all, if I knew the answer, I'd give it to you and we wouldn't be having this conversation, right?" She gave a soft, reassuring chuckle.

"Right. It's all your fault." Lucy tried to laugh.

"So Bowness-on-Windermere, huh? Are you sure?"

"That's what the postmark says, and I'm sure," Lucy announced with more conviction than she felt.

"How are you going to get there?"

"Mom . . ." Lucy closed her eyes. She could see her mother's face, hazel eyes narrowing at her as they had every time she'd caught her young daughter, her teenager, or her adult daughter in a lie or in an exaggeration or even telling a good story that wasn't quite true . . .

"It's a legitimate question, Lucy."

Lucy was tired of lying, making excuses,

backing out of fibs, or rewriting stories she'd already told. She was tired—so she gave the most honest answer she could. "It's not one I'm prepared to answer."

Lucy replayed her mother's words the entire weekend. What had felt serendipitous, even divinely ordained, now felt tainted and coerced—and it hadn't even been accomplished yet. She turned it over and over until the only answer she could find was to see it through. She unlocked the gallery's front door and noted the alarm's absence.

"Sid?" Lucy called loudly, glancing briefly at the antique standing mirror. *Ugh* . . . She slapped her cheeks, noting that the dark circles under her eyes seemed her most colorful and defining feature.

"Back here."

She hurried into the back room. "You're so early today."

"I thought you'd be busy planning and packing so I came in. See? I'm adaptable and will survive two short weeks."

"I didn't doubt it." Lucy stepped to the worktable where Sid sat hunched over a sketch. "What are you working on?"

"Designing a dressing room. It's right outside a full walk-in closet so it's more sanctuary than storage, but I can't get a feel for it. My concepts are too opulent for what I sense she wants and she isn't quite sure herself."

Lucy leaned over. The room was colored in pinks and greens with Baroque-style heavy hanging mirrors. "What's she like?"

"Good question. Claire Longreen is in her midforties, but her style is older. She volunteers at the library and her church, but never out front. She gives anonymously and fears she'll be irrelevant to her children someday." Sid looked up from his drawing. "She's reserved, but not insecure, and she's got a strength about her that's very appealing, especially because she's completely oblivious to it."

Lucy smiled. She was used to hearing Sid talk about his clients in such terms. He listened to them, searched for their essence, and created spaces that he believed could surprise and delight them because they simply *were* them. She laid a hand on his back; the physical connection soothed her heart. Sid had a good heart.

"What about covering the walls and even the doors in fabric? Flawlessly clean and understated, but beautiful, warmly tactile. Something pale, like a pink or lavender silk with hints of either gold or silver. Lavender and silver, I say."

Sid's head snapped back. "Nothing else. No hardware, no mirrors. Instead mount everything inside panels. Simple, elegant, and yet so sumptuous. Where'd you get the idea?"

"She doesn't sound like someone who'd want mirrors as a focal point, but they are necessary for a dressing room. And the lavender will be better—carries more gravitas than pink. You did something similar at Helen Carmichael's. Her guest room? But she needed the frivolity of the pink."

"I'd forgotten that. That room was such a treat. But look at you, taking it further and adapting it." He scraped the green pencil against his chin. "You've got an eye for this, Lucy. An inner eye if you'd trust it more." Sid flipped the page on his sketch pad and started anew.

Lucy tried to savor the compliment, but couldn't. While Sid worked on the Longreen home, she tackled the list of appointments and scheduling for London. She recorded the locations and hours of bookshops, antique stores, literary sites, tourist traps—anything and everything they might want to see—in London and Haworth.

She also canvassed all the necessary details for the Lake District, telling herself again and again that the addition was valid, it held personal and literary value for Helen, and it was best to be prepared.

Lucy secured the tickets and hotels then set to compiling the itinerary for Helen's son. Sid came and went and at some point dropped a sandwich on the corner of her desk.

"Sid?" Lucy crumpled the sandwich wrapper as

she reviewed the gallery business that she was leaving behind. She waited until he emerged from another sketch. "Can you handle all the sourcing while I'm gone? I don't want anything dropped with the time changes and I won't be able to stay on top of everything here."

He picked up another pencil. "I know that, but things will still get dropped. I don't have your touch or efficiency, but we'll survive."

Efficiency. Disdain curled the side of Lucy's mouth. "That's one word for it," she mumbled and leaned back in her chair. "'Go back to go forward'... A clean slate."

"Hmm...?" Sid didn't lift his head from his drawing.

Lucy called back, "Nothing. Thanks for handling all that." She tossed the sandwich wrapper into the bin. "And thanks for lunch."

"Hmm...?" Sid was deep within the Longreen home.

Chapter 11

Friday arrived more quickly than Lucy expected, especially considering she hadn't slept for the three nights leading to it. There had been no calls to make, little cleaning to do, and few things she needed to pack, but still, sleep had remained elusive.

So, wide awake, she had read. And rather than turning to her present favorites, she opened the pages of stories from her childhood: *The Tale of Ginger and Pickles*, *The Tale of Mrs. Tiggy-Winkle*, and, of course, *The Tale of Peter Rabbit* among other Potter stories; poetry by Wordsworth and Coleridge; and Ransome's *Swallows and Amazons*. All Lake District writers. She felt them drawing her closer and closer to her father and the latest Birthday Book buried in her suitcase.

She hadn't read it; she hadn't opened it. Part of her hated each book that arrived, with no note or message and probably sent book rate to save money, while another part, equally powerful, cherished each and eagerly awaited its arrival. That part she hated more. She climbed out of bed and slid the book free, rubbing her fingers across the envelope's postmark. *Bowness-on-Windermere.*

At six o'clock in the morning Lucy found herself dressed and stiff and nervous, standing in Helen's lobby. The bellman helped pull her rollerboard through the revolving door.

"Mrs. Carmichael's grandson is collecting her. He's taking you both to the airport." The door-man laid down the phone.

"Thank you." Lucy paced the small room, her feet wearing out the rug beneath her. She couldn't decide if it was anticipation over the trip or the certainty of seeing James that sent her pulse racing.

"You'll get dizzy."

She stilled at James's voice. He stood inches from her, looking down. She stepped back and caught her heel on the edge of the rug.

"Whoa." He steadied her by the elbow then dropped his hand again.

"I'm nervous." She captured his eyes then decided it was easier not to look there. "What are you doing here?" She tried to stop, but couldn't help herself and escalated the hurt swirling between them. "Still trying to convince her not to go?"

"Nothing I said had any effect." He looked down at her, no smile—no expression at all. "You could've helped."

Lucy felt her eyes flash in search of an answer or a retort, but she then noticed Helen exit the elevator, and relented.

Helen turned from the doorman and faced her. She stilled, her eyes flickering between Lucy and James. She crossed the lobby. "Are you two still at odds? Really, James."

James opened his mouth to speak, but Helen cut him off. "I said I'm not getting involved and I'm sorry I commented." She pressed her lips together to prove her point then parted them again. "Ask Ted for your car, dear, and we'll be on our way."

Once settled in James's car, Lucy found herself sitting directly behind him and able to catch glimpses of his eyes in the rearview mirror.

Rather than give in to the temptation to keep looking at him, she studiously observed Chicago slip by as they headed west. She also labored to block out the conversation in the front seat.

Yet as they approached the terminal, she couldn't avoid it. Helen reached over and squeezed James's hand. "I love you." The words came out low and soft. Lucy couldn't identify the layers beneath them, but they existed.

"I love you too, Grams."

"People aren't always what they appear, James. The gift is accepting them as who they are, not who we want them to be."

"Grams?"

Is she talking about me? Lucy missed Helen's reply as she shifted in her seat. The conversation ended as James pulled up to the terminal, and Lucy got out of the car, eager to create distance. But as she opened the trunk for the bags, she found herself lightly pushed aside.

James reached in. "You don't need to haul these."

"Thank you."

He didn't reply. Instead he set down the bags and then pulled his grandmother in for a last hug. He said softly to her, "Call me if you need anything."

"Don't fret. I wouldn't dream of bothering you at work."

"All the partners are in Hawaii. Disturb me all you want."

Lucy moved forward, but James avoided her, climbed back in his car, and drove away.

Lucy peeked at Helen. Her head listed to the side and her eyes were closed. The flight attendant removed the china bowl of warm nuts and pulled out Lucy's table. She then laid a dinner tray in front of her, complete with salad, bread, Chicken Piccata, and real silverware. Lucy stared at it until the flight attendant tapped her shoulder.

"Should we let her sleep?" She gestured to Helen.

"I'm not sure. She did order, so she must expect to eat." Lucy lightly laid her hand on Helen's arm.

Helen whispered, "I'm awake."

"Dinner's here if you're ready."

The attendant leaned over Lucy to help pull out Helen's lap table and lay down her tray.

"It smells wonderful." Lucy leaned over the steam. "I never imagined planes were like this."

"Is this your first flight?"

"Yes. When I was a kid, we took road trips. My dad loved driving and my mom doesn't take many vacations. She works in real estate and says it never sleeps."

Helen repositioned her silverware, straightening each piece. "Not now perhaps, but a few years ago I'll wager she thought it only slept."

"True. All the hard work in the world couldn't

move houses for a while." Lucy took a bite. "James didn't win the trip, did he?"

Helen shook her head as if replaying the moment he'd told her. It was a slow, sad motion. "He has the dubious honor, I gather, of being the number two associate."

"Is he okay?"

"I'm not sure. James has little tolerance for gray and there's been a lot of that in his life lately."

"You're talking about me."

"Not exclusively. I think there's a lot of gray at top law firms, and James wants everything to be clear and plain—transparent. He's like his father, most comfortable there. I think he's struggling with the complexity of reality."

Helen pushed her salad around the small plate. "I'm struggling with that myself. I should never have kept that watch, Lucy. Not because it belonged to someone else, but because of what it meant, deep inside me, for Charles, for us." She threw Lucy a sideways glance. "Can you tell I've been dwelling on this?"

"Did you tell James about it?"

"Goodness, no. He's struggling enough." Helen peeked over. "I know I told you this, but you really do have your grandfather's eyes. I find it strange to see him in you so strongly. I remember him now, far more powerfully than I've allowed myself in years. Only he had brown hair."

"My mom's a redhead." Lucy reached up and

patted her hair as if reassuring herself of the color. "We . . . We haven't had a chance to talk about all this."

"I'm sure you have a million questions."

"That's on the low side."

"Go slow." Helen laughed. "I'm not as quick as I used to be."

"Why did you keep it? You let Ollie go. You married Charles. Why wasn't the story done?"

"That would have been smart and healthy." Helen chewed as if processing her food and thoughts at an equal pace. "I took it as a carrot, a dare. I kept it as part-revenge, part-talisman. And for years, if we're going to be completely honest, part-hope. But the day I married Charles, the story should have ended. It wasn't fair to us. But I couldn't let go; I couldn't let go of Ollie."

Helen laid down her fork and dabbed her lips with the white cloth napkin. She held it inches from her lips. "I loved him with a crazy passion, Lucy, and it scared me. That was my ultimatum the night we fought. He needed a legitimate job— for us."

"And then *you* stole the watch?"

"When you say it like that it makes no sense at all," Helen agreed. "But it did at the time. I ran out of that garage with the watch clutched in my fist, feeling so powerful. It felt like I held Ollie's quintessence in my hands. He'd have to come for it, and for me."

Helen turned to the window. "You see, we . . ." She told of drinking gimlets while listening to Dizzy Gillespie at the Sutherland Show Lounge, dancing until dawn at a new club each night, and sneaking past her apartment building's doorman early each morning. She described her heightened state of anxiety, fearing Ollie's next crazy idea and fretting he'd become bored and not show up at all.

Food forgotten, her stories tripped into fall at school, when her red nail polish couldn't last more than a day or two because she chewed each nail to the quick waiting for him to come for her. Finally, she grew quiet as she relayed once again the desolation of the empty garage, her acquiescence to her father's plans, and the moment she met Charles Carmichael at a neighbor's New Year's Eve ball.

"There was nothing left to hope for. So after that Christmas, I did as told—stayed on the North Shore and married. I tucked the watch and that wild, carefree girl away . . . Until you . . . I'd forgotten about her—and she was bold and fun, and I miss her."

Helen continued, but as her stories drifted toward Charles, her eyes grew soft. They'd been electric blue, fierce and icy, flashing with mixed emotions and charged memories while she recalled Ollie. But talking about Charles softened those colors, deepened them, and soon Helen's blue eyes closed altogether.

Lucy's did not. The hope Helen had offered, *go back to go forward,* slipped away as the sun set and the plane charged east into darkness.

The new beginning, seeing her dad and setting everything right within her, suddenly felt too heavy and impossible. To go back a couple years and correct her muddled lies? *Maybe.* To go back a generation and find her father redeemed and restored? *Doubtful, but perhaps . . .* But to break from what Ollie had started—three generations of clearly wayward choices, manipulation, and hurt? *Not a chance.* Lucy lifted her arms in supplication and let them flop into her lap.

"I give up. I give up," she whispered and reached for *Villette.*

Chapter 12

As the plane touched down, Lucy reached across Helen to open the shade. The cabin slowly came to life with the soft rustle of blankets and pillows, pushed aside to stow books and organize bags. The flight attendants fluttered like hens, readying their chicks to leave the nest by delivering coats and hand wipes.

Helen touched Lucy's arm. "Did you rest at all?"

"No," Lucy huffed.

"Is your mind spinning?"

"There's no end to it."

"I can only imagine." Helen reached for her handbag at her feet. "Keep asking all the questions you want. Revisiting that time is good, like sweeping away cobwebs." She offered a soft smile. "I need them gone. They're so very old."

Lucy smiled back and tugged her bag from the overhead bin. As Helen touched up her lipstick and combed her hair and instantly appeared fresh and ready, Lucy sank farther into her seat. She dug around for a brush. She didn't have one. She searched for lipstick; she found Chapstick. She reached for the airline's small toiletry bag and squeezed a drop of toothpaste on her finger and slipped it into her mouth, hoping Helen wouldn't notice. She did.

"We'll check into the hotel and you can freshen up there. It's best to stay awake as long as possible to overcome jet lag, but I'm sure I'll need a nap. It's the only benefit to old age that I can find. You can sleep almost anywhere at any time."

The flight attendant brought their coats, and Lucy held Helen's for her then pushed her arms into her own sleeves.

Helen gently stretched her back. "Shall we?"

The pair made their way through Heathrow airport. It was darker than O'Hare. The signs no longer bright blue and white, but yellow and black; the terminal hallway not opening to the sky and decked with bright flags, but closed in and tunnel-like. It looked older, faster, more grounded, and frenetic.

"Where do we meet our driver?" Lucy asked.

"We collect our bags and go through there." Helen pointed to sliding doors, guards, and the long lines of Customs. "Can you grab them, dear?"

"Of course." Lucy moved to the conveyor belt and waited. Once they arrived, she pulled her black canvas bag alongside Helen's brown leather one and followed the crowd into line.

Passports stamped and questions answered, they passed the guards and spilled into the chaos. It felt as if thousands of people pressed into her outside the double doors of the International Hallway. They stood in rows, like people watching a sporting match, waving signs and calling to friends and family members in a cacophony of languages. Lucy paused to absorb it.

Helen stopped. "It's different, isn't it?"

"It's wonderful."

"Welcome to London." Helen waggled a finger to a black-clad young man standing a few feet away and walked toward him. His placard read "Mrs. Carmichael."

Lucy trailed, trying to pick out various languages and failing. She smiled ruefully; Sid would fare better.

She caught Helen's voice, speaking to the man who was probably her own age. He had straight brown hair, cut short, almost military-style, and light-brown eyes. Lucy couldn't help but compare them to James's—30 percent chocolate. And he was pale. *Welcome to England,* she thought.

Helen continued talking. "Delighted you're on time. Thank you. And what is your name?"

"Dillon, ma'am." He reached behind Lucy to take the bags, glancing quickly into her eyes.

"Hi, Dillon. I'm Lucy." She thrust out her hand.

"Nice to meet you, Lucy." He squeezed and winked before turning to the bags.

Lucy drew her hair over her shoulder, pulling it smooth through her fingertips. It felt nice, if a little silly, to have someone flirt with her.

"If you'll follow me this way, the car is parked right outside." Dillon nodded to Helen and wove them through the crowds.

The car wasn't like any limousine Lucy had ever seen—old, black, and always made by Lincoln. This was a deep-brown stretch Mercedes with cream leather seats that smelled like a fine, newly bound leather book and enveloped her just as thoroughly. Her body felt weary, but her mind buzzed as Dillon pulled out onto the highway on the wrong side of the road.

"This is so odd. I knew about it, but it's so . . . so wrong," Lucy said, her eyes glued to the traffic.

"You get used to it," Helen replied. "It's the right-hand turns, which feel like our lefts, that trip you up. Charles felt comfortable driving over here, but I never did. In fact, the only time I ever drove I went *ping, ping, ping* down a narrow street, popping off side view mirrors. It was horrible."

Lucy grinned at the image. "What happened?"

"Charles went door-to-door to make it right. It took him hours, but I was too humiliated to show my face. I didn't leave the hotel for two days until we flew out."

The day was bright and moving at full speed. The streets were soaked, but the morning sunshine burst through as if it had only recently escaped and wanted to flood down and assert its presence. Cars spit up water, horns blared, and as they approached Central London, the traffic tightened in a chaotic jumble. Motorcycles weaved between cars like pinballs shot through a machine.

"Are they allowed to do that?" Lucy exclaimed, diving back as one buzzed her window.

"If they can manage it. Some blokes are too bold though." Dillon turned and caught her eyes.

"It's crazy." Lucy watched another dodge through the traffic.

"We'll cross through Leicester Square then Regent Street to get to your hotel."

"The West End! We didn't even think of a show. Did you want to see any?" Lucy reached for her bag.

"I hadn't thought of it myself, but I think not. There is enough on our list."

The car then swung around a tight corner, passing between and underneath buildings. Lucy grasped her door's side rail and cringed, certain they wouldn't fit through the impossibly tight opening. Whizzing between the buildings, they emerged unscathed into a lovely courtyard.

"Here we are. Dukes Hotel." Dillon pulled alongside a Rolls-Royce. No other cars could fit into the tiny turn space.

A bellman materialized at Helen's door as Dillon shot from his seat. He waved the dark-blue stiffly clad man away and held Helen's door himself, reaching in to assist her onto the step. "Shall I wait to take you on to lunch, ma'am?"

The bellman walked around to open Lucy's door.

"I would like to rest a few hours, but then Lucy has our itinerary. She'll let you know."

Lucy noted Helen's drawn expression. Her eyes, usually flashing between sky and steel, seemed leached of color. Sid would call it #841 *Snow Angel,* a color he never chose. He'd once commented, *Lacks conviction. Is it white or blue?* when she'd suggested it.

"Go ahead and park, Dillon, while I check us in." Lucy dashed past them both and hurried into the hotel.

She expected something grand like The Four Seasons or many of the hotel lobbies that dotted Chicago's Michigan Avenue. Instead, the coziness of a lobby that could only hold a petite sofa and two delicate upholstered chairs enchanted her. The soft blues, bold yellows, and golds mixed with a few modern elements made it feel rich, intimate, and royal. She wanted to curl up and admire it.

After checking them in, she spun to find Helen seated in one of the chairs directly behind her.

"How are you doing?" Lucy perched in the chair next to her.

"I don't pull all-nighters like I used to," Helen quipped.

"Well, I'll carry your monstrosity of a key for you and we'll get you to your room." Lucy held up two oversize brass keys dangling from matching tags. "She said we should drop them in that box when we leave. Thank goodness we don't have to carry them around. They're larger than my phone."

"I always liked those. They feel special. Not like those key cards or how you use your cell phone some places."

"See, I kinda like that." Lucy stood and reached for Helen's arm. "Our rooms are right at the top| of those stairs or there's an elevator. Which would you prefer?"

"The stairs. I need to get some blood moving."

The bellman passed the elevator and escorted them to a single flight of stairs. He moved quickly, and Helen stopped halfway up.

Lucy stilled behind her.

"I just need to catch my breath." Helen's voice came out on a cough. She waved her hand to shoo Lucy on.

Lucy vacillated a moment before obeying. By the time the bellman had opened the door and rested her suitcase on the rack, Helen entered the room. She trembled slightly and her face looked a degree paler.

Lucy turned to the bellman and handed him a few pound coins as he backed out of the room. She quickly crossed the room to Helen. "Please sit. I'll get you a glass of water."

Helen dropped into the chair before the writing desk and cleared her throat. "I hate having everyone know I'm so old."

"I think you're remarkable." Lucy poured a glass of water, handed it to her, and waited for the color to return to her face. "When I sent your son our itinerary, he sent an e-mail back with a list of your medications."

"Did he?" Helen's voice held humor and a touch of annoyance.

"I'm sorry I didn't mention it."

"He worries well, doesn't he?"

"Is there anything I can do for you now? Let me recheck the list."

"I'm simply old and, yes, dying. Let's be honest enough to name it. But there's nothing to do. You don't need to recheck his list. I'll take my medications like a good girl and it will suffice."

She pressed her chest with one finger. "I'm aging more rapidly by the day. Do you think that happens? That time speeds up?"

Lucy plopped on the bed across from her. "I wouldn't mind that. The days seem interminably long to me."

Helen reached over and pushed Lucy's bangs aside, holding her head within her palm. "That's because you were in love."

"Still am." Lucy caught her words and her head shot straight up. "That's weird. I'm sorry I said that."

"It's not weird. After listening to James go on and on about you, I should hope you loved him. I'm simply sorry it turned out the way it did. And I did promise not to comment or play match-maker, so I'm safe." She zipped her lips. "No tattling to James."

"Good to know, but there's nothing to say. We're done."

Helen lifted her finger under Lucy's chin. "Keep your chin up. There's always a bend in the road."

Chapter 13

Why did you say that? Lucy repeated the question, the indictment, over and over as she unlocked the door to her room. What was Helen supposed to say to such an admission?

Defend her grandson? Tell her that James was better off without her? Admonish her for lying, for altering her books, and for anything else she might suspect? Instead, Helen had been kind and told her to have hope. *Hope.*

Lucy quietly shut her door and examined her room. It was a mirror image of Helen's with a double bed, a dresser, and a striking deep-red chair positioned before the petite writing desk. The cream walls and deep-blue carpet were so crisp and clean. The effect carried into the bathroom as well with its white marble and classic hardware. Lucy flopped down on the bed, spread her arms wide, and closed her eyes. With each inhalation, she willed the tension of the week to dissolve around her, into the ocean between home and here. Between James and herself.

You can reinvent yourself anywhere. She recalled how her dad had always closed his eyes when he said that, his voice carrying a dreamlike quality, as if he could see those new horizons. Lucy's eyes flickered open with the realization that the memories, of his voice and of this saying and others, were losing their fuzzy edges and softer notes. The colors of his accent and actions pressed dark and heavy on her.

Suddenly restless, Lucy popped up and pulled back the sheers. The room flooded with light. She quickly unpacked, brushed her teeth and hair, and placed her toiletries around the bathroom.

Satisfied with the job, she picked up her key and headed to the lobby.

Lucy walked out the hotel's front door ready for an adventure. The sun was high and she could see a patch of blue between the buildings . . . It was time to chase it. She strode three steps and stalled.

"May I fetch you a cab, miss?"

"I'd rather walk, but I realized I have nowhere particular to go. I've got tons of places marked on my phone, on my maps, but I . . . I want to see everything." She puffed out her cheeks then deflated them like a balloon. "I'm completely stymied."

The doorman pointed out the courtyard. "I recommend you start with something close. If you turn right you will catch Marlborough Road. It dead-ends at The Mall. If you turn right again, you can see the Changing of the Guard at Buckingham Palace." He pulled back his sleeve and examined his watch. "You've got twenty minutes. You don't need to rush."

"That's perfect. Thank you."

Lucy passed through the narrow opening and came to the corner. The street was much wider and she got an impression of the city. The air, crisp and sharp, blew away the damp and dried the streets right before her eyes, the cars acting like squeegees on a tennis court. So different from Chicago—foreign pollutants filled the air, diesel rather than gasoline; horns pitched to a higher tonality hit her eardrums; and the unfamiliar whirl of continuous motorcycles startled her. The cabs scurried like black beetles between lanes and stopped instantly the moment she stepped into the crosswalk. And in some ineffable fashion, it felt like home.

Lucy moved around St. James's Palace on Marlborough Road, crossing each street slowly and carefully. *Right. Left. Right.* At the second crosswalk, she realized her mistake and glanced in the opposite direction. *Left. Right. Left.* Then she laughed at herself—again—as the cars and cabs stopped so quickly she felt safe crossing regardless where she looked.

"Wait up. Lucy, wait up."

Lucy spun to find Dillon running behind her. "Hey, Dillon. Do you need me?"

"Not at all. I parked the car, but you hired me for the full two weeks. Do *you* need me?"

Lucy smiled, trying to decide if he was being solicitous or flirtatious—or both. "Not right now. Helen wanted a couple hours to rest so I'm headed to see the Changing of the Guard."

"Can I join you?" He tilted his head to the palace.

"Of course." She resumed walking and Dillon matched her stride.

"It's not so crowded now. This is actually one of the best times in the city. It'll start filling in the next month and be close to bursting all summer.

You won't get anywhere near the gates then. But now the weather can be touchy."

"I don't care; I think it's gorgeous." Lucy lifted her face to the sun.

"The rain won't keep you from much in the city, but Haworth might be different. I took some women to Bath a few weeks ago and they were spitting nails. They wanted a real Jane Austen walking experience and they caught a three-day gusher. Saw nothing and complained a blue streak. You need to be ready for the weather to ruin some plans, and I don't—"

Lucy stopped. "If I promise not to blame you for the weather, will you stop being the only gray cloud in sight?"

Dillon held up his hands in surrender. "Fair enough. I've given my disclaimers." They walked in silence for a few moments before he spoke again. "I'm sorry about that."

"You don't need to apologize; I get it. You don't want clients upset. Bosses too." Lucy nodded. "Believe me, that, I understand. I've just never been here and I want to see and experience everything and the weather isn't going to get in the way of that. Nothing is."

"Facing the wrong direction might." Dillon glimpsed past her shoulder. "You're about to miss the guards."

Lucy ran along the iron fence until she was near the front and could see the soldiers clearly.

Movement had already begun beyond the gates. She hopped on the stone base and held tight to the cold black rails. She pressed her face between the bars, mimicking those around her.

"It's better, bigger, when the Queen is in town."

"Dillon, again, if you want me to *not* complain, then you'll have to stop giving me things to complain about."

"Yes, ma'am," he agreed solemnly and climbed next to her.

Three officers on horseback rode into the courtyard beyond. A dozen foot soldiers followed. They marched in a line and turned at sharp angles, yelling calls back and forth until only three new guards remained by the gate.

At the end, Dillon jumped down and started walking toward the gate's outer post, following the blonde brick wall. "Follow me."

Lucy obeyed, noting the plaque as she passed. *The Mews.* And as she wondered what that might mean, she caught the faint scent of animals and hay, incongruent in the center of the city. "Horses?"

"This is where they house the Queen's horses and carriages. It's not big and there's no fee. Come on."

Lucy followed him through a door built within the large wooden gate. On the left was a small shop nestled into the wall with paddocks opening beyond and to the right. The cobblestones were perfectly clean and the smell was fresh, horse and hay. She passed the museum and shop and headed straight for the first of four stalls. A guard stood nearby. She reached her hand out.

"No touching the horses, miss."

Lucy pulled it back. "Sorry."

The guard made no acknowledgment.

"When we get to the country, I'm sure there'll be a horse to pet so you can experience that too." There was laughter in Dillon's whisper.

"You're making fun of me."

"I'm not really. Tourists are funny, but I understand. Trips like this are expensive. You want to see stuff and touch it. I went to New York a few years ago and made a right fool of myself, even posing for pictures with a foam Statue of Liberty on my head."

"Then you do get it."

"Is this your first time here?"

"Yes, but my dad lives here." Lucy said the words suddenly and without thinking. And now they hung in the air between her and this stranger. "He's up in the Lake District . . . I think."

"You don't know?"

"Not for certain. I guess I'll find out when we get there."

"My boss didn't tell me we were heading there. Is that after—?"

"Never mind." Lucy's confidence and hope slipped. She stepped away and whirled back.

"Please don't mention it to Mrs. Carmichael. It's not on the itinerary and I shouldn't have told you."

Dillon's eyes widened minutely, but he didn't comment.

"I plan to tell her. Ask her. I haven't yet. It isn't a big deal. Forget I said anything." Lucy clamped her mouth shut, annoyed by her own stammering, and ducked into the gift shop. *Never give unnecessary details*. Another of her father's favorite dictums. Her heartbeat ratcheted up a notch. Those were not the memories she wanted here and now. And he could have changed. Rehabilitation happened. Minimum-security prisons offered plenty of programs—reform was their whole purpose. Now her careless words were about to get her into trouble. The realization only elevated her pulse a degree more.

Lucy pushed away the frantic thoughts and wandered into the shop, perusing the displays. There was everything from books on royals and china statuettes and mugs to plastic Peter Rabbits and miniature carriages and horses. She touched everything she passed, much as James had done the day they met, and worked to remember the dad of her childhood—the one who told stories, loved make-believe, and held her when she awoke with nightmares. She focused on the dad who was worth seeking and the belief that anyone could change.

Once calm, she made her way back to the

front, clasping a small keychain with *The Mews* inscribed on one side and a brightly painted horse in full regalia on the other, and a small snow globe of Buckingham Palace. She grabbed a tied bouquet of pencils at the checkout.

"That's the worst waste of money I've ever seen."

"Ever? They're only eight pounds each."

"That's like thirteen American dollars."

"I was trying to forget that 'cause I'd like some souvenirs, and a friend of mine collects snow globes. The key chain is small and can fit in my suitcase. I thought I could pick one up everywhere we go and display them in a glass bowl or on a corkboard. And the pencils are made from bark from the royal woods—a great decorating small with a story."

"Small?"

"Little items that you put out on your coffee table or desktop. It's an aspect of my work I really like. You can bring a lot of a client's true personality out in the smalls." Lucy tapped her phone to reveal the time. "I should head back to wake Helen."

"Let's go." Dillon stretched his arm, inviting her to step through the shop door ahead of him and back through the gate onto Buckingham Palace Road.

As they walked, Lucy's phone rang. She stopped and answered it. "James?"

"I'm sorry to bother you, but Grams isn't answering her phone." His voice was flat and toneless, making it abundantly clear he took no enjoyment in calling her.

"She may be asleep. I'm heading back to the hotel to wake her." Lucy tried to mimic his tone. "Then we're headed to the National Gallery and Bloomsbury." Her final words burst out in a squeak.

A spontaneous chuckle met them. "Was that your idea or hers?"

"Hers originally, but I didn't protest. Then I upped the ante by finding a cozy tearoom nearby. It's right off—" She caught herself. The temptation to feel comfortable was so alluring.

James didn't reply for a moment as if he, too, was resetting their distance. "I simply wanted to touch base and make sure she arrived safely. Dad assigned me to the job, as it's a light week here."

"I know, and I'm sorry."

"Not your fault." His words were clipped, precise.

"But I know what it meant to you. Are you okay?"

She could envision James on the other end of the line. He rubbed his nose when bothered or concerned, when things didn't make sense to him or didn't fall within plan. Right now he was probably rubbing it right off.

"I have to go. There may not be any partners

and one less associate on site, but there's still work. Tell Grams I love her."

"Got it, and—"

The line died. Lucy slipped her phone back into her coat pocket. She noticed Dillon staring at her. "Helen's grandson. Calling to check on her."

"And?"

"And what?" Lucy's eyes narrowed.

"Is that something else she's not supposed to know about?"

Lucy laughed—at herself. "Oh no . . . She knows all about that."

Chapter 14

They stepped up. Again. And again. And every ten steps, they stopped. Helen caught her breath and Lucy drank in London. Below them sat Trafalgar Square, flanked by its great lions with Lord Nelson standing guard atop his tall column in the center. Tourists wandered without form or pattern, taking pictures and letting their kids climb the lions. Residents walked in determined lines across, through, around—their pace faster and full of purpose.

"I should have asked Dillon to drop us at the back. I believe there are fewer stairs." Lucy glanced at Helen with concern.

"Then we wouldn't have this view."

Lucy nodded as they watched the sun light Nelson's face. Helen turned and trudged a few more steps. Lucy jumped past her and pulled open the huge glass door. "What would you like to see first?"

"I've always loved this museum." Helen reviewed the map on the sidewall. "Let's see the Rembrandt exhibition first."

They walked through the galleries, absorbed in art, making small comments of no importance. Helen touched Lucy's arm. "What did you tell James?" At Lucy's blank expression, she added, "About the books?"

"Oh . . . Hey . . . I thought you weren't meddling."

"I've been thinking about that and I find I'm in an awkward position. While I am not getting involved, I can see you're both hurt. That concerns me and I'm a grandmother, I can't help myself."

Lucy kept strolling, her eyes fixed on the art. "I didn't tell him much. He knows about me and all my foibles really, but the books shocked him and I got muddled. There wasn't a quick answer."

"And now?"

"Still no quick answer and I doubt he'd listen even if I had one. I started doing it on Book Day. Maybe I got wrapped up in the stories. Maybe I am truly my father's daughter and I couldn't help myself. But writing names in books was never about the money . . . It just happened, like telling someone she looks beautiful when she doesn't. The history, those names, yes, they added value, but they also seemed to make people happy. They constituted a story in and of themselves."

Helen didn't reply and Lucy was grateful for that.

A few minutes later, Helen pointed to a bench in front of Jan van Eyck's *The Arnolfini Wedding Portrait* and sat. Lucy joined her.

Helen kept her eyes on the painting. "That painting has always been one of my favorites." She leaned forward. "See the one lit candle in the chandelier? That's a symbol for marriage. And note the way the man supports but does not hold the woman's hand, as if he's taking an oath; it makes the moment almost contractual. These two knew what they were about."

Helen stood and walked to the painting. Lucy followed. "They'd never reveal the truth of their lives. Few of us ever have that courage. And yet, if you pay attention to the details, you can understand."

"Symbols always carry the meaning, don't they?" Lucy shot Helen a knowing look. "If pressed, I'd have to say Book Day is probably reflective of my life—full of careful care, meticulous attention, and delving into the past far too much. It's like a wool sweater I washed last year; I'm embarrassed to wear it, ashamed it even exists and how I damaged it, but somehow I can't throw it away. If I throw it away, what's left?"

Lucy ambled to the next painting. Helen followed, her low heels clicking on the wood floor. "And after hearing about dear old Gramps, it feels even more hopeless. I certainly feel as if I've earned my place within the family fold."

"Nothing's that bleak, my dear. You're simply too young to see it."

Lucy didn't reply.

Helen said nothing more. Lucy's reaction to the older woman's silence shocked her. She *wanted* Helen to demand answers, throw down an ultimatum, threaten to tell Sid—something, anything, that would rip the wound further, make it hurt. Then, maybe, it could heal.

As the silence continued, Lucy's angst faded with the realization that no one could press the answers, force the change, or listen well enough to heal her.

She was on her own.

They walked on in silence and soon Helen's arm bore down on Lucy and her breath became shallow and labored, her throat clogging with each exhale. Lucy directed them toward the front doors.

Helen stood at the top of the stairs looking down to Trafalgar Square. "I think this is a new normal for me. Maybe one truly does lose the ability to heal. Or maybe that's what cancer does."

"I don't know, but you need to tell me what's too hard and what isn't," Lucy commented as she searched the square and side streets below for Dillon and the car. She finally found them—parked across the square. "Dillon and the car are too far away. I'll text him to come closer."

"I sound worse than I am. Let's walk to him." Helen gently tugged Lucy's arm. "This isn't too hard," she said, and started her descent. "Years ago this square was swarming with pigeons. It was great fun, but also truly disgusting."

"Where'd they go?"

"They quit allowing vendors to sell food and soon the birds disappeared. I have a picture of Charlie, when he was about six years old, completely covered in pigeons—at least a hundred of them. He was so scared, he couldn't scream. I had no idea he'd react that way, and I made it worse by laughing."

"That sounds very Hitchcockian of you."

"*The Birds* or the domineering mother in *Psycho*?"

Lucy blinked with surprise. "Probably a little of both."

They walked slowly through the park. Teenagers danced to rap music before an open box displaying a few seed coins; three kids sat piled atop one of the lions posing for a picture, one so small and round that he kept sliding off; a tourist group followed their leader like baby ducks;

139

and commuters crossed briskly in straight lines, not noting the scenery or the people surrounding them.

Rather than head toward Dillon, Lucy led Helen to a bench in the opposite direction. "There's someone I'd like you to meet."

Helen sat and twisted to the side, jumping slightly at the whimsical and grinning Oscar Wilde staring back at her. Only his bronze head, one hand, and what appeared to be a flowing scarf protruded from the bench, as if they'd burst out like lava and flowed in swirls and folds as his genius cooled on top of the granite.

"Ah . . . I've heard of this. I need to have a conversation with him, don't I?" Helen laughed to Lucy before turning back to Wilde. "I must say, Mr. Wilde, that I felt quite uncomfortable while reading *The Picture of Dorian Gray*. Such decadence, such duplicity—the depravity of it all. But *The Importance of Being Earnest* was delightful. You wrote fascinating studies on the human condition, my fine sir." She turned back to Lucy. "He's awfully quiet."

Lucy walked to the foot of the bench. "There's a quote here from *Lady Windermere's Fan*. It says 'We are all in the gutter, but some of us are looking at the stars.' "

"I'd say that's about right."

"Do you think you can sink so low that you can't see them anymore?"

"Goodness . . ." Helen patted the bench next to her. "Sit down here. You're going to make me worry about you. Where's all this coming from?"

"I'm thinking the answer is yes. And that makes me worry about me too."

"If it makes any difference, I disagree. It wouldn't allow for any hope or love and I won't accept that. Give yourself a moment, Lucy, and perhaps a touch of forgiveness."

Lucy gave herself a little shake as if slipping out of skin that was bound too tight. "You're right, and besides, all life's problems are across an ocean, and for now they need to stay there. You finish chatting with Oscar, then we'll head on to Bloomsbury. Unless you're not up for more walking."

"I think I am. This conversation has been quite restorative." Helen patted Oscar's head and stood. "Shall we?"

Chapter 15

Dillon pulled up to a corner off Bloomsbury Square. "Here you are, ladies." He caught Lucy's eye. "Text or call when you want to be picked up."

"Thank you, Dillon." Lucy held his gaze a moment longer to convey greater meaning. In returning to the hotel, gathering Helen, chatting about the trip and their plans, Haworth and the possibility of the Lake District, Dillon never once made a gesture, intonation, or suggestion that he knew something secret. Lucy wanted to hug him with gratitude.

She offered him a broad, deliberate smile and slid from the backseat behind Helen. He pulled away, leaving them on the end of a large square with a broad walking path straight through the center. "This is a lot of ground to cover."

"Then let's begin." Helen marched forward.

Lucy pulled out her phone. "It's a minefield of blue historical plaques and it'll be impossible to see them all, but I made my own little tour so we could catch the best, in my mind, with the least amount of walking. Unless you've already seen all this?"

"No one in my family reads like I do and it never interested them. This will be new for both of us."

"According to the notes I made, this is Bloomsbury Square, but it's not actually where all the action happened." Lucy lowered her voice. "Wait till I tell you . . . So much intrigue."

She led Helen across the square's center and headed for the opposite side. People filled the benches, sat on blankets, and strolled along the paths, enjoying the day. Lucy drew a breath in through her nose and caught the fresh scents of mulch, blooms, and cut grass. *New beginnings.* "This must be one of the first truly warm days of spring. Doesn't it feel that way? Like everything's waking up?"

"Absolutely lovely," Helen wheezed.

Lucy slowed the pace and they continued on to Bedford Place. "Everyone lived here, from writers to statesmen, from inventors to royalty. Dickens to the Bloomsbury Group and beyond . . . And there's our first Blue Plaque." Lucy surveyed her notes. "That one is for T. S. Eliot. He worked at a publishing house there for a number of years. That's where his crazy wife poured hot chocolate in the mail slot."

"She did?"

"I don't remember exactly what happened to her, but she either died or was committed, because he proposed to his second wife in those offices as well."

Lucy led on, through Russell Square, and upon reaching Gordon Square, she stopped. "Here it is. The heart of the Bloomsbury Group. You wouldn't believe who lived along here."

"Virginia Stephen and her sister, Vanessa, Clive Bell, Lytton Strachey, John Maynard Keynes . . . Shall I continue?" Helen winked.

"Of course you'd know."

"For many years, these were my favorite writers. They were daring and expressive—and their exploits even more so." She pointed to the

Blue Plaque for John Maynard Keynes. "Number 46. Did you read about this house?"

"I did. Before he owned it, Virginia Woolf and her sister lived here, when she was still a Stephen. Your 'Bloomsberries' had a very good time in this house."

Helen nodded. "I once read something that described them as 'couples who live in squares and have triangular relationships.' I don't remember who said it, but it stuck with me." Helen looked back into the square and turned to a bench on their left. "Do you mind if we sit?"

"Of course not." Lucy sat then bounced back up. "Wait here."

She raced back a few minutes later with a small brown bag. "I noticed a bookshop back there and thought we needed a little reading material." She pulled out a thin broad book, *Bloomsbury at Home*, and scanned the pages. Helen sat with her eyes closed.

"Oh . . . Listen to this. 'We were full of experiments and reforms. We were going to do without table napkins; we were going to paint; to write; to have coffee after dinner instead of tea at nine o'clock. Everything was going to be new; everything was going to be different. Everything was on trial.' Isn't that marvelous?" Lucy flipped to the back of the book. "The author, Todd, attributes this to Woolf's *Moments of Being*."

Lucy kept reading. "You know, some of this seems sad to me too."

"How so?"

"For all the creativity and the fun, there were lots of affairs and they . . . No one seems happy." Lucy scanned the pages.

"They were brilliant, but there was an edge to them too. Not sharp and clear, but sharp and pointed somehow. I think each was probably quite alone, but together at the same time."

Helen's quiet comment seeped deep into Lucy. She laid the book in her lap, leaned back, and watched clouds chase each other across the sky. Their movement made light dance through the leaves of trees above.

"Aloneness can creep up on you. Some is good and creative; I see that in Sid. He needs that time. But too much isn't a good thing. To have someone know you, really know you, that's a nice thing, I think." Lucy kept her gaze trained on the clouds and light.

"I agree."

"Can I ask a personal question?" Lucy shifted on the bench.

Helen leaned toward her. "Of course. Otherwise you and I won't have much to say, will we?"

"Were you alone? Is that why you question if Charles knew you loved him, because you kept something back and, therefore, you felt alone and by default he must have too?"

Helen held Lucy in a long, steady look. "That's exactly how it was."

Lucy slid the book inside her bag. "I can understand that."

"You seem a little young."

"I doubt age has much to do with it. I mean, can't one feel that way around parents or siblings or even out to dinner with good friends?"

"I suppose that's true." Helen faced the garden again. "Who would you say knows you?"

"I was just thinking about that and I'm not sure. My mom, I guess, but even there, we think so differently that I'm not sure she can. Sid, to a degree—a great degree. I have a few friends who do, one in particular. I've known her since we were eight—that's when my dad left and Mom and I stopped moving. And James . . . I'd hoped and, I think, I let him in." Lucy twisted toward Helen. "And you stepped into that one all on your own."

Helen laughed. "It was completely my fault and we will leave him here." She patted the bench beside her then stood. "Are you ready to press on?"

They crossed to Tavistock Square and headed toward Virginia Woolf's statue in the far corner.

"Look." Lucy pointed to a huge stone and redbrick building at the north end of the garden. "Tavistock House. Dickens lived there. He wrote . . ." She tapped open her phone. *"Bleak*

146

House, *Hard Times*, *Little Dorrit*, and *A Tale of Two Cities* all while living there.

"I blame my dad for my love of Dickens," Lucy continued. "Dickens was his favorite. We only read *A Christmas Carol* together, but he always said"—Lucy dropped her voice low—"'Dickens loved people best. He always gave the little man a way out.' When I read a bunch of Dickens in college, I finally got what he meant." She squeezed Helen's arm for emphasis. "Did you know Dickens never killed his bad guys? Well, he killed off one. The others were cowards, bullies, minor villains, and general degenerates, but they were worth something and they lived. If they didn't change on the page and find redemption, they lived with that promise still out there."

"I never made that connection."

"Hmm . . . Dad did. I suspect it's because he found comfort in it." Lucy peered down at Helen. "That's why I still contend the Lake District is a worthy stop for you. All those stories define us, and judging from your figurines, Beatrix Potter defined you."

"True . . ." Helen strolled on.

"I—" Lucy stopped. She couldn't bring herself to try again. She didn't want to. "Helen?" Lucy caught up in a step. "What did your PI tell you about my family? The one you hired to find the Parrish family."

"Nothing. He found the Parrishes from the

name on the front and all the initials scrolled inside." Helen must have caught Lucy's doubt. "Why?"

"I thought that, because of Ollie, you might have learned something, and I'd like to know something that's true. Proven true. Because I believe you. I believe you, but everything you tell me contradicts all my childhood stories. My dad told me my grandfather was a watchmaker, a craftsman, an artisan."

"Why can't that still be true?"

"Because he lied for a living." Lucy started walking again. "Didn't James tell you?" At Helen's confused head shake, she continued. "My dad was a con man. Hence the double emotional whammy of learning your version of my grandfather."

Helen stopped walking.

"My dad even spent some time in jail. I don't know what for, but I like to think it's because fact and fiction got mixed up with him and he got beyond his ability to straighten things out. My mom says that's an excuse. And it is, but . . ."

"But he's your father and that's what we do."

Lucy bit her lip. "I'm surprised James didn't tell you."

"Why would he? That was your father, not you. He said something about learning stories from your father and you've said something like that before, but I didn't quite understand."

"I learned a lot from my father." Lucy tried to remember that first moment. When had that first drop of ink fallen on a page? And why had she done it? She couldn't find it and wasn't sure what difference it might make now.

When Lucy returned her focus to the world, she found herself staring straight at the bust of Virginia Woolf. "She doesn't look very happy, does she?"

"I think we know she wasn't," Helen agreed.

"Enough." Lucy huffed. "I'm ready for food." She immediately regretted her hasty words and rude tone. "There's the sign for Tavistock Place. Bloomsbury Coffee House is right down the block. Would you like to get tea?"

"I might need coffee instead."

"Me too, really."

As they passed down the short residential block with a few unassuming storefronts and brightly painted doors, Lucy was determined to be light, bright, and stick to her role as consultant. Anything else wasn't her job and it wasn't helpful. And, she couldn't deny, all this thinking made her head hurt.

Helen stopped at a Blue Plaque above a red door. "Vladimir Lenin? Here?"

"Hang on a sec." Lucy pulled out her phone. "He lived here while reading at the British Museum in 1908, and the plaque went up, 'amongst great controversy,' in 2012."

"The red door is quite fitting, don't you think?" Helen quipped.

As Lucy pushed open the door of the Bloomsbury Coffee House, a rich warmth enveloped them. Smells of earthy coffee overlay sugar, yeast, and the sharp tang of sourdough. She ordered a slice of carrot cake with a rich cream cheese frosting and watched as Helen coated her toasted sourdough with bright homemade jam.

Lucy wiggled on the uncushioned chair, settling in, and regarded the small basement café. "It's charming, but not what I expected. It seems more like a hangout coffee shop down in Hyde Park—Chicago's, not London's."

"We're basically on a college campus here too, so that makes sense. I like it. I feel young." Helen took a bite. "And this is marvelous jam."

Lucy looked from her cake and found Helen staring. "Do I have cream cheese on my nose?" She touched it with her napkin then ran the napkin around her entire face.

"No. I think I've upset you and I'm sorry for that. I knew, at some level, this would be hard and maybe it was selfish of me to tell you and invite you on this trip, but you're a part of this somehow. You, not just your grandfather. After all, your green eyes brought us here." Helen smiled. "But I didn't anticipate it would cause you such pain."

Lucy played with the crumbs on her plate. Minutes passed. "Do you believe that generations can be bad? Emily Brontë did . . . And actually, if you look at all the Brontë stories, they each did to some degree."

Helen pressed her lips together.

Lucy slouched low and bonked her forehead on the table. "I sound ridiculous, but you're right, it does hurt—not hearing about my grandfather, but making all the connections down the generations to me. And I criticize my dad for living in stories and now I compare my life and family tree to *Wuthering Heights*. But that's what's upsetting. Where do they end and I begin? My family, not the stories."

"You are your own person and I wouldn't worry about the stories. We all compare our lives to them. That's why we love them; they help us understand ourselves."

"There is a line though." Lucy pulled herself up in the chair.

Helen reached to lift a long bang off Lucy's forehead and tuck it behind her ear. "Lucy, I'd like to ask you a favor."

"Of course."

"Before I die"—Helen held up her hand to Lucy's startled expression—"I want someone to know me, the real me. That's what this is all truly about. I want to be brave and meet that girl I knew long ago, before life and fear stifled her. May I start with you?" Helen rested her hands on the table. "I've shared this watch with you, we're on this trip, and there is so much in me that feels different and, while it scares me, I can't stop now. I need to see it through, find out who I am before . . . before I can't anymore. Would that be okay with you?"

"Yes," Lucy whispered. She had no other words.

"And if you'd like to do the same, I'd be honored by such trust."

That soft feeling crept over Lucy again. This time it wasn't *friendship or interview;* it felt like *friendship or therapy.* She sighed as she realized that sometimes they were perhaps the same. "I might like that."

Helen nodded her head slowly as if a secret pact had been formed. She then pushed back her chair to stand. "Let's finish our day. I'm fading and would like to add a few more plaques to our burgeoning Blue Plaque collection."

After another hour of ambling and chatting, they reached the northeast corner of Russell Square. Lucy had texted Dillon and he stood there waiting beside the car.

"Where to, ladies?"

"Back to the hotel. I think we've done the day proud." Helen rested her handbag in her lap. "Dillon, what time do you end with us each evening?"

"I don't. I'm at your command twenty-four-seven. Shall I take you on to dinner?"

"Not me, but would you mind taking Lucy? I'd rather not have her out alone, especially her first night in London."

Lucy chimed in, "I'm perfectly capable. Besides, I'm not leaving you. We can eat in the hotel or, if you're too tired, I'll eat there alone."

"Nonsense. You have only three days in London and I want you to experience all you can. I need my beauty sleep." She called back to the front in her own mix of cheer and command. "Dillon, I expect you to take her someplace nice, young man, very nice."

"Yes, ma'am. I can do that."

When they pulled into the courtyard, Dillon helped Helen from the car. She reached both hands out to him and whispered into his ear before continuing into the hotel.

He turned to Lucy. "That is the first time a woman has ever slipped me money."

"That's so wrong."

"It is, a little. She just handed me . . ." He slid the bills apart with his fingers. "Plenty, and I know where to spend it. Can you be ready in an hour? We don't have reservations, but we might snag a table early."

"You don't need to do this."

"I'd like to if you aren't too tired yourself."

"Oddly, I'm not."

"Good. One hour." Dillon ducked back into the car and drove away.

Chapter 16

Lucy headed into her room ready to let go of all the currents swirling around her, pull on her vintage fitted floral dress of blue and black splayed upon a bright-white background, and have an evening of fun. She loved that dress—one couldn't be sad while wearing such a happy dress.

She paired it with a thin black cashmere scarf, accented it all with deep red lipstick, and twirled in front of the bathroom's full mirror. She played with her hair and decided to leave it hanging in loose curls down her back—James always liked that. That reminder sent her searching for a hair band to pull it back into her ubiquitous low ponytail.

Too many opinions crowding this bathroom. With a half-laugh and a huff, Lucy grabbed the brass key off her bedside table and hurried down the steps.

Dillon stood waiting in the lobby. He whistled and she took a curtsy, pleased with the compliment.

"You're early," she said.

"Traffic was light and I live too far away to change. You'll have to deal with me in my livery here."

Lucy looked him up and down. He'd removed

154

his black tie and now stood before her as any casual city guy might, dressed in black pants, a matching black sports coat, and a white shirt, slightly rumpled and open at the collar. "You look great."

"Then let's be off." He held out his arm in an exaggerated fashion and led her out the door.

"Where's the car?"

"I dropped it back at the garage. We don't need it and I'd rather get it back early. The guys wash them down each night. This way, they can get outta there early. Most of the cars needed for the morning were already back."

"That's thoughtful of you."

Dillon brushed off the compliment and waved down at her shoes. "I thought a walk would be good; it's a nice night. But you've been walking all day and you've got heels . . ."

"These are actually very comfortable. Let's not give in yet." Lucy led the way from the courtyard and stopped on St. James Street. "Which way?"

Dillon pointed to the left. "Up to Piccadilly. We're going to an amazing Indian restaurant up Regent Street. Veeraswamy. I've never been, but clients rave about it. I think Mrs. Carmichael would approve."

"It sounds like an adventure. I believe she would."

They walked and talked the half-mile.

Finally Dillon reached for her hand and pulled

her up a last flight of stairs to the restaurant's second-floor home. "You've slowed down. I forgot about your jet lag. You shoulda stopped me. It's what? About noon your time?"

"But I've been awake since yesterday." She glanced down at her phone. "I think I'm going on thirty-five hours now."

"Give me a couple more, then we'll get you tucked into bed."

"Sounds good."

Dillon returned to the lobby a few moments later downcast. "No tables. It's my own fault; I should've at least called."

"Hang on. There are always tables."

Lucy walked slowly to the hostess stand and rested both hands on its high edge. "Is there any way you could squeeze us in? It's really important—not your problem, all mine, but if you could?"

The woman, tall and intimidatingly sleek, flashed a straight and humorless smile. "We are booked this evening. I have seating available for ten o'clock tonight for two or tomorrow evening at five."

Lucy leaned forward. "I'll be gone . . . But I posted on my blog that I was dining and reviewing here tonight. Again not your problem, but it's a popular site in the States, a series on summer travel and culinary highlights. This is my own fault; I'll think of another spot." She snapped her fingers at Dillon. "What was that other restaurant the Dukes Hotel concierge mentioned . . . You know . . . ?"

Dillon stared blankly at her.

The woman huffed. "Wait a moment."

As she walked away, Dillon touched Lucy's arm and whispered, "She knows you're playing her."

"Yes, but she's our age, and we know the power of social media. She's not sure what part's a lie and what's the truth, and she's not willing to risk making the wrong call."

An elderly man came to the stand and studied the computer screen. "I gather we are trying to find a table."

Lucy stepped around the stand and touched his arm. "We won't linger. You must have something this early. Something for a romantic dinner? For two?" Her voice softened.

He blinked, peeked at Dillon, then shifted his gaze back to the computer. "I think we can arrange something. Follow me."

He seated them at a corner window table overlooking Regent Street, darkening in the late evening light. It felt warm and opulent, toned in oranges and golds.

As soon as he walked away, Dillon laughed. "How on earth did you manage that?"

"Not hard, really. Clumsy, yes, but that's part of it too. She questioned the blog but didn't believe it, and he wouldn't have cared. I figured he'd be more swayed by batting my lashes. In the end, you tell them what they want to hear and you often get what you want because that's the most expeditious way to get rid of you."

Dillon raised his brow.

Why do I look at you and feel this compulsion to get all honest? Lucy's victory dissolved as she remembered her words to James as if spoken aloud. She opened the menu and concentrated on it, too embarrassed to look at Dillon or around the room. She felt a tap on her hand.

"I asked if you like it?"

Lucy took in the room. "I do. It's beautiful."

Dillon grinned and returned his attention to his menu.

Lucy surveyed the restaurant. The hostess was already occupied elsewhere and the older man had disappeared. She continued to look around. *Sumptuous.*

Dillon sat absorbed by the menu. "What shall we eat?"

Lucy leaned back in her chair. "I like that question. My boyfriend used to say that. Never what *he* or *I* should eat, but what *we* should, so we could share."

Dillon laid down the menu. "That'd be Mrs. Carmichael's grandson, I expect."

"You did not get that from one conversation."

"If your expressions and posture hadn't made it clear, listening would have. There's a tone . . .

Don't tell me you don't know what I'm talking about."

"I do."

"There you have it. Mrs. Carmichael's grandson. So?"

"We broke up a couple weeks ago."

"How does it work that *his* grandmother is taking you on a trip?"

"It's a little complicated." Lucy considered the many layers of complexity. "To summarize, I work in an interior arts gallery and, technically, I'm working as a consultant on a few purchases she wants to make." She lifted the menu. "So what shall we eat?"

She didn't know if Dillon was satisfied with the answer or not, but he didn't question and simply picked up his menu again. After a few minutes, he looked up. "A couple clients touted the Raj Kachori, and curries are my favorite. After that, I haven't a clue. You?"

"I've eaten very little Indian food."

With the server's help, they finally settled on Raj Kachori, neither fully understanding its description, the Kerala Prawn Curry, and a lentil dish neither dared to pronounce.

"Did he say 'filled with goodies'?" Lucy giggled.

"Maybe that's like an Indian version of haggis. I suggest you don't look too closely," Dillon mock-whispered.

"Oh no . . . My stomach is not up for your sense of humor."

"It'll be fine. I promise."

The food arrived with a variety of small ceramic dishes, each filled with nuts, chutneys, spices, cut-and-dried fruits, or other accouterments. The table soon overflowed with tiny bowls of exquisite colors and varied aromas and textures.

"Goodies." Lucy laughed as she picked over them and took her first bite of the Raj Kachori. "I think it's lobster and fish inside and the chutney's amazing."

Dillon scooped a spoonful and moaned. "This is killing my favorite pub."

"An Indian pub?"

"English, but it's got an Indian restaurant out of the back. I'm there like four days a week and now I'm gonna be disappointed." He scooped out lentils from another dish as he flicked his hand to her. "Hand me your plate and try this." He glanced at the next table and whispered, "Swipe your naan in it. That's what they're doing."

Lucy tore a piece of the thin hot bread. She dipped it into the lentils and tucked it into her mouth as some dripped down. She scrambled for her napkin. "So yummy. I may fall asleep soon."

"Not yet." Dillon downed another prawn. "I need to go back to this grandson a minute. If my ex-girlfriend went on a trip with my gran, I'd be sore. You break up with a guy; he keeps his own family."

"One would think. Honestly, I can't explain this one."

"More secrets? I already know your master plan in the Lake District. What's one more?"

"I can't decide if I should laugh or get nervous."

Dillon hiked a shoulder. "I'm only curious."

Lucy watched him. His eyes were hazel and clear and it struck her how much one could see in another's eyes. They shadowed under the strains of lies; they drifted in dreams or peace; they widened in surprise and fear; they darkened in tension; and worst of all, they sharpened in manipulation. She knew that one, had seen it in others and felt it within herself. Dillon's eyes carried nothing beyond open interest and innocent curiosity.

"He broke up with me, but Helen thinks I can help her in a way her family can't right now. And that one I really can't explain other than to say that she and I seem to share some common history."

"You are a mystery." Dillon took a sip of water and regarded her over the glass's rim.

"Part of it's Helen's story and not mine, or at this point I'd blab it all."

Dillon nodded as if accepting the answer. He waited a beat then asked, "Was he *the one?*"

Lucy smirked, but her voice remained light. "You go for the gut."

"Ah . . . *the one.*" Dillon laid his hands on the table, fingers spread wide on either side of his plate. "I had this girlfriend. We were just dating, but one day she says we're done 'cause she's found *the one.*" He bracketed the word with stiff hands. "Now she's married in Kingston with two kids."

"Prior to James, I wouldn't have said there was only one. But now . . . He made me better. That's the best description I can give. He challenged me, in a good way, and I respected him."

Dillon rolled his eyes, making Lucy laugh.

"Cliché, but it's all true. We brought out each other's best and I didn't want to let him, or us, down. It was like a road opened before me and I wasn't alone on it."

"What happened?"

"I let us down."

"That's too vague." Dillon leaned forward.

For a split second Lucy pondered the intrusiveness of Dillon's questions and a sense of relief rather than annoyance filled her. Dillon wanted to know, was curious, and on first assessment, had proven trustworthy. But more to the point, Lucy wanted to talk. And someone was finally listening.

"James is a truthful guy. He's smart and funny, mission-oriented. One of your good guys. It's one of the things I loved about him, but I made some bad decisions along those lines." Lucy looked back to the hostess. "He caught me in a lie and that was the end of our story."

"Except it's not the end."

Lucy faced him again. "He won't come back. I'd hoped, but I can tell now. I know him."

"Still not the end."

"Ah . . . You know something that I don't?"

"It's obvious." Dillon waited a beat. "You're here with his grandmother."

"She's not playing matchmaker. This trip isn't about anything like that. And I wouldn't want her to. What I did was wrong, and while I wish he'd forgive me, I don't want him manipulated into it. Then it's not real and we'll just break up again. If we're only headed for that, we were better off ending it two weeks ago. Helen knows that."

"I'm simply saying that you being here with his grandmother is a game changer."

After dinner, dessert, and a small glass of Chenin Blanc, Dillon offered a bus then a cab, but Lucy refused, preferring to walk and gently lean on his arm. They ambled down Regent Street back toward Piccadilly and turned to the right. They chatted about everything and nothing, but with the unspoken and seemingly mutual agreement that James needn't be canvassed further.

They simply enjoyed the cool night and the soft breeze that carried the scents of fish and chips, spices and ale, mixing with the warmed stuffy air blowing from the street grates leading to the

Underground. Despite the lateness, the streets felt as crowded as they had during rush hour, but the tenor had changed from bustling traffic to the evening's frenetic sounds of boisterous laughter as friends streamed out of restaurants and pubs, shouting plans overly loud and slightly drunk.

Before Lucy knew it, she stood wobbling on the hotel's front step.

Dillon gave her a squeeze around the shoulder. "I think your feet finally hurt."

"They do." She shifted her weight. "And I'm exhausted."

"Sleep well, Lucy." Dillon backed away.

"Thanks, Dillon." She called after him, "See you in the morning."

Chapter 17

The morning was dark and rainy. Lucy sensed it the instant before she opened her eyes. She wondered if rolling over would make the day, and all reality, drift away in a dream—a Brontë dream, preferably, overlaying reality with romance and filled with a larger-than-life hero stomping to her rescue through the storm. *Who would come? Probably a Heathcliff* . . . She jumped out of bed.

She drew the shades, wondering what to do next. She found a starting point. *Smile. You're in London.* She quickly pulled on a black knit skirt, black tights, and ballet slippers. The sweater proved more difficult. She touched the dark orange V-neck. The one James said lit her hair on fire—in a good way. She then fingered the softness of a light purple cashmere crewneck. It seemed a purple day, veering to a soft lavender, so she pulled it over a crisp white blouse, tugging the cuffs and collar out stark and proud. She plugged in her straightening iron, but without a proper convertor, it was searing hot within seconds. She unplugged it, let it cool, and used it as best she could without singeing each strand before tying it all back in her usual ponytail.

Grabbing her bag, her coat, and the monstrously large brass key, she was heading to the door when her phone rang.

"Sid?"

"Good morning, *mein sonnenschein*."

"German?"

"I wondered if it'd be my next language, but I'm not liking the roll off the tongue."

"Stick with the Romance languages. You've got what—only Portuguese left?" Lucy plopped onto the corner of her bed.

"Romanian too, but that's not what I called about . . . Your itinerary says you're headed to the Silver Vaults today."

"We are."

"Did you get the information I sent you?"

"Got it."

"Do you know what she's after? Because silver services are a strength for Barring and Shepherd. I've also been watching trends, and your best value will be in early to mid-Victorian. Later and you may get too fussy for her sensibility. Earlier and I doubt the value—are you getting all this down?"

"Are you aware it's two o'clock in the morning?"

"Not for you and I didn't want to miss you." Sid paused. "I'm well aware that I'm hovering, but isn't it exciting? Your first trip. Guiding someone to find something special. I only want to help."

Lucy lay back. "Thank you, Sid. You just did."

"That was easy."

So easy. Lucy smiled at the ceiling.

Sid continued, "You also have the War Rooms, Westminster Abbey, and Portobello Road marked for today. The market will be very crowded. Are you sure she's up for the walking?"

"She's remarkable. We walked all Bloomsbury yesterday."

"Did she really? I find people defy my expectations all the time."

"True." Lucy sat up. "Thanks for calling, Sid."

"Of course."

Exiting her room, Lucy knocked on Helen's door. *No answer.* She quickly padded down the thick-carpeted stairs to the lobby below. *Empty.* She crossed to the small dining room opposite the bar. Amidst an intimate space of soft blue and gray, silks and pale velvets, she found Helen sitting alone at a white-linen-covered table. A cup of tea, a glass of bright juice, and a bowl of yogurt and granola sat in front of her. The entire picture evoked a sense of luxury, warmth, and longevity. Lucy pressed her hand against her stomach to squelch a rumble. *Hunger.*

She hurried forward. "Have you been here long? I'm sorry if I'm late."

Helen laid down her spoon. "We didn't arrange a time and we're not in a rush."

Lucy touched her iPad, bringing up the day's calendar. "I've rearranged our day. The rain is to clear out by this afternoon. Let's do our underground things this morning."

"Put that contraption away and enjoy breakfast." Helen softened her words with a laugh.

Lucy dropped the tablet into her lap. "Sorry."

"No need to be sorry, but my grandchildren do that all the time. James is the worst."

"He is, isn't he?" Lucy sparked at the memory then redirected herself. "I'll pull it back out after breakfast."

A waitress came and poured Lucy a cup of coffee. "Oatmeal, please." She then turned back to Helen and searched for a topic. "Did you sleep well?"

"I did. Thank you. And you?"

"No." Lucy pursed her lips and absently tapped

the iPad under her napkin. "I tossed around all night."

"Jet lag can do that to you. It'll get better."

And it did get better as breakfast was spent sharing stories. Lucy told a few childhood tales, but focused primarily on Sid, the only friend they held in common. Most of Helen's included her grandchildren, James especially, and Lucy found she could not stop her and remind her of their pact to keep James "off-limits." She didn't want to.

As the waitress removed their plates, Helen laid her napkin on the table in front of her. "You said 'underground things' this morning."

"We put the War Rooms and the Silver Vaults on the list for this afternoon, but I thought we'd move them to this morning because of the rain."

"Perfect." Helen fingered the napkin. "What then is switched to the afternoon?"

"Being Saturday, it's a perfect day for Portobello Market. The stalls are open all along the street and if we walk up rather than down, we'll be only a few blocks from Peel Street at the end."

"And there we are. All roads lead to Peel Street."

The rain didn't keep anyone from the streets. They were full of bustling, noise, people, and chaos.

Every time Dillon dashed through a roundabout, Lucy hung on, not understanding how the mass of cars careening in the circle didn't collide. But they didn't. Each darted on and off as if scripted in a choreographed dance. Dillon even changed lanes within the circles, amidst motorcycles roaring around them, unconcerned.

Helen requested an indirect route so Lucy could get the "lay of the land," as Helen called it. And from the window, Lucy spied many of the landmarks she'd marked in her notes: Tower of London, St. Paul's Cathedral, Covent Garden . . .

Lucy read the street sign as Dillon turned down Drury Lane.

"Hey, the Muffin Man lives here."

"Hah. Never heard that one before," Dillon called back.

He drove past the Silver Vaults with an "I'll have you right back here later" and double-backed toward the Thames, passing the Royal Opera House, before cutting down Whitehall to Churchill's War Rooms. He slid into a spot outside a massive stone building. "You're in the heart of it now. Treasury, Foreign and Common-wealth Offices across there, and Downing Street is a block that way if you want to drive by after."

"What will you do while we're here?" Lucy looked around.

"Park the car and stay close. This exhibit's not big. It won't take you long."

Lucy and Helen walked into the building and followed the signs to a flight of stairs leading to Churchill's underground offices. Helen stopped in front of her and didn't move.

"This is a trip into history I don't feel like taking. I added it to the list, I know, but it doesn't fit somehow. Charles and I toured it right after it opened in '84 and I don't want to go again. I'll wait if you want to see it."

"No. Let's go onward and upward."

"'Come further up, come further in,'" Helen quoted softly. "I haven't thought of that recently." She peered up at Lucy, still standing two steps above her. "Westminster Abbey is across the square. I'd like to go there now, if you don't mind walking in the drizzle."

"The nice woman at the desk gave me this as we headed out." Lucy reached into her bag and pulled out a compact umbrella. "We're prepared."

They walked outside and Lucy opened the midnight-blue umbrella with a bold *Dukes Hotel* logo on the side. She held it above their heads with one arm and supported Helen's hand with the other. Within a few minutes and two traffic lights, Lucy gaped at the Abbey's famous west entrance—its massive wooden doors recessed into huge stone arches, topped by detailed sculptures and flanked by two imposing towers.

"The height of Gothic architecture." Helen's eyes flickered over the entire structure.

"It's almost overwhelming."

"Wait until you see inside." Helen stepped forward and Lucy rushed to pull open the door.

She stalled as the nave stretched before her.

The sun pierced through the clouds and shot bolts of light through the stained glass windows. It danced across the flagstones and off the gold of the center altar, far away. It reminded her of the MacMillan vases and sent a burst of joy, then a shadow of regret through her.

She shifted her gaze to take in the rest of the Abbey. Choir stalls flanked each side, close to the altar, built from dark wood and lit by antique red-shaded lamps. The narrow sides arched up and high with flags draped every few feet. The walls and floors were covered in stone memorials and plaques. Every square inch burst with history, memory, and sculpture.

"Every monarch since 1066 has been crowned here," Helen whispered. "Would you like to take a tour? It's as much a national museum as it is a church. The tombs and monuments are astounding."

"Not a formal tour. I'd rather roam on my own."

Helen nodded. "You go where you'd like and we'll meet back here when you're finished."

Lucy wandered around the space and, for the first time, felt something holy, outside time and larger than anything she'd ever known or understood. It wasn't peace. Peace was calm. This was active and vibrant. *Anticipation? Expectation?* She couldn't find a descriptor so she stopped trying to classify it and instead delighted in it.

As she approached the central altar, she imagined royals, dignitaries, and choirs sitting in the side-facing seats. The sun's rays made the wood glow gold and brown with shafts of red as light reflected off the cushions and lampshades. It was rich, polished, tended to, and loved. In her mind, it instantly contrasted with the dry chest left neglected in her apartment.

Lucy absorbed every detail, including the dust dancing in the sunlight. She noted each flag, each coat of arms, and each plaque. The oldest she found dated back seven hundred years, but she knew some were older. The history of this place reached farther and deeper than that. The Abbey felt solid and she wanted to sit, stay, and let the feeling grow and take root—as if she, too, could become more solid, more defined, simply by spending time beneath its arches. She sat in one of the pews and rested.

After a few moments, the active feeling compelled her forward. She moved through an arch, around a statue, and turned the corner to find a small sign hanging from a rope: *Poet's Corner*. It was packed: the walls peppered in plaques and reliefs; the floors covered in special stones with names and designs of all shapes, fonts, and sizes; and the stained glass window inscribed with names in center panels of white amidst the bright blue, red, and green. Her writers, her beloved, all immortalized here with their stories and words that reached high, dug deep, and soared with wind and clouds.

Shakespeare stood fully formed front andcenter, with Jane Austen's name scrolled clearly beside him in a clean, precise font that matched her writing, and Keats and Shelley provided anchors for a wreath above Johnson and Campbell. Lucy gazed at the window and found Elizabeth Gaskell before noting Henry James, T. S. Eliot, Tennyson, Browning, Thomas, Carroll—the list went on and on—scattered like manna at her feet.

Her eye caught Charlotte, Emily, and Anne Brontë's stone, each named individually but grouped together, as sisters should be. The words *WITH COURAGE TO ENDURE* were written in all capital letters, strong and commanding, beneath them. Lucy couldn't move.

"I thought I might find you here," Helen whispered.

"I like that quote. It fits them . . . It's exactly what should be said."

"True." Helen nodded, thinking. "It fits their stories and their short lives. Each heroine made choices, faced her consequences, and endured. Helen Graham. Shirley Keeldar. Agnes Grey. Cathy Earnshaw." She gestured to Lucy. "Lucy Snowe. Jane Eyre always strikes me the most, but I'm biased to that story."

"I don't know that Cathy fits."

"Ah . . . But the children endure, and that's

when the imagined story ends and perhaps th real one begins. New life. I think there's courage and endurance there too. And I think of those sisters, becoming who they were and what they did at such young ages, in such changing times but in their relative isolation."

Helen took a few steps forward and pointed to the stone floor plaques. "That quote I mentioned earlier? 'Come further up, come further in.' It's one of his. *That's* who I came to see."

"C. S. Lewis? My father started the Narnia books with me. We didn't get past one or two."

"He wrote others too. They were such a blessing to Charles in his last months. He was often too tired to talk so I sat in a chair and read. *The Four Loves*, *The Great Divorce*, *The Screwtape Letters*. Oh, how that one made me laugh and cringe. It ends something like 'Your increasingly and ravenously affectionate uncle, Screwtape.' He's going to eat his nephew, a junior devil, who let one slip through his fingers." Helen waved her fingers in the air. "It's diabolically delicious."

The gleam in her eyes faded. "They aren't all funny, though. We read *A Grief Observed* last and I did not like that. It's excerpts from Lewis's diary after his wife died, and I think that was Charles's way of preparing me."

Lucy's smile faded as well.

Helen continued with a slight shrug of a single shoulder. "He was right; it did prepare me. But it was *The Great Divorce* that meant the most. That's where I get the idea of going further up and further in. The quote is from *The Last Battle*, but it's the very journey in *The Great Divorce*. That's how I see Charles now, journeying further and further in, getting ever closer to God."

"That's a nice image."

Helen slowly walked back toward the Great West Door. "It's a part of my journey here too."

"You're planning to journey further up?"

Helen blew a soft sigh. "Someday; but for now, I'm working on my choices. There are things I have to lay down and others I need to embrace. Right choices that are good—they hit your heart. We are wired to know what they are and they make us solid. We can stand on them. And that's what I want, Lucy. I want to stand firm. I want my family to know me, and I'm not sure they really do. I was so bold and daring and then somewhere along the way, I shrank. I became frightened, and I hid behind rules and manners and other things that weren't true."

She pursed her lips as if the memory tasted sour. "If Ollie had chosen me, I would've followed him anywhere. And that would have been a disaster. Somehow I do know that. We weren't good and right for each other. But in stepping back from that ledge, I raced too fast and too far in the opposite direction." She clasped Lucy's arm. "I'm so tired, Lucy. So tired of regrets."

Lucy stopped walking. "Was my grandfather that bad?"

Helen slid her hand to Lucy's and held tight. "We were young. He had ambition and I was rebelling—against everything. But we all grow up. I expect he did too."

"Not everyone changes for the better as they age."

Helen stared, possibly catching Lucy's deeper question. "Look back at that corner." She waited until Lucy turned her head before continuing. "Do you see all those poets, writers, thinkers, and philosophers?"

"Yes."

"Like Lenin, few of them got their names on those plaques or their faces carved in that stone without controversy. All real lives hold controversy, trials, mistakes, and regrets. What matters is what you do next."

Lucy couldn't speak—unsure of what *next* might entail or what it might cost.

Helen looped her arm through Lucy's and patted her hand. "Don't hang on to the past so tightly that you taint the future. And that advice, I give from experience." She glanced at her watch. "It's still too early for lunch and I ruined your schedule by skipping the War Rooms."

Lucy pulled herself back to the present. "Not at all. Shall we knock out your shopping? The Vaults are closer to here than Portobello Road, where we'll be this afternoon. That is, if you'd still like to buy flatware sets for Sophie and Molly."

"I would. Not that they'll appreciate them." Helen stepped out the doors and into the sunshine. The sidewalk was packed with pedestrians, some locals and some tourists, taking photos—more of themselves than of the Abbey. "My grand-daughters do that."

Lucy didn't comment.

"Those girls are so different than I was at their age." Helen tilted her head toward a group of teenagers not listening to their tour leader. "I take that back. Molly is perhaps quite like I was, which is why she has her father in fits." She faced Lucy. "I wonder if they'll even understand why I'm giving them flatware. Is it too dated?"

"I don't think so. People want good silver in their home, still entertain, and Sid's clients are constantly buying it for children and grandchildren. There is a sense of enduring across generations, but please don't purchase anything because you think Sid expects a commission."

"I'm buying these gifts as much for me as I am for them. Something to remember me by. It felt right when I thought it up, so let's stick with it."

Dillon dropped them moments later at a nondescript entrance. Merely a wooden door and Lucite plaque noting *The London Silver Vaults*. Lucy had read that it was the world's largest collection of silver for sale. At the bottom of the stairs she quickly reviewed her notes—a listing of which "booths" sold what and expected valuations.

Within moments, a set caught Helen's eye. "This is so similar to mine. I hadn't thought of leaving one of the girls mine. What do you think?"

"It's a wonderful idea."

"But then James's wife . . ."

Lucy quirked a half-smile and Helen raised a hand. "That was thoughtless of me. It's just I shouldn't give the girls something so significant and not think of him, simply because he's a man."

"Of course not. And of course he's going to marry someday."

Helen studied the room. "Lucy, I want to do this. I want to give a gift that has meaning and lasts, but suddenly this feels staid. Like the War Rooms, it's somewhere I've been or something I've done and it stifles now. I don't want that."

"You want something new and different, and to put everything on trial." Lucy paraphrased Virginia Woolf's words.

Helen's penciled eyebrows shot up as she caught the reference. "Exactly."

"Then let's accomplish both." Lucy felt something new unfurl inside her, similar to the anticipation that crept within her at the Abbey. She spun slowly, scanning her options. "Sid always says to pay attention to who someone is and not who she wants to be. So I say we're on track with the silver, but the early to mid-Victorian is not going to satisfy you. Not the real you."

Helen's face lit with excitement. "Find me something fun. Something my girls will love."

"Let's go searching." Lucy led Helen down the central aisle. She took in all the gorgeous silver work—intricate scrolls on trays, latticework climbing candlesticks, flatware sets, some smooth and clean, others filigreed and infinitely detailed.

Lucy noticed Helen fall behind. After a few minutes, she found her again. "Remembering?"

"That's the true gift of old age, not the sleeping. It's the ability to drift away into memory at any time and in any place," Helen lamented. "Some of this reminds me of Ollie's work. He was an engraver too, Lucy. Your father was right when he said Ollie was an artist." She strummed her fingers together. "These hands can't even hold a pen without pain anymore."

Lucy felt a shadow spread with her grand-father's name. She pushed it away. "Come see what I've found."

Helen followed her to a far booth where a slim woman in her midsixties stood waiting. "She picked out some lovely sets."

Helen laughed with delight.

"If you're sure . . ." Lucy paused, but at Helen's eager expression, she tapped on the glass-topped case below her selections. "Those are what you say you don't want. They range from very simple, early 1700s and a very nice value"—she dragged her finger across the glass—"to very ornate, the height of the opulent scrolls. But these are different." She positioned the black velvet blotters directly in front of Helen and grasped the first fork. "These sets are both Danish and they're bold. Crazy bold when compared to what we've been talking about."

"I love them." Helen picked up a knife, the handle fashioned from a thin, long stem that folded under and rested on a flower's bloom. "It's alive and fresh, like it's growing out of the handle."

"That's by Orla Vagn Mogensen, late 1950s, and terribly innovative. Still considered some of the finest Danish work." The woman lifted a knife from the other blotter. "This set is by Georg Jensen. The master. His Blossom pattern from 1919."

"I might like this even better." Helen reached for the fork and let her fingers trail along a strong flower growing from the silver and bursting on top of the handle rather than dipping beneath—the gorgeous bud forever poised on the brink of opening. "There's nothing passive about these. They feel fresh, young, and beautiful."

"Are you sure? I don't want you to regret these choices."

"I'll never regret this." Helen ran her finger over each and every flower.

"Okay then." Lucy addressed the woman, who slid a piece of linen paper across the counter.

Helen gestured for Lucy to look first.

Lucy looked, bit her lip, and then slid the paper to Helen. "It's quite a sum, but they're priced well."

The woman behind the counter accepted the compliment with a short nod.

"I agree. I'll take them both." Helen pushed the paper back to the woman. "Lucy will handle the details. I'd like them shipped to her gallery."

The woman laid several forms in front of Lucy along with a slim black fountain pen as Helen continued. "And while she's handling that, I need something for my daughter-in-law." She scanned the glass display cases and the lit shelves. "I want something equally fresh and fun. What do you suggest?"

"It's not old, but recently I acquired a cut crystal vase with silver inlay that I think is magnificent." The woman reached into a deep cabinet behind her and pulled out a heavy vase at least twenty inches high with silver laid into deep grooves like vines reaching up and around.

Lucy set down the pen. Light bounced off the cuts in the glass and the silver, refracting in a shooting of rainbow colors off each edge and glowing warm off the silver. "Sid tells me all the time that decorating should evoke a response. I trusted him, but never felt it. Then he got some vases by an English artist, MacMillan . . . And this." She reached out and traced one silver vine with a delicate finger. "There is something so personally meaningful here, isn't there? When you get it. When it speaks to you."

"I think so. We're relational creatures and I don't think those connections are made exclusively with people." Helen traced another vine. "Artists create things that point us to beauty, to truth, to God."

"I agree, but I've only ever felt it with books. Not true . . . My drapery panels . . ." Lucy stilled. "Helen . . ."

"I agree. It's stunning." Helen turned back to the woman. "This is perfect. In years to come, I want my daughter-in-law to remember me like this."

A few minutes later, with purchases made, the pair headed to the elevator. Helen gripped Lucy's elbow and leaned hard. "I'm oddly spent. I came here to buy gifts, and I did, but there's a piece of me in those selections that I haven't spent time with in many years."

Lucy smiled with understanding. "I think that was the most fun I've had in a really long time too. Those selections were you. All you. It was extraordinary to be a part of that." Lucy felt herself expand.

Helen exhaled, a mixture of release and exhaustion. "Now let's go get a bite to eat and wander Portobello Road. It's time to be in the sunshine."

Chapter 18

D illon dropped them at a small courtyard opening onto Borough High Street.

"This is going to be special," Lucy commented as they wove through the black picnic tables to the front door. "You mentioned this place. Have you been here before?"

"I have. We brought Charlie here before his senior year in high school, and while Charles was off somewhere, the two of us ate fish and chips and he enjoyed his first pint. At least, he told me it was his first. It was a wonderful afternoon."

"Well, you're back and I pulled up lots of little fun tidbits for inside." Lucy slid her phone out of her bag and as they ventured through the inn's front room, she noted the signs marking it as London's *last galleried coaching inn*. Another sign indicated that The Middle Bar had been a coffee room in Dickens's day.

Helen tapped the wall next to Dickens's life insurance policy framed near the fireplace and whispered, "Mine's with my lawyer."

The hostess led the way up a slender turning staircase to the restaurant above. It was snug and comfortable with plastered walls and rough-hewn beams, red and cream carpets, and wood furniture that didn't look any less cozy because the benches and chairs were simple and uncushioned. The room was only half-filled, but the air buzzed with excitement as if diners were munching on history and remembrance as well as fish and chips.

Soon full and picking at the remnants of a Neal's Yard cheese platter and George's ale-battered cod, Lucy watched the light playing off of the raindrops still sticking to the window mullions.

"Does your father have green eyes too?"

"He does. I remember them well." She turned back to Helen. "What was Ollie like? You made him sound very exciting, then at the Abbey today, almost scary, like he was some Heathcliff who tormented you."

"Not that at all. He was more Rochester than anyone."

Lucy groaned. "That's hardly better."

"I disagree." Helen laughed. "Edward Rochester had some fine qualities in the end. He simply had lessons to learn, and I expect your grandfather grew up nicely too.

"My dad had to learn deception from somewhere . . . It seems history just repeats itself."

"That's an easy out. It exonerates your dad from responsibility. Maybe your dad needed some stability, emotional support, or something else completely and he found it in stories, but what he did with those stories was his affair."

Helen laid a slice of cheese on an apple wedge

and handed it to Lucy. "As for Ollie, we met when I was only twenty-one and he twenty-four. We were young. He had plenty of time to mature. He may have been everything your father told you."

"That's not that young."

"You aren't looking back at those years across a gap of sixty-five. You'll see." Helen smiled softly. "At twenty-four, he was bold, exciting, and annoyingly confident. He kissed me within ten minutes of our meeting, right there in the jewelry store when Mr. Jones stepped to the back, and was so certain, so sure."

"But earlier you mentioned a ledge?"

"He was bold and a risk-taker. I was only playing at it, trying to keep up in a game I didn't understand. But he took care of me and I do think he truly loved me. When I walked out that last night, I didn't know it was the end, but he did. Letting me keep the watch was a conscious choice on his part." Helen set down her glass. "Yes, if anyone could reinvent himself, Ollie could."

Lucy sat back and closed her eyes. She felt herself at a crossroads, and the need to make a choice pressed upon her. The lightness of helping Helen find gifts and discover herself, of joining in a moment that had brought Helen laughter and delight, felt strangely distant. Heaviness and shadow had replaced it, as if footsteps echoed down a dark corridor and, against her will, Lucy followed.

She opened her eyes. "I feel as though, in many ways, I'm a trial run before you share with your family. I'm safe." Lucy slowed her voice. "I can't judge you, but this is hard."

Helen considered her statement. "You're right. I think if we hadn't met, I wouldn't be here. James mentioned your name, and it niggled and grew and wouldn't leave me alone. Then once we met, waves of memory rolled over me, and there wasn't a choice but to accept it all."

Helen sighed. "I hadn't thought what it would mean for you, but I knew, somehow I knew you needed to be here. So why not let it work both ways? As I said at the coffee shop, you can talk about your life and your dad with me." She slowed her voice to mirror Lucy's. "I won't judge you."

Lucy leaned back. "So much about my dad is coming back to me and I don't know what's true. The only thing I know for certain is Dad called England home. His mother was from here, died here, and his best memories came from here, never Chicago. And I only know that because he never had to say it. He'd get this glow when he talked about it, and his accent, all Chicago, would morph into a beautiful, lilting English one. I used to make him tell me stories or read English authors so he'd slip into it. Even then I knew that was honest. Beatrix Potter was the best, I think, because his own mother read them to him as a child."

"That's lovely and sad at the same time."

"I learned to watch him, watch people really, and learn the cues rather than listen to their words. And now, I feel, rather than using that ability to discern truth, I use it to get my way. I'm more like him than not."

"Childhood lessons, favorites, skills . . . They shape us."

"They do."

Helen laid her hands on the table. "I said this was *our* trip and I sense Beatrix Potter was important in your life as well. Perhaps I was too hasty. Shall we add the Lake District to our itinerary after all?"

Lucy startled. "No. I was only reminiscing. I— Let's enjoy today. We can talk about that later." The bread crumb she'd inadvertently dropped fell squarely on the trail to Bowness, and it felt ugly, dirty, and obtrusive. She swept it away.

Lucy looked up the street. The slight hill allowed her to see all the way to the bend at the top. It was Saturday and the center of Portobello Road was full of carts and vendors. People spilled from the shops along the road and wove through the center stalls.

"This isn't the place for books, not like Charing Cross Road, but I did find a few shops. Do you mind?"

"Not at all. And I want to look for gifts."

"Me too. I've only found a snow globe for one friend and it won't go over well if she's the only one who gets a gift."

"That never goes well. My grandchildren won't understand if there isn't a little something in my suitcase either."

They wandered up the street in a lazy fashion. Lucy snacked on crepes from a vendor and Helen purchased a blue cashmere scarf that matched Molly's eyes.

"Here's one of the booksellers." Lucy squinted as the bright light of the street dimmed inside the door of the antique emporium—a series of booths arranged in hallways within connected buildings.

"Look here." Lucy picked up a tan leather-bound book. "*The Vicar of Wakefield*. I love this one. It's so over-the-top and delightfully formal." She ran her hand over the worn cover. It was well moisturized and the scratches had been rubbed and softened.

An elderly gentleman in a wrinkled oxford and cardigan sweater stepped toward her. She waved the book to him. "You take good care of these."

"I love each and every one."

She ran her finger over another title. "I can tell."

"Do you collect books?"

"I read them. I sell them, much like you do, in Chicago, but no, I don't collect them."

"If you love them, that's all that matters." He laid another on the counter.

"I do . . . I do love them." The admission wasn't new, but it brought James to mind and the night he'd told her that she devalued them.

As she held the tan volume in her hands, she recognized that, while she'd said she loved them, she hadn't in fact enjoyed books for a long while. Somewhere along the way, they had become commodities to sell and perhaps forging inscriptions had also been more about their monetary value than she thought or was willing to accept. How much changed in a life, in a person, when one wasn't paying attention?

The man had continued, unaware he'd lost her. ". . . I can't make as much profit on them as I used to." He gestured to the shelf behind him. "There's much more interest in silver, glass, and trinkets like this." He picked up a silver and leather snuffbox. "Very popular in the late nineteenth century and coming back in the last several years."

"You'd think we'd all know better about tobacco." Lucy noted several thimbles within his collection. "Those are lovely. May I see the one on the far right?"

He reached in and pulled out the tiny thimble. It had simple scrolling above the dimples and barely fit on her pinky finger.

Lucy whispered to Helen, "Sid would like these . . . Displayed in a wooden dish or something like a nineteenth-century needle box."

"I used to love to sew . . . You're good at this. I understand why Sid raved about you on the phone that day."

"I always thought my gift lay in procurement, in the books and keeping him organized, but now . . ." As Lucy fingered the thimble and turned back to the books, her eye caught a whiskey pourer.

"James!" She picked up the delicate glass bottle by its tiny circular handle and flipped the sterling lid up and down. "He'd love this. Did you know he drinks scotch? Only single malt. He's sort of snobby about it, really."

"That's my fault. Charles and I gave him a bottle for his twenty-first birthday."

Helen pointed to the bottle. "Do you have two of these?"

The gentleman's face lit. "I have a matched set." He bent down and pulled two from the display case. Small engraved plaques hung from delicate silver chains around the bottlenecks.

"Perfect." Helen touched the plaques. "I think Charlie might enjoy one too."

As Lucy handled the purchase details, Helen walked farther into the emporium. She was almost out the other end by the time Lucy caught up with her, carrying a small bag. "I didn't have them shipped. He wasn't equipped for that and I have plenty of room in my suitcase."

"Did you get your little book too?"

"I did. It's so lovely. I'll end up putting it in our

case for sale, but I'll get to read it first. There's even a small picture of when Burchell makes his great reveal and solves everyone's problems. I adore that moment."

"I've never read it."

"Well, during our drive to Haworth, we can start." Lucy grinned. "I'll read to you."

"I'd like that." Helen stopped at the top of the street. "Is it that way?"

Lucy knew exactly what she meant. "About five blocks. Long ones though. If you want to walk, we should start. Or I could text Dillon."

"Let's walk. It'll settle my nerves."

They crossed Notting Hill Gate and turned onto Kensington Church Street. They walked two more blocks, without talking, and soon they found themselves standing in front of a small flat.

Lucy chuckled. "I think when it's four floors high, it should be called a 'vertical,' don't you?"

Helen stared at the house. "This has been a good day, Lucy, two good days. I feel as though they've led me to this moment and I thank you for that." She peered at Lucy. "I'm sorry for the pain I've caused, but I needed you here."

"You're welcome." Lucy drew her eyes from the building and leveled them at Helen. "Are you ready?"

"I am." Helen nodded. "It's a shame I didn't do this years ago. I wonder what might have been."

"What do you mean?"

"Secrets always have a price, even if only for ourselves. And this one has cost me. I don't think I knew how much until . . . recently. That's the very sad part." She lifted the heavy knocker and let it fall.

"What will you tell them?"

"I haven't decided. Nothing sounds right."

The bright-blue door opened immediately and there stood a man in his midforties sporting an anxious expression. "Mrs. Carmichael?"

"You must be Edward. Edward Parrish?"

"I am. Come in. Come in." He retreated into the narrow hallway. To the right it opened into a large living room with a beautiful enclosed garden behind the French doors. The room was pale lavender with a yellow, purple, and grey Aubusson rug. "My wife will be right up. She's in the kitchen preparing tea."

"You didn't need to go to any trouble for us."

"Trouble? If what you wrote was true, it's worth some trouble." He led them into the room. "Please. Please sit."

Lucy sat in a small straight-back chair by the door, letting Helen cross in front of her to the couch. "Your home is lovely."

"Thank you. We moved here about five years ago after our son left for school. It's become a wonderful home for us. The kitchen is downstairs with a small parlor. Clara and I spend most of our time there or above in the study . . ." He paused.

"I don't think I've sat in here since Christmas."

Edward's wife entered with a delicate teapot and four cups and saucers resting on an enameled tray. A small plate of cookies tilted on the edge.

Lucy jumped up. "May I?"

"Oh . . . I thought I was going to lose that. Thank you." She set the tray down with a clatter as Lucy caught the cookie plate. Edward made hasty introductions then fell silent as Lucy helped Clara pass tea and cookies.

Once everyone was settled, all eyes turned to Helen. "I should begin." She laid down her cup and Lucy heard it gently rattle within the saucer. Helen reached into her handbag and pulled out the gold watch, dangling it from its chain.

Edward reached out his hand and then drew it back. "May I?"

"Of course." Helen offered the watch to him. "Your family name is on the cover, and if I'm correct, all the initials inside line up with your ancestors."

Edward ran his fingers over the case, opened it, shut it, opened it again, and finally looked up with moist eyes. "AGP. Augustus Grant. EDP. Edward Dunning. TMP. Theodore Moore, my grand-father. My own father's aren't here. The watch went missing during the war and he . . . He was born in '43."

"Did they lose their home in the bombings?"

"No, but they moved, probably five or six times,

during those years. Things were lost." He held the watch in his palm. "But this is it. He never saw it, but he described it to me as his father had to him." Edward passed the watch to his wife. "I could've described it perfectly. And Daniel, my son, knows it too. How silly is it that three generations have never seen that watch and yet we all know every scroll and every line?" He reached to pull it back as if it might become lost again. "But it's here. It's here."

"Is your father alive? The private investigator I hired found only you."

"He passed away in '04." He traced the initials with his finger. "He would have loved to have seen this. He never gave up hope that it would find its way back to us . . . I'll still add his initials."

As Edward sat gaping at the watch, Lucy noticed that Clara watched Helen.

Clara took a sip of tea, then spoke. "How did you find it? And your letter said you hired a private investigator?"

Fair questions, Lucy thought. She, too, turned to Helen, wondering what she'd say. How much truth was enough truth?

"I've thought long and hard about how to answer . . . I've had the watch for sixty-five years and, yes, I knew from the first day that it didn't belong to the person from whom I acquired it." She dropped her eyes to her lap, took a deep breath, and met their gaze again.

The whole truth.

"I was in love with a young man who sold stolen property in the States." Helen gazed at Lucy. "And when we parted ways, I took that from him. Part talisman, part revenge, and wholly wrong, but I never studied it so I didn't know about the name and the initials inside. I simply hid it away."

She rubbed her fingers together as if kneading out the story. "Then recently I was reminded of it and that's when I noticed the markings. It became very important to me to end the story and return it, if I could." She addressed Clara. "I'm only sorry it's taken so long."

"All this time." Edward's face reddened. "You knew it was stolen? And you kept it?"

"I didn't realize I could find the proper owners. It wasn't like that . . ." Helen pressed her lips together.

"Then how was it?" Edward's voice pitched higher. "This was a piece of our family. Our history. My father—" His voice cut out as if he couldn't bring himself to finish the sentence.

"I sincerely apologize and I have no real excuse to give." Helen sat with her hands in her lap and her face blank—as if willing to accept anything that came next.

"You said you loved the man who stole it. Was he your husband? Did he steal it?"

Edward's anger surprised Lucy. She glanced at Helen.

"Never." Helen's eyes darkened to steel. "This was before I met my husband. He didn't know it existed at all."

Edward peeked at his wife; she took up the questioning. "What made you come here?"

Helen's visible anger faded and a new emotion flitted through her eyes, gone before Lucy could identify it. "Some things you must do in person, and my time to see those through is . . . ending."

Edward opened his mouth but caught a gesture from his wife before speaking. Watching, Lucy felt as if an entire conversation passed between the couple without a single word spoken. Hurt, anger, acceptance, forgiveness, and then joy flashed between them—one leading, one questioning, one answering, and one accepting. It was impossible to tell who led the volley, but Lucy could discern when the last emotion settled. Clara blinked and nodded so slightly, so minutely, that Lucy wondered if only she had caught it.

But Edward had caught it as well. He gave his wife a brief and intimate smile before turning to Helen. "Forgive me. It's home now and I truly do thank you for the efforts you took to find us." His words came out stiff and clipped, but Lucy felt as if he wanted them to be sincere—as if he knew what was right and, by saying it, he could make it so.

He closed the watch between his palms. "It's a good idea, I think. I'll add my father's initials and mine. Daniel's too, soon." Edward's voice trailed off.

Clara picked up the thread. "I sense this is about more than the watch, but we thank you for that part. Even I could've told you what it looked like." She laughed.

"It was the perfect reason for a little trip." Helen stood as Edward sat rubbing his finger over the watch's delicate casing.

"We should go now. Thank you for your kindness and the lovely tea, Clara. I wish you both the very best."

Lucy stood as well and Clara led them to the door.

They'd covered only a few steps to the sidewalk before Helen stopped and clutched the wrought-iron railing. Lucy grabbed at her arm, unable to fully see her face in the dim light until she stood inches from her. "Helen?"

Helen released a deep sigh that ended in a cough, a laugh, and a hiccup simultaneously. "Oh . . . That took much too long, Lucy. Much too long. And there was a moment there. Oh . . . His father, Lucy, there's no making that right. I had a piece of their history, their story, this whole time. And poor Charles. I couldn't bear that . . . Clara got me out of that, don't you think? I could've hugged her right then. Ahh . . . I'm so glad she was there." She grabbed for Lucy's wrist.

"Bless that woman! Did you see his face? Beet

red? And his hair? It stood up a little, like a cat. How did he do that?" Helen started to laugh, frantic and watery, then hiccupped again. She let go of the fence, but not Lucy's wrist, and started to walk. "It's over. It's all finally over."

At the street corner, they both stopped.

"Shall I call Dillon?"

"I suppose so . . ." Helen stepped forward. "Look, Lucy, Sally Clarke's. It's still here."

"What is it?"

"A sheer delight. Don't bother with Dillon yet." She pulled at Lucy's hand. "Come on. I feel like celebrating."

Chapter 19

Lucy followed Helen into the small provisions shop bursting with beautiful jars of culinary delights, baked goods, cheeses, and pastas. There were biscuits, tins filled with candies, and a small display of fresh vegetables and fruits in baskets. She kept glancing at Helen, not quite sure what to think of her new giddiness. She was touching every package and every piece of fruit as if seeing things, seeing color, for the first time.

"There's a restaurant attached. Will you see if we can get a table?"

"I'll be right back." Lucy ducked back out of the shop to the restaurant next door.

A young woman, a few years younger than herself, was making notes on paper while dragging her finger across a computer track pad. Her face was drawn tight, her eyes upset rather than annoyed.

Lucy watched her as she crossed the small waiting area. "We have a reservation for Carmichael at six, but we're a few minutes early and we'd like to be seated now if possible."

The woman's face fell and she looked back to her screen, to her notebook, and to her screen again. "I don't have any reservations for Carmichael this evening." She slid her finger across the track pad once, then again.

"I confirmed this reservation. Twice. And I am not going to tell my eighty-five-year-old grandmother you lost it." Lucy flattened out her accent, making herself even more American and louder. "Do you know how far she's traveled? Just give us whatever you have available. I requested a window table."

"I don't have any notes down and we don't have—"

"Find something. Now."

The young woman glared at her, then relented in the next beat. "Please excuse me."

She hurried away and talked to a server who pointed to a center table. She came back and said, "We can seat you now but not at the window. It's the best I can offer."

"That'll do." Lucy smiled. "You made me nervous for a minute. I did not want to tell her that her favorite restaurant wasn't going to happen tonight after all."

"No, of course not." The woman gripped the edge of the hostess stand before erasing something in her notes.

Within minutes, Lucy led Helen into the candlelit dining room where the hostess awaited them at the small central table.

Lucy ran her hand across the linen tablecloth. "She forgot our menus."

"If it's like it used to be, there are no menus. It's a set three-course meal." Helen leaned forward. "I feel good, Lucy. I hadn't realized how deep that reached, how important that was to me."

Lucy straightened her napkin in her lap. "James called me questioning our trip, you told Charlie it couldn't wait until summer, you've dropped comments here and there, and you just told Clara that your time is ending."

"Is there a question there?"

"There's a story. James told me you had—*have*—time." Lucy felt the currents gaining strength. She also felt the curtain draped in front of her, velvet, thick and dark, providing the tension and movement, just like it did in every good story.

But suddenly she wanted a Burchell—an honest and humble young man—to step forward and, as in *The Vicar of Wakefield*, announce he was Sir William Thornhill and he possessed the authority and the desire to set all to rights. No secrets, no shadows, no curtain . . . No Brontë wife in the attic. Clear and beautiful transparency.

Helen stared straight into Lucy's eyes. No blinking. "Getting old is not for the faint of heart, Lucy. It's a trial unlike any I've known, to be constantly betrayed by my body. That's what's happening to me. I'm not strong enough for more treatment. So, yes, my time is ending and no one is fully aware of that yet."

"Why haven't you told your son?"

"I needed to see this through, and the moment Charlie knows, I'll be put on lockdown and may never make another decision for myself again."

"That's a little dramatic." Lucy threw Helen's words back at her.

"Only slightly."

"Then time matters, Helen. We should go home now. You need to be with your family."

"Yes, time matters to me very much. I've used it exactly the way I wanted to, and if it costs me in the end, it will be worth it." Helen's jaw flexed and Lucy noted her remarkable eyes cooling in color. #821 *Blue Ice* would best describe them now. "I won't regret this, ever. I finally feel like I can be present and real and me, and even if it's only for a little while, I need that. My family needs that."

"I don't have the power to drag you home, do I?"

"Not really," Helen agreed.

"Excellent. Now I'm an accomplice. Edward was so upset that you'd withheld a watch from them—and that's a watch! Your family is going to be hurt far worse. And when James finds out that I know . . . He already hates me."

"He doesn't hate you."

"Helen, I hate me right now."

Helen shifted her gaze. "I should've been honest with you about how bad my cancer is."

"What will you do?"

"I'll go home and be honest with Charlie— honest about so many things, which is why this needed to come first." Helen scanned the restaurant. "Part of me is sad you could get us in here."

"Why?"

"You used to have to make reservations months in advance. To get one so easily must mean that it's gone downhill."

Lucy didn't reply.

"Let's order champagne. Don't you think that's fitting?"

"No. It doesn't feel fitting at all."

"I feel better than I have in years. Please, Lucy, celebrate with me." Helen sat back. "And I think we should cut a day from Haworth and one from London and visit the Lake District. It won't add any time to the trip."

Lucy shook her head. "Forget it. Please. Let's just get back to Chicago."

Helen reached across the table. "A few days now won't matter. This is part of it too, Lucy. I'm not done yet. I'm here and I'm seeing this through. We've done the hard part; now I want to have a little fun. Stay at an inn and sit by a fire. I won't come this way again, please."

"You didn't even want to—"

"Lucy, Haworth and the Lake District."

Lucy knew a command when she heard one and didn't protest. Jane Eyre's refusal to marry St. John floated before her—the double-edged moment, the acquiescence with stipulations. Two paths. One choice. *I am ready to go to India, if I may go free.*

Could she say the same? Lucy tried. "We stay two days in Haworth, one in the Lake District, then straight home. No coming back here. Cutting three days off in total is my final offer."

"Very well."

"I'll make the arrangements," Lucy conceded.

"Now that everything is settled, it's time we ordered that champagne."

Helen was right: once the champagne was ordered, there were no decisions left. A beautiful arugula and pear salad arrived, followed by a Dover sole and light tart for dessert. And although every bite was delicate and delicious, Lucy felt herself tasting little and flitting in and out of the conversation.

Helen talked of blues clubs, staying out all night

drinking French 75s, watching sunrises, and who knows what else . . . But she seemed younger, lighter, and more alive. She wrinkled her nose and her eyes widened and softened. "He used to get so mad and tell me to loosen up. If he only knew the fun I'd had. I wanted him to get into his own scrapes, make his own bad decisions, and wallow around youth. But he was right, I reined him in. I should've told him, 'run mad as often as you choose; but do not faint,' and left it at that."

"Who? Charlie?" A smile finally reached Lucy's eyes as she returned to Helen's story. "I remember that line. Jane Austen is a font of good advice."

"And yet, I followed another's. 'I set to right everything. Myself and him by setting his task from hour to hour, standing by him always and helping, controlling him really, from moment to moment.'"

"What's that from?"

"I'm not surprised you don't recognize it. It's very random, but it struck me and I read it over and over until I memorized it. Do you know what effort that takes at my age?"

Helen nodded encouragement. "Come now." One corner of her mouth tilted up. "You can give me one guess."

"I see where your grandson gets it." Lucy relented and waggled a finger at Helen's smile. "James's lips curve up that same way when he feels superior."

"As well I should. *Jane Eyre*. I must say it was hard to see myself so clearly in such a character."

"It's got to be St. John. No one else is so truculent."

Helen tapped her nose. "Yes. Me and St. John. It's when he's trying to convince Jane to marry him."

"What?" Lucy was surprised it was the very scene she had pondered moments ago.

"You know that part. He wants her to marry him, but she'll only travel to India if she can go unattached." Helen continued, "He was so set, couldn't see things another way, but not me. Not any longer. Spring is coming and I'm thawing. And in all sincerity, I can't bring myself to care about what comes next."

Lucy sat back in her chair and studied the room. Helen followed her gaze. It held a handful of white-linen-draped tables and only a few of them were filled so early in the evening. Small nosegays of tight white roses sat in the center with two or three lit votives casting a warm glow on their petals. The air was faintly sweet. To catch the perfume, she had to drag in the air and savor it.

I do, Lucy thought. *I care what comes next.*

"Helen?" Lucy called.

Helen's head bounced up, startled by Lucy's anxious tone.

"I came over here and told the hostess that she'd lost our reservation. I bullied my way to this table. The restaurant hasn't gone downhill at all."

"Lucy!"

"I know." Lucy let her hands flutter. "Sometimes a soft word gets you what you want. And sometimes, pressing your advantage works." Her eyes trailed to the hostess stand. The young woman rapped her pencil against her notebook, perhaps rearranging tables for that very evening or perhaps too angry to lift her head.

"Excuse me." Lucy stood and walked toward her. The hostess glanced up at her approach and frowned. Lucy noticed her fingers whiten as she gripped the pencil. It bent, ready to snap.

"I owe you an apology. I . . . We didn't have a reservation. I didn't want to disappoint my boss, but that wasn't your concern. I acted badly, really badly, and I'm sorry."

The woman's eyes rounded then narrowed. "Am I to make you feel better?"

"I simply wanted to apologize."

"You've apologized. Please enjoy your table."

Lucy was impressed with the biting delivery. Every inflection screamed that she, in fact, wished Lucy would choke on her fruit tart and expire immediately, and with excruciating pain. Lucy offered a small gesture of agreement that she deserved no better. The hostess returned her focus to her notepad and Lucy returned to the table.

"And?" Helen took a quick sip of champagne

and pushed Lucy's toward her. "You should finish that before we have to leave."

"We get to stay. She said to enjoy our table, but I suspect she meant only you."

"What on earth did you say?" Helen stifled a giggle.

"I apologized." Lucy took a quick sip. "It didn't go over well, but I can't blame her."

"I'll say not." Helen clicked her champagne glass against Lucy's and sipped again. "How do you feel?"

"A bit like you earlier. Completely shredded." Lucy blew out a shaky laugh. "But I think you're a little responsible for that too."

Upon reaching Dukes, Lucy found herself unwilling to go to bed, but not eager to walk around London, even in the bright lights of Piccadilly, alone. She kissed Helen's cheek good night in the lobby and headed to the bar, settling in a bright yellow armchair in the front window. She watched the octogenarian Italian bartender, whom a guest called Gilberto, pour drinks and entertain the few men standing near him. Realizing she was staring, Lucy opened her book, more to have something to do with her eyes and her hands than to read.

"An espresso?"

Lucy looked up to find him leaning above her. "Thank you, but it'll keep me awake tonight."

Gilberto bowed and stepped back behind the

bar. Lucy laid her book down, remembering Bowness-on-Windermere and the change in plans. She opened her computer and secured reservations at the inn she'd found. Clicking the final key for "confirmation" felt far from a victory. As she sent a quick text to Dillon to tell him of the change in their plans as well, she felt Gilberto's presence once more.

This time he held a small wooden table with bottles, a lemon, and a frozen glass resting on its top. He set it down and, with a "Martini, *molto bene*," proceeded to pour vermouth from a small silver shaker into the ice-clouded martini glass. He then added thick frozen vodka until it bubbled at the top.

"You watch this." He peeled a small strip of lemon zest and, with a quick flick of his wrist and hip, put his full weight and effort behind cracking the peel lengthwise. The oil mist exploded over the glass and dotted Lucy's face.

She closed her eyes and drew in the fresh, bright smell. "That's amazing."

Gilberto held the peel high then slid it, never breaking the vodka's surface tension, down the side of the glass, pushing the liquid's bubble up farther.

"It's above the rim. I won't be able to move that," Lucy exclaimed.

"You take your first sip here. Then you move the drink."

Lucy leaned over and took a sip, the lemon oil moistening her lips and tickling her nose. "I've never had anything like this."

"And you only have one. On me." He picked up the drink and carefully placed it on her side table. "My specialty."

"Thank you."

He bowed again and picked up his little table to move back behind the bar.

Lucy took slow sips, thinking of Helen and her gimlets, her dancing, and what was now ahead . . . *James.* Unable to follow that further, she directed her mind back to the day and other niggling images surfaced. The sun bursting through the window at Westminster Abbey. *With Courage to Endure.* The extraordinary vase Helen purchased at the Silver Vaults. The tantalizing feeling of helping Helen express her true self for her granddaughters, for her daughter-in-law. The honesty with which Helen approached Edward Parrish. His anger, his vulnerability, his loss, Sally Clarke's . . . *Oh my . . .*

Lucy picked up her phone and tapped Sid's number. He answered immediately.

"I was hoping you'd call. How was today?"

"It's been a big day . . . She purchased two full flatware sets and a spectacular crystal vase with silver inlays. I meant to send you pictures of everything, but forgot. I'll do that as soon as we hang up."

"Excellent. Did you stay early 1700s? Or was her style more like yours?"

"Victorian? Fussy?" Lucy tried to lighten her tone. Sid would question otherwise and where would she begin? Where could she end?

"I didn't say that." Sid's tone carried a smile.

"She said she felt daring and wanted to step out. I think that's the true Helen Carmichael so I showed her some bold early-twentieth-century designs, both Danish. She adored them. Purchased them then and there."

"I'm impressed, Lucy, and I trust you. Well done."

Trust. Lucy closed her eyes. "Sid? Do you still have all three MacMillan vases?" She opened them as her question hung across the line.

"I do. I thought I might reach out to the Palmers saying I have a surprise, but I haven't gotten around to it. I'm enjoying them too much. And they're stirring up your walk-ins. Two lamps and a lovely bronze Norton have sold because folks needed a closer view of the vase, that one you said was your favorite. And there's interest in the Pol piece. If that sells, it'll top your record. The prospective buyer was in here for only five minutes." Sid paused. "Why do you ask?"

"I . . . I really want to see them again." Lucy opened her mouth to say more as Sid chuckled in reply.

"Considering I think you're responsible for

getting them here so quick, I'll certainly keep them. We're not in a rush."

"Thank you." Lucy noted a large party enter the bar as the volume rose. "I have to go, Sid. I'll send you the pictures."

She tapped off the phone.

"Enough," she whispered to herself as she dropped her phone into her bag and took a last sip of her drink. As she discreetly waved a thank-you to Gilberto, her eye caught the painting above his head, Nelson defeating Napoleon at Waterloo. "Skirmish lost. Further down and further out."

Chapter 20

Early the next afternoon as Lucy settled into the car, she bumped into a huge wicker basket resting between her seat and Helen's. "What is this?"

"While you were out gallivanting, I asked Dillon to procure a picnic for us from Fortnum & Mason." Helen raised her brows and Lucy noticed they were penciled more lightly, giving her a wide-eyed doe appearance.

She directed her gaze back to the basket. "May I peek?"

"Of course."

Lucy opened the top panel and pushed boxes and jars around in an attempt to see everything.

"Olives, shortbread, sparkling water, nuts, lemon cookies, fruit, chocolates . . . What isn't in here?"

"There had better be some cheeses. I requested a good Stilton." Helen pulled at the basket's lid.

"There are at least three cheeses, and crackers too."

"Lovely." Helen leaned back as Dillon started the engine. "Tell me about your morning."

"My gallivanting? It was incredible. I raced around and saw everything I wanted to see."

"If you'd let us come back . . ."

"I think you're teasing me and you don't really want to come back." Lucy sat back. "You must know it's time to go. Even these few days feel like we're stealing from your family."

"I'm not ready. You may not understand this, Lucy, but to go back, I need to feel strong. And I don't yet, physically or emotionally. I'm not delaying our return frivolously. I need this, and the calm of Haworth and now the Lake District appeals to me."

Lucy studied her and accepted the truth of her statement. "Then I won't question again."

"Thank you." Helen reached over the basket and patted Lucy's shoulder. "Did you get to the British Library?"

"I beelined only through the Ritblat Gallery to glimpse the *Jane Eyre* and it was lovely."

"But you also caught the Magna Carta." Helen chortled at Lucy's head shake. "The Gutenberg

Bible? Shakespeare's first folio? Handel's original *Messiah*, in his own hand?"

"When you ask that way, you make it sound like those are more important," Lucy droned.

"Goodness, never." Helen laughed. "I'm glad you went and glad you had fun."

"I did. I also took the Tube to the Baker Street Station and visited Sherlock Holmes. The museum is everything you'd want it to be—kitschy, authentic, touristy, and marvelous. It made me want to reread all those stories again . . . I'm sorry you couldn't join me."

"You needed to see everything you could." Helen offered a small smile. "I move more slowly regardless of other factors."

Dillon pulled onto the highway, and as the start-stop and sharp turns of city driving smoothed straight, with the engine at a constant soft thrum, Helen's eyes drifted shut and her breathing slowed and deepened.

Lucy grabbed onto the headrest of the passenger seat and leaned toward Dillon.

"Hello."

"I overheard your morning. Did you see Da Vinci's notebook at the Library?" Dillon asked wryly.

"Ha! I actually saw that. I didn't pause, but I did pass it."

"That's good . . . Are you excited?" He threw her a wink.

"About Haworth?"

"No, about sitting in a car for three hours and watching cows pass by."

Lucy thumped the top of his head. "Sarcasm does not become you."

"Yes, Haworth."

"I'm not sure." Lucy watched Helen. Her head had listed toward the window. "There's so much going on, Dillon. This trip is not what I expected."

Dillon flickered a glance into his rearview mirror. "She was in a rare mood when I picked you up last night."

"She was and I wish I could tell you about it—about all of it—but it's not my story to tell." Lucy sat back again. "Haworth will be slower. That'll be good for her. Did you get my text about the Lake District?"

"I did. I told my boss and brought some more clothing. Thank you for that." Dillon peeked again into the rearview mirror. "She had me put a cane in the boot. I didn't know she used one."

"Neither did I."

Hours and a good meal later, the car climbed the hill into Haworth, vibrating lightly on the cobblestone street. Lucy could feel the wind kick up and push the car in sideways bursts.

She leaned forward. "Do you feel that?"

Dillon kept his eyes on the road. "You should feel how I'm tugging on this wheel to compensate. The wind's always blowing around here this time

214

of year, but this is strong. Look at those signs."

Lucy looked out the window to find the colorful hand-painted signs, meant to hang over the doors, swing parallel to the ground. She also saw several placards that had been blown down or scooted sideways in the wind. Only the light lace or calico draperies hanging inside the windows draped still and peaceful.

Dillon slowed to let another car scuttle past. The shops hugged the curb, never allowing for expansion of the narrow street, and two cars made for a tight fit.

"Welcome to Haworth," Dillon whispered into the backseat.

Lucy drew herself out of her thoughts. "Even with the wind, it's like a postcard."

"Did you catch some of the names?"

"You mean the Brontë Falls? The sale on Jane Eyre's bath salts? Or the sign for the Brontë Bakery?"

"The Wildfell Hall Tea was always my favorite. It had a little book painted in the corner with a teacup resting on it, but it's probably blown all the way to Thornfield Tasty Treats by now."

"Stop it. There's no Thornfield Tasty Treats."

"You Americans aren't the only brash commercialists," Dillon quipped.

"I'd hardly call this brash commercialism."

"Wait until you buy the Cathy tea cozy or Jane Eyre knitting needles, or drink that Wildfell Hall tea. It'll feel like Disney World." Dillon pointed out the window. "But for all that, I love it up here. I like the North. I'm from a town just northwest of here and it's very different from the South. Better, I say."

"You sound like a book I love."

"Let me guess, Civil War story?"

"I'm kind of a fiction girl. This one's an English love story, actually, titled *North and South*. Margaret from the South looks down on the industrialist, John, from the North, until she falls in love with him. No war, just a couple skirmishes and plenty of sparks."

"It's a little that way in reality too. The South still looks down its nose at the North. But I say, let 'em. We get the work done." Dillon rapped his window. "A group I brought up here last year raved about that shop. You should go."

"Bainbridge Books? Hey . . . I've purchased from them. They have a wonderful antique book collection."

Dillon slowed into a tight driveway framed by large stone pillars and parked directly in front of a massive wooden door. The inn was a manor house such as Lucy imagined an eighteenth-century squire owning. It was yellow stone and broad, with lead-paned windows, bays on both floors, and huge stone urns bursting with spring flowers and plantings straddling the front stoop.

Lucy squeezed Helen's wrist. "We're here. Are you awake?"

She opened her eyes. "I am. I can't imagine why I'm so sluggish. It's hard to keep my eyes open. Do you have any Advil?"

"I do." Lucy dug into her handbag and tipped two Advil from a small bottle. She handed them to Helen with a water bottle as Dillon walked around the car to open the door.

He handed Helen out as a young woman bustled through the inn's front door. Lucy caught a glimpse and got the general impression of pale. The young woman was slightly plump and dressed in a white blouse with an equally crisp apron tied over it. Her blonde hair whipped across her face, obscuring any further details.

"Welcome. I'm Bette." She shook Helen's hand first then turned to Lucy as she stepped from the car. "Thank you so much for calling this morning and letting me know your arrival time. It was such a help." She then reached out to Dillon. "If you drive the car around to the garden, the car park has plenty of room."

Dillon stood still until Helen nudged past him. He grabbed the bags and flashed Bette a thousand-watt smile. "Let me take care of these first and I'll get right to that."

Bette held her hair back with her hand as two bright spots of rose burst on her cheeks in reply to Dillon's eagerness. She appeared flustered as she directed Lucy. "Please walk through to the Great Room. I've set out pâté and wine."

Lucy led Helen up the few stone steps to the foyer, which served as the inn's lobby and opened up into the second floor. The stairs traveled up the far wall, turned, and continued to the floor above in a circling hallway. There was a fireplace on the right wall with a heavy wooden mantel that matched the exposed beams of the ceiling. Lucy took a deep breath, pulling in the smell of past fires, wood polish, and flowers. "This is beautiful."

"Thank you. The house originally belonged to the Northrup family and was built in 1679, but it was taken over and added to in the mid-1800s by Thomas Seaton, a textile manufacturer. His family sold it to my great-grandparents in 1913 and it's been an inn ever since World War I, following its days as an infirmary."

"What an amazing story, but then again, I bet most old houses have interesting stories to tell." Helen sounded groggy.

Bette nodded. "When you're standing for over three hundred years, a lot is bound to happen to you. I can give you a tour tomorrow if you'd like."

Bette led them to a love seat and an armchair set before the fire. She picked up a tiny placard on the small center table. "I reserved this for you as I thought you might be tired, even a little chilled."

"Thank you." Helen moved slowly toward the chair.

"Rest here while I check you in and get your keys. Mum is finishing your rooms and we'll take your bags straight up."

"Thank you, Bette." Lucy sat across from Helen and pushed the table out from between them. "Helen, may I see your foot?"

"A lady doesn't show her ankles." Helen's voice was too drained to carry off her joke.

Lucy reached for her right foot and slowly lifted it. "You were limping. Your shoes are too tight." She slid off Helen's Belgian-style loafer. "It's cutting into your foot. Was it like this yesterday? We walked too much. Why didn't you say anything?"

Helen leaned forward and gaped at her foot, which was slightly purple under her sheer stocking. "It didn't hurt. It doesn't hurt even now, but I do notice the shoe is off. That feels better."

"Have you lost feeling?"

"It was simply cramped. It's fine now."

Lucy put Helen's foot back on the floor and slid the shoe next to it. She removed the shoe from Helen's other foot as well. "You can slip them back on when we go upstairs, but do you have something bigger?"

"I have a pair of loafers I wear with socks. They're a half size larger. I can wear those."

Lucy sat back and bit her lip. "This isn't right, Helen. I'm over my head here."

"You're not. My feet are tired and swollen. That's hardly surprising with all we've done. Why don't you hand me a little of that pâté? Perhaps a small glass of wine?"

"Of course." Lucy acquiesced and slid the small table back between them.

The sun dipped behind the hill and instantly the room chilled. Lucy poured Helen a glass of wine. "That was nice of her to save the fire seats for us. She must have known that would happen." She gestured to the window and the last rays of light receding from the hill.

"I imagined the moors were like this. Wild and wintry out of the sun. In all the books, there's always a fire burning." Helen snuggled deeper into her seat.

Lucy poured herself a glass and sat back as well, watching the dark wine take on tones of ruby and raspberry in the firelight. She lifted her gaze and found they weren't alone. A few guests were scattered about enjoying tea or wine, whispering, reading, or simply looking out the large windows to the field behind.

Bette returned with two keys dangling from purple tassels. Lucy flicked her hand toward the window. "That would be called a moor?"

"Yes. And that particular moor leads right to Top Withens, Wuthering Heights, if you're up for a walk. I have maps at the front desk."

"Now we're in the thick of it." Lucy motioned

to Helen. "Wuthering Heights, right here. Shall we wander in search of Cathy tomorrow?"

"You certainly should."

Lucy dropped her eyes to Helen's feet and saw her discreetly tuck them farther under the love seat's skirt. She returned her attention to Bette. "Is the Brontë Parsonage open too?"

"Every day from nine to five o'clock." Bette surveyed the room. "Would you excuse me? I apologize, but there are a few dinner details left. We had someone call in sick and we're short staffed."

"Absolutely." Lucy took both keys from her. "Where do we find our rooms?"

"You're at the top of the stairs to the right. Your driver offered to carry your cases up, so I showed him the rooms and everything is all situated for you."

"Thank you. We'll sit here a few more minutes and then head up. I believe we have dinner reservations for seven o'clock." Lucy glanced to Helen as if asking if that plan still suited her.

"We'll be ready whenever you'd like to eat. The dining room is through that doorway behind you and there will only be two other couples besides yourselves tonight, so please come whenever you wish."

"Thank you," Helen chimed into the conversation as Bette hurried away. "She's working hard, that one."

"Sure looks like it. I feel like I should be helping somehow."

Helen smiled. "I got the impression Dillon will make himself available. Didn't you?"

"You caught that too?" Lucy grinned. "I thought he was going to fall over himself right there on the front stoop."

"He did and don't you dare tease him. He's a good boy."

"Fine," Lucy mock-moaned. "I hardly think that's— Hello."

Dillon strode into the room right to them. "Your bags are in your rooms and I thought I'd go . . ." He stalled.

"Come join us." Helen opened her hand languidly to the seat next to Lucy as if she had all day and simply wanted to chat.

"Thank you." Dillon sat and rubbed his knees. He shifted in his seat.

"Tell me. How are the rooms?" Helen's voice was light—and fake.

"They're real comfortable. You'll be pleased." He shifted again.

"Dillon, would you mind asking that nice young woman . . . I can't remember her name . . ."

"Bette," Dillon offered.

"Yes. Would you mind asking Bette if there's any help you might give? She seems over-whelmed this evening and—"

"Be glad to, ma'am." And he was off.

"You said I couldn't tease him." Lucy laid a hand over her forehead and simpered, "I simply can't remember her name."

"I couldn't resist."

"You are having fun, aren't you?" Lucy studied Helen. Even if Helen was feeling unwell, she seemed lighter. "I know all that's ahead . . . but you seem happy. Your eyes . . . It's hard to describe. They're clearer. Sid would call them 'Mountain Blue' right now. Even in the firelight, they're bright, and he says the deepest, clearest skies are only above mountains."

"I like that. To me, they feel wider too. Do they look it?"

"They do."

Helen sighed. "I'm unwinding in a way I don't think I ever have before. I think I'd grant every favor asked right now, so don't call my grand-daughters." She winked and raised her glass in salute.

Lucy took a sip of wine and knew what she should ask . . . *Can we go home now?* Helen needed it, Charlie needed it, James needed it—they all did. But she asked nothing.

Chapter 21

The next morning, Lucy felt it again. Wind, rain, cold. It whirled out her window and rattled the pane. She closed her eyes and, rather than wish it away, snuggled deeper into the pillows and the soft down comforter. *Perfect.*

She thought how marvelous it would be to sit by the fire all day and read. She'd put away *The Vicar of Wakefield* and read Helen passages from Brontë novels. Maybe the scene from *The Tenant of Wildfell Hall* when Markham goes to visit Helen in the winter and she gives him the rose and tries to discreetly woo him. Or the one in *Jane Eyre* when Jane first arrives and meets Mrs. Fairfax by the fire and, of course, the reader senses the beginning of a great adventure tinged with dark mystery. So many gems to share by the fireside.

After indulging in a few passages, Lucy dug into her suitcase for leggings, a deep brown tunic sweater, and patent leather walking loafers. This was not a day for skirts, ballet flats, or heeled boots. This was a day for soft wool, warm socks, loafers, and literature. She pulled her hair into a high ponytail and skipped down the stairs to find Bette at the desk.

"Good morning. Has Helen come down yet?"

"She hasn't passed me. There's a full breakfast in the dining room and a fire already laid in the Great Room." She nodded at the tablet in Lucy's hands. "You've some books in there, I expect."

"Over a hundred. If I could carry them all around I would because I love the touch and the smell of the paper, but this is the best way to carry mass quantities. I thought I'd entice Helen into a slow day of reading next to the fire. I don't want to even suggest going to the Parsonage. She'd probably say yes and the weather seems pretty rough right now."

"It's supposed to clear," Bette wailed.

"We're not upset."

"I don't know why not. Everyone else is." Bette chuckled and seemed to relax. "Thank you for not blaming me. Come have some breakfast." She tilted her head toward the dining room then cast her eyes up and over Lucy, who turned to follow her gaze.

Helen walked slowly down the stairs dressed in dark wool pants and an aubergine turtleneck sweater. Lucy immediately noted that the colors were new for her; Helen usually wore clear, pale colors. Lucy also caught a glimpse of Helen's loafers, large, black, and most likely, much more comfortable. She concentrated on each step and only looked up as Lucy called to greet her.

"Good morning. I thought we'd stay here and sit—"

"I—" Helen reached out her hand, and as if someone opened a drain, she and all the color in her face slipped together.

In slow motion, Lucy watched as the figurative hole opened and sucked Helen inside. She crumpled and fell down the steps just as Lucy sprang up to catch her.

"Helen, Helen!" Lucy caught her before she slid down the three remaining steps.

Bette rushed forward and held Lucy up so that she didn't topple under Helen's weight.

Lucy's voice strained under her efforts. "I've got her. Call for help. Is there 911?"

"Are you sure you've got her?"

"Yes. Go. Go."

Lucy felt Bette's hands release her shoulders. She swayed back before pushing forward with her feet to stabilize Helen.

Footsteps pounded behind her. "We thought we heard— What happened?"

Lucy released her hold on Helen as two men gently lifted her from the steps and carried her to the long sofa in the Great Room. The taller one sat on the sofa's edge and patted Helen's hand. "What is her name?"

Lucy glanced between them.

"Miles is a doctor," the other offered.

"Helen Carmichael."

"Can you hear me, Helen? It's time to wake." He said something quick, deep, and, Lucy presumed, German to his friend, who left the room.

"Is she okay?"

"She is waking now. Wil is bringing her a glass of water."

Moments later, Bette led a tall young man with a large black bag into the room as Wil returned with the water. Both men went straight to the sofa. Bette stood with Lucy.

"That was so frightening." Bette twisted her hands in front of her. "But Dr. Matthews will know what to do."

Lucy noticed Bette's flushed face and rapid breathing. "You ran?"

"It was faster than calling. His office is down the street."

Impulsively Lucy threw an arm around her. "Thank you so much."

Within a few minutes, Dr. Matthews, with the help of Wil and Dr. Miles, had Helen safely tucked into bed. When Lucy entered Helen's room, she was propped against the pillows with an IV flowing into the top of her wrist.

"Are you sure she shouldn't be at a hospital?" Lucy's semi-belligerent tone caught everyone's attention—including her own. "I'm sorry, but are you *sure?* I mean, how do you know she's okay?"

Dr. Matthews regarded Helen before addressing Lucy. "Her vitals are strong and other than fatigue and extreme dehydration, she's fine."

He clasped Helen's hand. "You can see the effects of dehydration in her hands and swollen feet."

Helen pulled her hand away with a huff of annoyance.

Lucy caught it, but directed her focus to the doctor. "Her feet were swollen last night. We . . . I didn't know that's what that meant. Are you sure about the hospital?"

"I'll give her two bags of fluid and I recommend a few days' rest. I suspect the antibiotics contributed to this and, that said, her immune system is weak. Sometimes hospitals aren't the best places to be."

"You're sure?"

"If you insist—" came from the doctor simultaneously with a sharp "Lucy!" from Helen.

Lucy held up her hands. "I'm sorry. I'm nervous." She leaned around the doctor. "I'm not telling James if something happens to you."

Helen laughed. "That's what you're worried about?"

"Wouldn't you be?"

"I'd be more scared of Charlie." Helen closed her eyes. "Now could you all please leave? I'm done in and there's nothing more to do. A trip to the hospital is not up for discussion."

The doctor chuckled. "We will leave, but I'll be back in a couple hours to switch your fluids. And if you need to use the bathroom, please ask—"

He stopped at Helen's raised hand. "We are not discussing that. Thank you, young man."

Shaking his head, he followed Lucy from the room.

She turned toward him as soon as the door clicked shut. "You are sure she's okay? Really sure? There is nothing you're not telling us?"

"She is exhausted and she's dehydrated and"—he gave Lucy a significant look—"that is the extent to which she's allowing me to treat her and the extent to which I could regardless."

With a slight bow, he ducked around her and loped down the stairs. He waved to Bette and called back to her from the front door, "I'll be back in a couple hours to check on Mrs. Carmichael."

Lucy stood holding the railing and staring down until the heavy front door slammed shut.

Bette lifted her head. "He's a very good doctor."

"He'd better be."

Lucy had secured the armchair near the fireplace by leaving her book in it every time she ventured up to Helen's room. Hours later, Helen remained fast asleep; Lucy still checked regularly.

By one o'clock, she felt as if she'd already worn a path along the plush Wilton carpet and sank once more into the chair. She palmed her phone and ran her finger across the blank black face to turn it on. But this time, she tapped James's number.

Lucy listened as it rang and rang. Right before it would've jumped to voice mail, she heard a brusque, "Lucy? What's up?"

She wanted a softer intro, but this was what she had to deal with. She dove in. "Your grandmother fainted walking down some stairs this morning. She's fine. They were carpeted and I caught her, but I needed to call and I don't have your dad's number."

"What happened?"

"She just fell. The doctor says she's suffering from exhaustion and severe dehydration."

"Are you in London?" James asked with a slight bang and a groan. "Darn desk drawer."

"We arrived in Haworth last night."

"What hospital is she at?"

Lucy closed her eyes. "She isn't in one."

"What?"

"I asked, but the doctor said she was fine. I asked again and he said the same thing. He even said a hospital wouldn't be good after her cold, that her immune system might still be compromised."

"Nevertheless, if she needs—"

"She agrees with the doctor. She won't go."

"She doesn't get a choice," James growled.

Lucy pulled her phone from her ear, as if it had relayed something wrong, as if James could not have said that—and in that tone.

"I'm the one without a choice, James. She won't go and the doctor agrees with her. I agree with

you, but that doesn't count. She's perfectly lucid."
Lucy heard James suck in air as if he was about
to start yelling.

She spoke before he could. "He hooked her up
to an IV and he's just left after switching her to a
second bag. He'll be back in a couple hours and
promises to come by again when his office hours
end."

"She's eighty-five. He can't give her a glass of
water and think that's enough."

"James." Lucy pressed her lips tight, refusing to
argue or plead.

"What?" His voice calmed.

"I can't force her to do anything. I'm not
family." Lucy pulled a card from her bag's side
pocket. "I'm going to text you his number. He
told me to pass it along so that your dad or her
doctor, or anyone, can call him. I didn't want to
text it to you without talking to you first."

"I appreciate that. I'll pass it along to my dad."
James paused. "Lucy?"

"Yes?"

"Take care of her."

"Always." Lucy let the word, and all the meaning
it once carried, linger. James hung up. She texted
the doctor's number then slid the phone into her
bag and wandered toward the stairs again.

"It's only been ten minutes since you checked."
Bette's soft voice surprised her.

"I didn't see you there."

"The wind has died down. Go for a walk. I'll keep an eye on her." Bette walked around the desk and stood near her.

"You're so busy."

"I'm not too busy to dash up there for a few minutes." Bette tilted her head to the front door. "Go."

Lucy accepted the offer. She needed out. She grabbed her coat and strode toward Main Street, thinking she'd be eager to see the town, explore the shops, and relish all things Brontë. But as she approached the first door with the tempting sign, *Thornfield Luncheon Special*, she found herself racing on. Helen had brought her to Haworth and was such a fundamental part of the experience that to see, smell, or touch anything now felt like a betrayal. The discomfort of the cobblestones and gravel under her feet felt fitting as she pushed to the edge of town.

By the time Lucy found Main Street again, her feet were sore and numb. The sky had turned dark gray and her stomach made gurgling noises, audible to passersby. She was late and anxious.

She found Bette descending the stairs. "Perfect timing. She and Mum had a lovely time over a bowl of soup and now she's wide awake."

Lucy started up the stairs. "Thank you, Bette, and thank your mom too." She knocked on Helen's door and entered without waiting for a reply. Helen sat up in bed with a pale-pink satin bed jacket draped over her shoulders. Her cheeks matched the jacket's soft tone. Lucy smiled. "You look lovely."

"You sound relieved."

"I am." She walked over to the bed and squeezed Helen's hand. "I was really worried. You were so pale. I pushed you too hard."

"Don't be silly. This has nothing to do with you. I think I had more invested in returning that watch than I thought. All systems seem to be letting go." Helen smiled and added, "Resting. All systems need rest. Nothing more."

She handed Lucy *The Vicar of Wakefield.* "Here, you take over reading now."

"Where are you?"

"The Primroses have just been thrown in jail."

"How?"

"I skipped some. There was a lot of foolishness. I needed to cut to the chase."

"You came to the right place. You're closing in on the glorious reveal." Lucy plopped into the chair and opened it to her bookmark. "I forgot I left this in here." She pulled out the laminated index card and flicked it in her hand. "I guess you saw this too."

"I used to make up those poems all the time for Charlie and my grandkids. 'Roses are red, Violets are blue, Eat your green beans, or no cake for you.'"

"Then that's where he gets it. James wrote this one."

"Oh . . . I'm sorry I read it." Helen burst out a quick laugh. "I expected more elegance, intelligence . . . Something more from him for a love note."

"No criticizing. That's exactly why I like it." Lucy slid the card into the front of the book. "It was silly to bring it, though. . . . On to our happy ending."

Lucy trained her eyes on the book as if the physical action could keep her emotionally anchored to the hope of a glorious reveal and a satisfying ending.

Chapter 22

Lucy spent the night tossing and turning and regretting her poor reading choice. She had thought it a delectable idea to read *Dracula* within her heavily curtained bed, the wind whistling in the windows. But hours later as she jumped at every creak and clink, and was sure she caught a whiff of death and decay seeping under her door, she knew she'd been wrong. Six times she softly padded to Helen's room, creeping across the floorboards, to listen for her soft snores. And when she did fall asleep, she only found herself in a worse state—running frantically and banging on locked doors, unable to escape, unable to breathe, and shrinking from the sun.

The next morning, Lucy marched into Helen's room with *Wives and Daughters* pulled up on her tablet and started to read.

"No hello?" Helen laughed. "And I thought we agreed on *The Tenant of Wildfell Hall* next."

"I can't. I went for that walk yesterday afternoon, then last night . . ." Lucy moaned and slouched into the armchair. "I know we're here and this is Brontë country, but Stoker got involved and I can't deal with any wives in attics, dark secrets, rotten, violent husbands, or window banging. Gaskell was a friend of Charlotte's, wrote her biography, so I figure that's close enough, and there's nothing creepy in Gaskell. Everything happens right in the open—arguments, yearnings, class warfare, misunderstandings— all in daytime and with the appropriate amount of angst and romance."

"I think you need to get outside. Get some fresh air today."

"I think I need to exorcise Dracula, and he's always indoors." She nodded to the cup of broth Helen was sipping. "As soon as you finish that and I finish a couple chapters, I'll let you rest and go wandering. You can even read *The Tenent of Wildfell Hall* on your own."

Helen narrowed her eyes. "Have you had breakfast yet?"

"A bite."

"Go get some more or go for a walk. It's gorgeous out that window and you need to have some fun today. I'm sorry my frailty has gotten in our way."

"Don't say that." Lucy stood and handed Helen the tablet. "But I will take your advice and go. It wasn't a good night. I could use the food . . . and a walk."

As Lucy headed to the stairs, a *thump* stopped her. She peeked in the cracked doorway to the bedroom next to Helen's.

Bette sat on the floor. Perfectly still.

"What are you doing?" Lucy pushed the door open.

Bette scrambled to stand. "The sheet slipped from my hand and *kerplop*."

"Do you want some help?"

"I can't have a guest help change the sheets." Bette pulled the sheet tight and groaned with the effort to secure it on the underside of the mattress.

"Yes, you can." Lucy stepped into the room.

Bette groaned again. "We replaced all the mattresses last month and they're thicker now. The bottom sheets don't fit."

"They're super comfy."

"I'm glad, but they're impossible to make." Bette gripped the sheet again. "You wouldn't believe the cost of fine linens and I refuse to buy anything less. This old house, it deserves good linens." She dropped her voice and started mumbling to herself. "Of all the things I need to do . . ."

Lucy couldn't hear the rest as she looked around the room. She noted the quality fabrics, the heavy drapes on the four-poster bed, the nineteenth-century dresser and side table. Bette was right. Everything here was of the first quality. "What else do you need to do?"

Bette dropped to the floor again. Lucy caught the moment when Bette decided to trust her; it was accompanied by a huff and sagging shoulders. "The whole place needs renovation. Tourism has been slow for a few years—your economy, our economy, and three cool summers in a row."

She rubbed her hand over her eyes. "Last year we had 92 percent occupancy of the year before and that was 89 percent of the previous year. I'm trying to take some of the management off Mum's and Dad's shoulders and they haven't updated these rooms since Thatcher." Bette gripped the edge of the fitted sheet again and pulled. "That alone is probably responsible for a 5 percent drop."

Lucy laid a hand on her shoulder. "You're going to rip it. Hang on a second." She walked to the opposite corner and released the sheet. "Let's set the corners at the same time; sometimes that helps."

Lucy held up her corner. Bette did the same. Simultaneously they fitted them under the mattress.

"How'd you know to do that?"

"Like you said, fine linens are a must." Lucy spread the sheet smooth. "The interior decorator I work for . . . Sometimes we actually make the beds for clients so that their first night in their newly decorated room is perfect. Sid can't abide a poorly made bed." Lucy joined Bette on the antique carpet and surveyed the room again. "What do you want to do in here?"

"What don't I want to do? New curtains, new coverings. It needs to be fresher, lighter. Doesn't it feel stuffy? Oppressive?"

"I wouldn't say that." Lucy stood and walked around. She ran her hand across the dresser. "It's tempting to want to pitch it all, but . . ." She patted the armchair, noting it was firm and well filled. She then circled the huge bed. "Envision this. What if you remove the heavy drapery on the bed? I kind of agree the fabrics are old and the first thing I think of are allergens, but that's just me. And then what about moving the bed to this wall?"

Lucy spread her arm across a long, unbroken wall on the door side of the room, across from the double window. "Facing the fireplace is nice, but over here, guests will not only catch all the light from that huge window in the afternoon, most likely when they're seeing it for the first time after check-in, but you also create a better sitting area in front of the fire."

She pulled the legs of the armchair toward the fireplace. "What do you think of this here? And do you have a stool someplace? It can serve as a side table with a tray atop or second seating without. And if you have a spare chair, this room can handle it."

"There's tons of spare furniture in a few of the outbuildings."

"If you have a wood straight-back chair, I'd paint it this color green." She turned to the armchair. "See the thread woven on the bias? It's a gorgeous color. Pick it up in the chair and add a few throw pillows."

"I never noticed that green."

"If you put that on pillows, in something light— like a twill or a linen—it will wake up the color palette and lighten the aesthetic. So in here? Mini face-lift done with three to five pillows, a chair you already own, and a stool."

Bette's jaw hung open.

"Bette?"

She furrowed her brow. "Horrible idea?"

Bette scampered atop the bed. "It's brilliant. Here. Help me?"

"What are you doing?"

"Pulling down the curtains."

Lucy giggled. "I didn't mean now."

"I do. This has defeated me, but no more. We've got six empty rooms today and if I'm going to make them up, I'm going to do it right." She stopped and stared down at Lucy. "Get up here, you're taller."

Lucy pulled off her shoes, climbed up on the bed, and bounced slightly. "This is so tempting."

"You will not break this bed." Bette pointed at her, but softened the command with a smirk.

Lucy reached up to push the curtain rod. "It'dbe easier to hold the bars off their rests and slide the rings, but I'm not strong enough."

Bette's arms dropped. "Then how are we ever going to move it too?"

"We need help." Lucy laughed. "Wait here. I'll go rustle up Dillon."

Three sets of bed curtains, five armchairs, two desks, a bowfront dresser, and two rugs later, Dillon begged for a break. Lucy and Bette, also exhausted, agreed—especially as Bette discovered she was late for lunch preparations.

"You go. We'll clean all this up." Dillon gently pushed her from the room.

Lucy gathered an armful of the bed curtains and headed to a back storage room where they'd been stacking them. Upon her return, Dillon had vacuumed the room, straightened everything, and was backing out.

"You're amazing, you know that? I don't know a guy in a million who would do what you did today." She leaned against the doorjamb. Her memory drifted to James. *Two guys in a million.*

"It was fun." Dillon wrapped the cord around the vacuum's holding hooks. "And she needs the help . . . She's sorta like sunshine, isn't she?"

"That's just what I was thinking," Lucy teased.

"Go on with you." Dillon shoved against her shoulder. "I'm serious."

Lucy was about to push Dillon back when his words stopped her. "I know you are. And yes, she's like sunshine."

Bette's mother and another woman were clearing the tables and preparing the dining room for tea as Lucy finished her lunch. Dillon had already left to go dig more furniture out of an outbuilding for Bette.

"Do you want me out of here?" Lucy called across the room.

Bette's mother, a short woman with blonde hair, came over. Lucy imagined Bette looking much the same in twenty years—a little plumper, a touch of gray, but still gentle and still like sunshine.

"You're fine." She tucked the chair across from Lucy farther beneath the table. "Bette took me up to the rooms you and Dillon helped her with."

Lucy laid down her fork. "I hope you don't mind. Do you like the changes?"

"I like them very much. It's hard to see what needs changing when you've lived with them one way for so long. I don't even see the rooms anymore."

"I think that's true. As long as you're happy . . ."

"I am and Bette's thrilled. I'm so pleased to have her excited about this place. We're not getting any younger and it's time she felt it was hers." Bette's mom touched the rim of Lucy's plate. "You enjoy the rest of your lunch and I'll finish clearing the buffet. Those tomatoes are from last year's garden. Bette and I canned all last fall and Robert grills them up well, I think."

"They're amazing. Thank you." Lucy returned her attention to her plate.

"Hey."

Lucy choked on the tomato, squirting seeds onto her plate.

James stood above her.

"Whoa . . . Not a good idea." He reached for her then dropped his arm.

"Hot," she gasped, swallowing the tomato whole. She jumped up, pressing her napkin against her mouth.

James held her gaze, his hair dipping over one eye, five o'clock shadow darkening his chin, and the sun hitting his eyes at just the right angle to highlight the fine lines at their corners.

Lucy took in his tired expression, his green waxed coat, blue oxford shirt tucked into jeans, and decided that, yes, he was still cute. Every gothic hero of old came to mind. *Valancourt,*

Tilney, and *Markham*—those were James's speed. *Heathcliff?* She couldn't make a demon out of James or a man out of Heathcliff. *Rochester?* Despite Helen's assertion, he didn't work any better. *Thornton. Hamley. That's it. Hamley!* Her eyes widened farther with the realization that she'd perhaps spent too much time with Gaskell's *Wives and Daughters* already.

She lowered the napkin. "What are you doing here?"

"Little work . . ." He shrugged and she pinned him with a glare. "I wanted to come. I didn't think . . . I didn't feel you should handle this alone."

"You came for me?" Lucy heard the wonder in her voice and tried to cover it by clearing her throat. "I mean, Helen will be thrilled."

James twisted. "Where is she?"

"In her room. Asleep." She stumbled back against her chair. "Come on. I'll take you up."

As they passed by the front desk, Lucy noted Bette's absence. "Did you check in?"

"Yes. Bette? She told me where to find you."

As they walked up the stairs, Lucy couldn't help peeking James's way. To have him so close, but in many ways so far away, was an exquisite torture. She wanted to tell him about the past few days, all she'd done, all she'd felt, and how she wanted to be different and new, "break the mold" as Helen had done.

She knocked on Helen's door and, when no

answer came, pushed it open to let James enter first.

"Not locked?" he whispered.

"I asked her not to so I can check on her."

James leaned around the door. He pulled back. "She's asleep."

"You can wake her." Lucy nudged him forward.

"That feels a little counterproductive."

James's tone scraped down Lucy's spine. "We wouldn't want that," she retorted, and backed from the doorway and headed down the stairs.

"Why are you annoyed by that?" James clicked the door shut and called after her.

Lucy spun at the landing. "You've flown across the ocean to see her and yet you won't wake her to tell her you're here?"

"What's the point? She needs the sleep and she'll be awake soon enough."

Lucy clenched her fists at her sides. "You're right and that's very logical. But on the other hand, after all she's been through, she'd love the treat of having you here and sharing the last few days, everything, with you. She'll be upset when she finds out you've been here for hours and she missed that time. The thing to do sometimes is not what's right, but what's best."

"She'll have plenty—"

"You don't know that." Lucy held up her hand. "I get it." She marched down the stairs. "And it's not my business," she mumbled.

"What did you say?"

Lucy didn't reply.

James called over the stair rail, "Where are you going?"

Lucy looked straight up. "I'm heading out for a walk. You wait for Helen to wake. I'll be back soon."

"Can I come with you?"

"Why?" Lucy stopped in complete confusion.

James stared down at her. His hair flopping in front of his eyes gave the distinct impression that he'd surprised himself with his request. "I've been on a plane . . . Forever."

She debated then nodded. "Come on."

She walked out the door and heard him follow her moments later, his feet shuffling along the gravel driveway. As she turned onto Main Street, he drew up beside her and they walked in silence to the bottom of the hill to where she'd seen a sign for Stanbury Moor.

"A moor?"

"They're everywhere." She trudged through the gate.

"Why are you acting like you're mad at me?" James called after her.

"Because I am."

"You're mad at me? Are you serious?" His tone changed from sincere inquiry to sarcasm. It grated.

Lucy twisted, both feet planted on the ground.

"Very. You came all the way here and I know it's for her, but I thought it was for me too, which was completely stupid because you made it very clear that I'm not worth your effort, but if all you're thinking is that I'm harming her, keeping her from the hospital, I'm not."

"I never felt that and that's not what I think."

James's tone incensed her more.

"But you must be here to judge my care for her. Because there's nothing between us and if you'd come for more than that, to actually spend time with her, you would've woken her."

"That's what this is about? Because I let her sleep? Do you hear yourself?" James took a step toward her.

Lucy marched away, calling back, "Then why bother flying across an ocean? I'd have had her back in Chicago within forty-eight hours. If she was up to it, I was going to press for a flight out of Heathrow tomorrow, just like I told your father yesterday. He was fine with that. Why weren't you?"

James caught up to her. "I came to make sure she's up to it. You said yourself that you're not family. You shouldn't bear all the responsibility."

"And yet your father was fine with it . . . Somehow, James, that's not ringing true."

"Fine." James stopped again. "I did come for you. Happy? I came because you owe me."

Lucy stopped. "I owe you?"

"You owe me an explanation. After all our time together, you owe me something."

"That was weeks ago, James. You had plenty of time to ask and when I tried to talk to you, you wouldn't listen. Twice you wouldn't listen." Lucy stilled, trying to read his face. "Why now? And a phone call is much cheaper."

"Some things are better done face-to-face, Lucy, and you never tried. You stood there and flat out told me you'd forged those inscriptions and who knows what else and you never came to see me. You never came to explain. And you tried only once, on the phone."

"I tried that night and you walked out on me. And what was wrong with trying again on the phone?"

"I deserved more. We deserved more. And of course I walked out. What'd you expect me to do? You just stood there."

"That's not how it went down, but have it your way." Lucy marched away.

"This isn't my way!" James yelled. He didn't sound angry. He sounded like a boy, a young boy, denied something promised, something he'd desperately wanted.

Lucy dropped her hands. "What do you want from me?"

"I want us to be what we were. I want to go back. I want to look at you and see . . ." His hands dropped. "I loved you . . . And that was hard . . ."

"What was hard? Me?" Lucy watched him and it dawned, slowly. "Telling them. Telling your dad and your grandmother. For you, that was hardest."

"It's more than that. It's all so messed up." James continued in a soft exhale, "I want to not be such a fool."

She stepped toward him, just out of reach. "You aren't that."

"Sure feels like it."

"Come on." Lucy tilted her head down the path and started walking. James walked beside her and for a few minutes neither spoke. The brown grasses were beginning to turn green and lengthen—some already long enough to bend in the breeze. The landscape was scrubby and stark with only a few trees breaking the sterility. Even secrets couldn't hide here.

Lucy started softly. "Do you know how to boil a frog?" At James's blank expression, she continued. "I've never tried it, but I gather you start with cool water and slowly raise the temperature. The frog never jumps out. Forging inscriptions started that way. It made a good story and the client liked it. Yes, it also added value and Sid liked that. He didn't know what I'd done, but was pleased with the sales. So the temperature kept rising. I didn't pause to notice and that's the problem."

Lucy quirked a smile. It wasn't returned so she faced ahead, kept walking, and continued.

"To be honest, it probably didn't even start then. It felt like forging my mom's name as a kid so she wouldn't get angry at a bad grade, or making up a good story to cover for a friend in high school, or writing friends' literature papers in college 'cause I knew the novels best. Didn't you ever do that stuff?" She peeked at James. He didn't pull his eyes from the path.

She continued, "You probably didn't, but none of that ever felt wrong. It was what you did for a friend and those things made people happy or helped keep them from pain . . . And the books sold well and I . . . I enjoyed the stories. In many ways, I felt that same sense of excitement that I did with my dad when he'd weave stories for me. I loved imagining who might have owned the books and who they'd passed them on to. It's not an excuse, but it's the start of an explanation."

"What's the rest?" James peered at her. "Of the explanation."

"A warped worldview?" Lucy threw it out and checked to see how James received it. He clenched his jaw as if her reply was an evasion and it bothered him.

"I've thought a lot about that in the past couple days. A person's worldview. Helen took me to Westminster Abbey and we found a plaque for her favorite writer, or one of them, and there's this quote wrapped around his name. Here, I took a picture . . ."

Lucy stopped and pulled out her phone. "It said, 'I believe in Christianity as I believe that the sun has risen, not only because I see it, but because by it, I see everything else.' It struck me because we all see the world through a lens, a unique lens. For C. S. Lewis, it was Christianity. You have yours; I have mine. They're different, and for you to understand me at all, you first have to accept that."

"You can't have a lens that makes what you did right."

"I'm not saying that." Lucy closed her eyes and willed her face not to blaze the color of her hair. "Are you going to listen? 'Cause if not, I'd prefer to walk by myself."

"Go on."

Lucy started to walk again. "My dad was a con man, James. You know that. He told lies, stories, and convinced people to sign over stuff or sell him things cheap because they didn't know their true value. Weaving lies was his gift. I always said he left me the books, but what if that's not all he left? Maybe he trained me in ways I'm only now fully understanding." She laughed, a low, bitter sound. "Those forgeries, those lies, aren't any different from what he did. Not really. Like father like daughter."

"What are you doing about it? You can't keep deceiving people." James laid a hand on her arm.

"That's obvious." Lucy pulled away. "And that's

what I'm trying to figure out, but I can't give you the nice neat bow you need."

"What do you mean?" James stepped back.

"That's why you came, isn't it? That's what was hard. Feeling vulnerable in front of your father and your grandmother. Their expectations. And you had no answer for me, for what I'd done." Lucy resumed walking.

"You can be so frustrating," James called after her.

"So can you. But I'm trying to figure this out, James. Do you think I like what I've become? I hurt you. I hurt Helen. And Sid? Do you not think that keeps me awake at night now? None of this is easy, but I've got to sort it out, and dealing with your expectations and your burdens is too much. You walked away from me, James, and we need to keep it that way. Because I can't take on your issues as well as my own."

She walked back to him. "You've got your own mess. Find out who you are and what you want. Not what they want for you, but what you want, because life is short and, as your grandmother says, regrets are exhausting. And I can tell you, they're also very, very heavy."

Somewhere in her speech, James's jaw had dropped open. Lucy resisted the temptation to flick it shut with her finger. Instead, she sighed again and continued her walk to the gate. "I'm going to head back to see if Bette wants any more help today. You should come too and wake your grandmother, because even if it's 'counter-productive,' it's the nice thing to do, James, the relational thing, the kind thing."

As Lucy stalked up Main Street, she looked back repeatedly. James didn't follow. She found her anger and frustration building with ever step, along with a crushing sense of loss that upset her more, until she practically hurtled herself through the front door and ran into Bette.

"What happened to you?"

"Nothing. Why?" Lucy stopped.

A smirk spread across Bette's face. "Go look in the mirror." She opened the door to the tiny hall restroom tucked under the staircase.

Lucy followed inside, shutting the door before she flipped on the light. Once on, however, she debated flipping it back off. "This can't be . . ." She covered her face in her hands.

When she pulled them down moments later, all she could see was Sid's paint deck, splayed out on his worktable as they'd debated a selection of red and orange tones for Veronica Laughton's home. Lucy reached up and pulled at her hair. Usually so neatly tied back, it curled wildly à la Albert Einstein around her face and the color seemed to have burnished to a striking resemblance to Benjamin Moore's #1309 *Moroccan Red*.

Her face was worse, but at least she could see it cooling from a #1307 *Geranium* to a #1304

All-a-Blaze. Lucy glanced down at her sweater and moaned. She hadn't even realized that she'd worn James's favorite, the one he said lit her hair on fire; now it clashed against all the other reds at war. It had morphed to a dull #1322 *Ladybug Red* and lit nothing well. "Why? Why can't I just be a lovely #1329 *Drop-Dead Gorgeous*?"

There was a soft tap at the door. "Lucy?" Bette called in with a little laugh. "Are you okay in there?"

"I'm humiliated."

"Open the door."

Lucy unlocked the door and plopped onto the closed toilet seat. "I imagined it all so differently. I stood out on that moor and I told James everything I'd wanted to say." She waved her hand. "It didn't come out as I imagined, but it wasn't too bad either. I got to tell some of it . . . And he saw all this." She dropped her head in her hands. "There's no recovery from this much red."

Bette started laughing.

"Go ahead. I'd do it, too, if it were you."

"I'm so sorry. It's not even all the red; you're so dramatic about it. I just meant your hair went a little crazy."

"Nice try."

They both heard a noise in the hallway. Bette peeked her head out the bathroom door. "He's standing at the desk. I've got to go."

"Don't you dare."

"Lucy, I'm going to the desk. Lock the door behind me until your face turns all creamy pale again."

"My face is creamy pale?"

Bette rolled her eyes and slipped out of the bathroom. Lucy twisted the lock behind her.

Chapter 23

L ucy didn't see James again. She and Dillon spent the afternoon with Bette, moving more furniture, and he spent the time with Helen, had even eaten dinner at her bedside. And when Lucy went up to grab a sweater and her tablet after dinner, she heard them laughing behind the closed door. She paused to listen and had to admit that, despite being angry with him, she was glad he had come. Helen needed him and was probably shocking and delighting him in equal measure with all the stories of her youthful exploits and saddening him with what lay before her, before their entire family.

As Lucy entered the Great Room to read by the fire, she found Dillon had already stolen her favorite chair. She slipped off her loafers and tucked into a corner of the love seat across from him.

"Bette told me to wait here," he said.

"Do you want me to go? I don't want to interrupt something."

"You're not interrupting anything. This is for the three of us," Bette called as she entered from the dining room. She carried a silver tray with a wine bottle and three glasses.

"One of Dad's best." She poured out the wine. "In honor of his two favorite guests and my heroes."

Bette noted the guest reading in the corner then sat next to Lucy on the love seat and lifted her glass. "Cheers," she whispered.

"I can't move my glass," Dillon moaned.

Lucy reached across the table. "If it's too tough, pour it in mine."

Dillon drew back. "Forget it. I earned this. Cheers."

They raised their wineglasses in unison and flopped into the cushions.

Bette lifted her glass once more. "Thank you both so much. I can't tell you what today meant. I took my mom up again while you were out to dinner to show her the two new rooms and she cried."

"That bad?" Lucy quipped.

Bette swatted her arm. "That good. She loved it. And tonight I'll upload the pictures we took onto the website. It's a whole new look."

"Let's name them too," Lucy added.

Bette took another sip and considered Lucy's

suggestion. "We've never done that. Dad thought it was tacky to play into all that."

"I think it'd be fun. I get what he's saying but I also see that every sign out there works. They create links to our favorite stories and people come here to be a part of that. You don't come here to see a moor. You come here to see Cathy's moor and get a glimpse of gothic love at its finest and ponder the incongruence of three lonely girls writing some of the most provocative literature of their age." Lucy felt herself getting swept up in her sales pitch.

"Tell us how you really feel?" Dillon sent her a cheeky smile.

"I'm serious and I think naming a room, like the one at the top of the landing, 'Earnshaw Suite' would be fun and not cheesy at all. Maybe 'Varens' for that pink room we overhauled this afternoon or 'Millcote' for the one with that huge apothecary cabinet. That's the village where Rochester went to buy all those gifts for Jane and all those drawers kinda reminded me of that. Like they'd be full of little treasures for purchase."

Lucy put her fingers together like she was pulling out little drawers. Dillon laughed at her and she shot an "Enough from you" at him before she turned back to Bette.

"The names can be less obvious than you might find at other inns and it'll give you a chance to tell a good story about the town or the room when you check people in."

"Creating emotional attachment," Bette whispered.

"Exactly. It's all about emotional attachment." Lucy tapped Bette's leg. "Decorating 101."

"Psychology B-Levels." Bette reached over and clinked her glass against Lucy's. "I think you're right. You were right about everything else today. The rooms look great. You have a real gift."

"Thank you. I've always thought of myself as the nuts and bolts at work: procurement, billing, scheduling, and stuff. But today felt really good." She sipped her wine and watched the fire dance. "More than good."

"Not me." Dillon reached his right arm far over his left shoulder and pulled at his back. "This really hurts."

Lucy opened her mouth to tease him, but stopped as Bette jumped up and nestled on the edge of his armchair.

"Turn," she gently ordered him.

He threw Lucy a grin and scooted forward as Bette set to work on his shoulder.

"You're going to spoil him," Lucy remarked. "He's not worth it."

"Quiet down over there," Dillon tried to bark, but a moan escaped. "Right there. Do you feel that knot?"

"Turn a little more." Bette pushed harder until Dillon closed his eyes and visibly melted under her hands.

Lucy waited a beat before asking, "What are we moving tomorrow?"

Dillon's eyes flew open. "We're done." He twisted to face Bette. "Please tell me we're done."

She pursed her lips. "If you don't leave, two more rooms open up tomorrow and Lucy said we could work on hers too."

"I'll let you in mine as well." Dillon moaned. "Four rooms left."

Bette squeaked and threw her arms around him in a hug.

Lucy grinned. Whether Bette knew it or not, her pursed lips did the trick. There was no way Dillon was going to turn her down when the slightest hint of a kiss was presented.

Lucy chatted a few minutes more then decided to give them a little privacy. After all, the distinct possibility remained that there would be no four rooms and no reward kiss, because Dillon would be driving them to London in the morning.

As she reached the top of the stairs, she decided to check on Helen. It felt odd, after all their time together, not to know how her day had gone . . . how she felt . . . what she and James had laughed about . . . She knocked on the door. When no one answered, she twisted the knob and opened it a crack into darkness. She heard Helen's soft breathing. Every other inhale caught on a light snore. Lucy shut the door.

At her own room, she flipped on the light and took in the space. They could move the dresser, find another armchair, and maybe use a paler covering on the bed. And once the bed curtains came down—it'd be lovely.

Lucy lay back against her pillows and tapped Sid's number.

He answered at the first ring. "Hello. I got your e-mail. You must be loving Yorkshire."

"Helen fainted yesterday and fell down the stairs, so our trip has taken a turn." Lucy noted that she was rubbing her own shoulder just had Dillon had done minutes before. "The doctor said she's suffering exhaustion and dehydration. I think we'll head back to London tomorrow or the day after and catch a flight straight home."

"I'm sorry . . . How is she now?"

"She rested all day yesterday and today. Well, I haven't seen her since this morning. James arrived."

"Your James?"

"No, Sid, her James."

"You really must write all this down someday. How is *that* going?"

Lucy snuggled deeper into the pillows, recalling her conversation with James. It was similar to a conversation she'd need to have with Sid soon.

But not now . . . "It's okay. He's been with her all afternoon. I've barely seen him."

"This means no Lake District."

"You're right. I'd forgotten that . . ." Lucy pinched the bridge of her nose.

Sid continued, "A couple books arrived today. Two Thomas Hardy's."

"Could you put them in my drawer and not in the case? I don't want to keep them."

"Why?"

"I . . . I thought hard about what you said. About questionable buyers? Right now I need to manage what we have and reassess my priorities for the business. I don't want to add any more books for a while."

"I thought it was doing well."

"It is. It's just that . . ."

"It's your business and you've managed it well, Lucy."

Lucy shook her head, rejecting the compliment. "I don't know—I can't believe I'd forgotten about the Lake District." As soon as the words escaped, she recognized how desperate and nonsensical they sounded. She rushed on. "Speaking of business, guess what I did today?"

"I'd say romped on the moors, but I'm not sure that relates to business."

"I spent the afternoon doing a little decorating here at the inn. It was amazing, Sid. Bette, the manager, and I updated the rooms by moving furniture, removing old, heavy curtains, and generally clearing out the clutter. I also made her a list of what I thought she needed to freshen the spaces and it was all stuff that'll fit in her budget: a few throw pillows, repainting some end tables and chairs in bright colors, small stuff. She was thrilled and it led me to an idea . . . Remember how you told me it was time to develop my own clientele?"

"Go on."

She heard Sid's enthusiasm and pushed up on the pillows. "What about attracting young urban professionals on a budget and not ready to pay your prices, but still looking for great stuff? Clients for you someday, but for me today?"

"I'm not following you."

"I was thinking about offering something like a 'Design Session' or a full plan in which I set up the vision up front, with visuals, numbers, sourcing, and the budget—all within a computer file. My age group works much more comfortably in that format and I can add pictures and links to a lot of the stuff I recommend so they can execute the plan whenever they're able—in the middle of the night on their laptop or when a bonus comes in. And the budget is also set up so when they input the price, it all trickles in real time to the bottom line."

"My first thought is that you've put a lot of power in your client's hands. After the first meeting, they don't need you. You've given them the access points, everything."

"Is that wrong?"

"It's simply a different model. I love the idea, but it takes you out of the equation."

"Often people like that control. They're busy and they need time to let ideas sit without pressure." She frowned. "But you're right, I'd need to bill up front and it'd be good to track loyalty somehow and see how often they re-engage . . . Is it too weird? Unworkable?"

"It's client focused and that's what matters. It's new and different and very you. I like it a lot. Keep developing it and we'll talk about it when you get back."

"Thank you, Sid. And thanks also for not putting those books out."

"They are already in your desk drawer. Sleep well, *meu pequenino*."

"You've lost me. Back to Spanish?"

"I took your advice and am sticking with the Romance languages. That's 'little one' in Portuguese."

"Sid, when I grow up, I want to be just like you." She heard him chuckle before he tapped off his phone.

Lucy did the same then sat listening to the wind rattle the windows.

Chapter 24

Lucy approached Helen's room, wondering if she was awake but still unwilling to intrude—or encounter James. She walked softly past it and down the stairs in search of Bette and breakfast.

James was leaving the dining room just as she rounded the corner.

"How's Helen?" Lucy blurted.

"You haven't seen her?"

"You're here." She scrunched her nose, realizing how immature she sounded. "I didn't want to intrude."

"Oh . . . Well, I'm heading there now." James looked as if he was about to invite her to join him. Instead he said, "You two have had an interesting time."

Lucy started to nod then fully realized what that meant and why his tone had dipped with such weight.

He knows.

He knew about Helen's summer and the watch . . . He knew of Helen's health . . . He knew of Lucy's grandfather . . . He knew more about Lucy's family . . . What else did he know about her?

"Are you okay?" She tried to keep her tone light as if quantity of information was the only issue in question.

"Are you?" He studied her.

Lucy pursed her lips, unable to discern if she caught condescension or simply expected it to be there. Either way, she felt the hair at the base of her skull prick her.

"I'm fine." She turned her head toward the doorway. "You should go on up and say good morning." She passed him then spun back. "Since you told Dillon that we're leaving tomorrow, he and I are helping Bette today. Please find me if Helen needs anything." She heard a soft "Fine" drift toward her as she walked away.

Lucy noticed Bette standing in the kitchen doorway, watching.

She tilted her head up, as if looking over Lucy's shoulder, before facing her. "You don't look at all like I expected."

Lucy slapped her hands to her cheeks. "Please tell me I'm not red like yesterday."

"You're not red at all, but I kinda thought you'd look happier somehow. I don't think all that fire yesterday was just embarrassment and annoyance."

"Whatever it was, it's gone now."

"Mmm-hmm . . ." Bette smiled and put her basket of baked goods on the buffet.

"What?"

"Nothing. Come grab some breakfast. Dillon said you two are all mine."

"So we are." Lucy grabbed a delicate china plate

and a scone. "Did he say why James chose to stay? Is Helen not doing well?"

Bette flicked a finger toward the door to the Great Room. "He was just here. Why didn't you ask him?"

"He'd have told me if it was something serious. I suspect he wants to give Helen another day of rest."

Bette shook her head and passed through the swinging door to the kitchen. She returned five minutes later as Lucy was eating the last of her scone and a small fruit salad. "Are you ready?"

Lucy stood and fell into step behind her. "Where to today?"

"Two rooms at the back of the house are empty. The first is the Markham Room. Do you like it? It overlooks the yard and he was a farmer."

Lucy nodded. "I like that name a lot."

"Then come on; it's one we haven't tackled yet." Bette looped her arm through Lucy's and pulled her along. "I felt a little guilty about yesterday. You can't do all the rooms, okay? Help me with a couple then head to the Parsonage. What if you'd left today without seeing it?"

"I would've survived. Helen is more important, and somehow, seeing it without her felt like a betrayal."

"And yet you haven't seen her since James arrived."

Lucy didn't reply, knowing that all excuses

sounded small and selfish—because they were. She'd avoided Helen because of James. At first, because looking at him hurt. Now, looking at him was impossible. He knew everything about her family now. Everything.

They headed to the Markham Room in silence and started pushing and pulling at the furniture. Within minutes, Dillon joined them and the work moved faster. Another hour and they moved to the third room and Lucy felt herself unwind.

At the two-hour mark, as Dillon carried an unwanted chair to an outside building, Bette threw up her hands. "Enough. Why don't you go next door, look around, and tell me your ideas? You can't stay here doing all the work. My dad and I can get it done while you go to lunch and the Parsonage."

"Alone?"

"Take Dillon." Bette stood straight. "You've got to get out."

"Dillon won't leave you, not if you're still working." Lucy raised her eyebrows.

"He won't, will he?" Bette's cheeks blossomed.

Lucy picked up the end of an early-twentieth-century desk and scooted it to the other side of the window. She pulled the brown cushion from its chair. "Let's put a new turquoise velvet cushion on your seamstress list." She glanced up. Bette stared into space. "Bette?"

Bette blushed deeper. "Got it. Cushion." She

pulled out her pad and wrote down the new addition.

Lucy laughed and stepped back to the desk, polishing rag in hand.

"What happened between you and James? Can I ask?" Bette softly called from across the room.

Lucy stilled and mentally calculated the distance—one floor and five rooms—between her and James. Something in Bette called out an honesty in her and she wanted to respect that. She moved closer, too embarrassed to say the words above a whisper.

She picked up the fitted sheet laying folded on the bed and motioned to Bette to grab a corner. "I did something wrong and he took it as a betrayal." She tugged her corner. "I forged inscriptions in some books. They sell for a little more that way and I . . . He found out and that was it. It's not quite that simple, but that's what it boils down to."

Lucy pulled her end of the top sheet, tucked it under, and made a hospital corner. She ran her hand across the smooth bed. "Before that, I was all smooth and perfect and then I wasn't. I'm not."

Bette tossed her an edge of the comforter. "No one is smooth and perfect. You made a mistake."

"It wasn't just that. It's a life of mistakes—three lives of mistakes."

"I don't follow you."

Lucy positioned the pillows and peered out

the window. The sun was now high in the sky. "Do you want to know why Helen brought me along—?"

"Hello?" A soft tap on the open door preceded James's head poking in. "I've been looking for you."

They both froze.

Bette spoke first. "How's your grandmother this morning?"

"She's doing great. She kicked me out for a nap and she asked about you." James addressed Lucy. "What are you two doing?"

"Lucy's helping me freshen the rooms." Bette's expression asked if she used the word correctly. Lucy blinked as if to say *I'm impressed* and she continued. "We're updating their looks."

James's eyes flickered to Lucy's then away. "She's good at that."

"Will you help us move something?" Bette motioned toward the bed.

James stepped into the room and pushed up his sleeves.

"You don't have to do that. Let me go find Dillon." Lucy rushed out of the room and down the hallway.

Within minutes, she'd hurried Dillon from a storage shed and was back outside the room. James and Bette were laughing within.

"Set it down here," Bette said. "What do you think?"

"I like it, but you'd have to ask Lucy—she's the expert."

"Speaking of Lucy, what do you—"

Lucy burst into the room.

Bette threw her a wink. "We were just talking about you" floated in the air alongside James's "How do you like what we've done?"

"It looks great." Lucy addressed James and ignored Bette. "Let's scoot the bed a little farther and call this room done."

James tossed Bette a crooked grin. "Told you."

They pushed the bed into place and moved on to another room. Lucy directed the men where to move the furniture and Bette took notes on fabrics and ideas.

Bette then called it quits.

"Send me your notes, Bette, and I'll put them on a spreadsheet with approximate costs. I'll also send you pictures of fabrics that would work well and their numbers so you can order them with someone local. I would guess you've only got about $3,000 invested in all the changes." Lucy positioned the last armchair in front of the window.

"Two thousand pounds? I was trying to find at least twenty thousand in the budget over the next couple years. This is unbelievable!" Bette flopped into the armchair. "I can't thank you all enough, but now you need to go. It's past noon and you've hardly been out of this inn in two days. You too, James."

"I'll go check on Grams." James scanned the room. "It really does look wonderful. I like it, Bette." He left the room without another word.

"And I'll go grab some food." Lucy straightened her back. "Wanna come?"

"Dad manned the front desk so I could come up here, but I need to go help. Mum made a fantastic Italian wedding soup this morning that she passes off as northern English; I'll take some to Helen and James. You two go."

"Dillon?"

He turned to Bette, who gave him a quick smile before he answered, "I'm game."

"I'll tell James where you've gone when I deliver their lunch."

"Don't." Lucy stopped. "Only if he asks."

Bette huffed. "Only if he asks."

Chapter 25

Lucy and Dillon had just stepped into the gravel drive when James called to them.

"Where are you going?" He skipped down the three steps and skidded to a stop beside them.

"We're heading to lunch and the Brontë Parsonage. Bette said she was taking Helen soup. Aren't you eating with her?"

"She kicked me out—again. She says I need to

see the town before we go." James looked between them. "Can I join you?"

Lucy turned to the drive, but Dillon backed away. "Since you won't be alone now, do you mind if I head back in? I told Bette I'd paint some of that furniture this afternoon and the Brontës aren't my thing."

Lucy gave him a pointed look, which he met with a smirk before he sauntered away.

"Did I interrupt something?"

The question sounded innocent, but Lucy enjoyed the hint, the slight uplift of James's curiosity at the end. "The Brontës aren't his thing, but Bette sure is. You helped a brother out."

"So that's how it is." James fell into step beside her. "I wondered."

"From the moment she came out to welcome the car." Lucy walked down the lane. "You'd really like those two. They are who they are—kind and straightforward."

"I do like those two."

"You did get a good introduction this morning." Lucy threw him a glance. "Sorry to drag you into that. You could've said no."

"Why would I? It was fun. Besides, I'm quite good at moving furniture."

His light tone dropped heavy as a stone. Lucy saw the leather armchair and empty shelves in front of her. "Speaking of that, I have—"

"Don't." James didn't turn to her. "We'll have to discuss it sometime, but I'm not interested in figuring out how I'm going to get my stuff back right now."

They crossed onto the slate sidewalk and headed down the hill into town. "Where are we going?" he asked.

"I'll tell you, but you can't laugh."

James held his palms out with feigned innocence.

"I'm headed to the Wuthering Heights Inn for lunch. Bette says there are better spots, but . . ."

"Sorry . . ." James chuckled. "But I agree; it's the only place to go."

The conversation died once again. Considering the time he'd spent with Helen and her new loquacious nature, Lucy was certain every morsel of their trip had been shared, dissected, and thoroughly masticated. She walked on, wondering how they'd survive lunch and why he had come at all. The silence was deafening.

"You're going to have to speak, you know." Lucy blurted.

"Why me?"

"Because you're the one who's been with Helen for the past day and there are things you know now and to not say anything is just cruel." She stopped. "You aren't that." She focused on the sidewalk, unable to meet his eyes.

He touched her arm. "I think the biggest takeaway from the past twenty-four hours is that we aren't related."

Lucy's head bounced up. "I know, right?"

"Right." James walked on. "Everything else, honestly, is overwhelming—not the facts, the sheer quantity. No wonder the woman fainted. Has she drawn breath since you two landed in London?"

"She's very sick, James. She told you that too, didn't she?"

James studied the shop signs, as if refusing to look at Lucy or directly face her question. "She did, and that was my other takeaway."

"I'm sorry."

"Me too."

James pulled the door open. A puff of warm air, full of grains, hops, yeast, and fish, welcomed them. "Perfect." He sighed.

Lucy inhaled in agreement. There was something so comforting, so elemental, about the atmosphere. The Inn was crowded with patrons and decorated with beer placards and awards lining the walls. Lucy read a few food reviews pinned among them. "Bette must have some serious standards. These reviews are great. The fish and chips seem to be their crowning glory."

"Isn't it every pub's crowning glory?"

"You're stereotyping," Lucy joked. "Some favor bangers and mash."

"You order that then and I'll get the fish and chips."

In the end, they both ordered the fish and chips. There was no talk of sharing and the absence felt like a chasm between them. And in that empty space all their words seemed to fall—for there was nothing to say. Lucy thought to ask a question. She decided against it. She opened her mouth to make a comment, then closed it when she realized how silly it would sound. She soon quit trying to bridge it at all.

Their food arrived and still they sat. Lucy finally couldn't stand it and tipped her half-pint of ale toward James. "Your grandmother told me they call these 'bedwetters.' I have no idea if that's true, but it's a great name."

James swirled his glass. "You want to know what I don't get?"

"Please," Lucy exclaimed then checked herself.

"She's acting like this 'Summer of Love' was the defining moment of her life. It was a summer, big deal. Relationships end. You don't hang on for sixty-five years."

Lucy wanted to recant her "please," deciding that she would rather not know what James was thinking after all. She closed her eyes to imagine if James could be right. Could a feeling, unrequited, last for so long?

Like a movie reel, scenes played before her and she saw James the first day they met and a flash of every moment after. She saw the gleam in Dillon's eyes as Bette raced to greet their car. That spark was real and she doubted time diminished it.

She opened her eyes. "I think one could. Even if the relationship ends, some are that defining. Don't you believe in soul mates? Love at first sight?"

She watched James ponder the question over one fry, two fries . . .

"One person you're destined to meet and love? No."

Lucy leaned back in her chair and let her fantasies go. Cathy slipped away from the window. Heathcliff called in vain. Jane stepped away from the tree and Rochester paid her passage to Ireland, perhaps he even married Blanche Ingram. Dillon and Bette drifted apart as he returned to London, deciding that she was *one of* and not *the one,* as Bette struggled alone at the inn. And James still walked away from the gallery that last evening, and even though he was right here, right now, he never returned.

James continued, "I grew up seven miles from my grandparents' house, Lucy. I was over there after school and stayed with them on weekends. Grams loved Gramps as much as he loved her. So, while I get revisiting one's youth, especially now, I'm not going to get too undone over it and I'm not going to believe that your grandfather was her one true love." James dunked his fish in the tartar sauce with such force it broke apart.

He dug out the pieces with his fork. "I don't

think she was trying to hurt you. But negating the past sixty-five years of her life? And our entire family with it?" His eyes trailed over her shoulder and into the past. "It's selfish."

"She's changing, James. I think it's surprising her as much as it is you. She isn't trying to be selfish, just the opposite; she's trying to let you in."

"People don't change, remember?" James poked his fork at her.

"I wish you'd stop saying that. It's not true." Lucy's conviction startled her. She quickly searched for something, anything, to back her claim. "Look at the stories. Jane and Edward? Huge change for both of them. Catherine and Henry from *Northanger Abbey*? Both grew up. Admittedly she had more growing to do. Heathcliff and Cathy? Okay, bad example. That one kinda makes your point. But John Thornton and Margaret Hale? Huge divisions and huge changes in understanding . . . Writers wouldn't write about change and true love unless they were real, and if they did, we wouldn't read the stories because we'd know they were writing lies."

She heard a soft chuckle. "What?"

"There you go, one full run-on sentence, trying to vindicate my grandmother's choices with fiction."

"I don't have any real-world examples and you're making me nervous."

James's eyes softened at her admission. "Only because I'm right. To twist a line from another book—all your examples are from stories written by women. Of course they make sense to you."

"You're completely ruining Jane Austen and deliberately missing my point!"

James threw out the same self-satisfied grin Helen had recently used.

"You are so like her," she spat out. His eyes immediately clouded and she regretted her words.

"I know," he whispered back. "That's why I don't like being told she should've taken another road."

"Then you haven't been listening, because I know she didn't say that. Never once has she said that she and Ollie were any good together or that she wished it had turned out differently. Quite honestly, he sounds dreadful. The only thing she says is that when she walked away from him, she lost some vital, alive part of her personality that she's withheld from you all."

James's eyes widened.

"What now?"

"I hadn't thought about that." He chuckled without a trace of humor. "She rewrote your family history too, didn't she?"

"That's beneath you."

James reached across the table and grabbed Lucy's hand. "I didn't mean it like that. I promise you. It was thoughtless. I only meant that I feel hurt about my grandfather, my family—almost betrayed—and you must feel the same. That's all. I'm so sorry."

"Let's get our check and go."

James reached for the bill and paid. She avoided any eye contact with him and simply got up and left the restaurant.

He was beside her within half a block. "Sincerely, Lucy, I didn't mean it like that."

"Please, let's not talk about it anymore . . ." She stopped. "No. I'll say one thing. Every story I told you about my family, while I may have embellished here and there, they were true as far as I knew them. Now I know they were probably all lies. Knowing my dad, I figured some might have been, but now it's so much worse. There's a whole new generation of bad in my family tree. Okay? And that was my takeaway—that maybe there are things that just *are* and you can't change them."

"That makes no sense," James countered. "You just told me people *can* change. You even cited literature and now you're switching sides?"

"Don't be such a lawyer, James."

"Witty retort." He twisted, facing back down the hill. "Did you know, on the flight over, I read that the Parsonage was considered healthy because it was at the top of the street and all the sewage drained downward?" He glanced to Lucy, who refused to engage. "But considering how young they all died, I'm thinking 'healthy' is a relative term."

Lucy cracked a smile and leapt up the parsonage steps. "I know what you're doing and I thank you for that, but . . ." She pressed her lips together as if stopping herself from qualifying her statement. Then she met his eyes. "Do you want to come in? Or do we part ways now?"

James, two steps below, regarded her at eye-level and from only a few inches away. "I feel like we should talk."

Lucy backed up the last step and pointed to the door. "I can't . . . I am going to walk in this door and visit the place that produced some of my favorite books in the whole world and you aren't going to ruin it. You in or not?"

"I'm all in."

Lucy tugged open the white wooden door to the Brontë Parsonage Museum. A large Lucite sign within the door described the family and their lives and times in the house from 1820 to 1861. Lucy read every word twice before an older woman welcomed them and offered a tour of the house. Lucy could hear footsteps above and all around.

"We'd rather just wander, if we may." James spoke before Lucy could. "Is that good with you?"

Lucy nodded and they crossed the front hall into the dining room. She could feel a different vibration in the floor now—the footsteps of three girls, three young women walking round and round the delicate mahogany table. She could almost smell the melting wax and the closed stuffiness of the room as the sisters paced, reading aloud, brainstorming, editing, and creating their stories.

It was the same table around which, after Emily and Anne's deaths, Charlotte paced alone. The thought pricked Lucy's heart. It felt familiar as if she, too, had paced alone for far too long.

Lucy started talking, not caring if James was listening or not. There were simply things to say. Things she needed to share.

"My dad always read to me. That's about all I truly remember about him. Every night and sometimes after school while I ate a snack. After he left I continued. I started reading the Brontës' books when I was in middle school. Part of me thought it'd bring him back; he'd sense that those moments were going on without him and miss them. It was silly, but I was just a kid."

She walked around the table. "He lived through books, through story. That's partly why I loved our reading time together. Fiction and reality blurred and it felt magical. I could *be* Cinderella or the mice, or Peter Rabbit and his sisters, or Frog and Toad . . . And that's all he sends, like you said, those books that pull the strings annually. And I dread each birthday and each book, fearing he'll either ruin another story by tying it between us or he's finally forgotten me and won't send one at all."

At the landing, Lucy stopped and turned back to the dining room. "I read that their father, Patrick, would stop here each evening to wind this clock and use the moment to yell a reminder to not stay up too late. It was his ritual, but it was also theirs—that late-night creative time."

"That sounds like you." James raised his eyebrows. "You used to call me when you couldn't sleep and were bored of reading."

"I shouldn't have woken you. Sorry about that."

"I liked it." James didn't wait for her to reply, but climbed the stairs to the second floor. There they entered a larger room at the front of the house. It boasted two windows facing the street.

Lucy read the sign. "Charlotte moved in here after her brother died. Her father gave it to her and he stayed in the back bedroom. She was the breadwinner by then and, I think, he was paying her respect."

James squeezed her arm and wandered away alone.

Lucy stayed. She let her eyes roam the room with its small desk, stiff, straight chair, and bed, and she thought of all the stories penned here. *Jane Eyre*, a journey of self-realization, passion, and promise . . . *Shirley*, emotionally distant with more of an eye to social change rather than to the heart . . . *Villette*, with its pervading sense of isolation and search for one's place. How could the Brontës, all the sisters, write such characters, write of such change and of such loss, unless they'd felt it, endured it, and suffered through it? *With Courage to Endure.*

As Lucy stepped down the stairs, going carefully over each shallow step and turning her feet sideways so as not to slide over the edge, she let the stories drift through her, and as she reached the bottom step, she recalled another statement Charlotte wrote. *Human beings never enjoy complete happiness in this world.* Again, most likely true.

Lucy found herself stepping into the Parsonage's garden. James stood a few feet away, staring at a statue of the three sisters. The small notice stated that the garden remained as it was during the sisters' lifetime. Well over one hundred years and something could stay the same. *Endure.*

James didn't turn as she came to stand beside him. "It's not all so black and white, is it?"

Lucy knew he wasn't talking about the Parsonage. "I guess not."

He meandered across the lawn to an empty bench and sat. He dropped his head into his hands. "She told me a lot more too." James rested his forearms on his knees.

"She told me that my dad wanted to be a math teacher and join the Peace Corps, but that she didn't let him. She told me that she didn't talk to my mom for the first three years of their marriage because she had wanted my dad to marry some family friend. She told me that she was too hard on her husband and my father, and even me and my sisters when we were children, because she wanted us all to learn responsibility and respect, but that maybe she'd gone too far and there were things she'd forgotten and she was sorry. She . . ."

Lucy laid her hand on his back and he let his words drift away. After a moment of silence, she asked, "What'd you say?"

"I asked if the doctor had given her any pain meds."

"You didn't." Lucy pursed her lips to stop a laugh as she dropped onto the bench next to him.

The left side of James's mouth curled up. "I did and her eyes shot daggers. Have you seen when they actually change colors?"

"Sky to steel and back again. Happens in a heartbeat."

"Exactly." James spun to her. "It took a few minutes and an apology for them to morph back to sky. But what did she expect? I'm not her confessor; I'm her grandson."

Lucy realized her hand still rested on his back. She slowly removed it and placed it in her lap. "You should have seen her after we returned the watch. She practically floated down the block and then we went to her favorite restaurant and drank champagne."

"Grams?"

"Grams." Lucy tilted her head. "Look, I'm not the best judge between truth and fiction, but this is all very real to her and she wants to share it with you. There's definitely going to be a little bad with all that good because, as you say, it's not so black and white. But, James?"

She waited until he sat straight and locked eyes on her. "When she fainted, it was scary. She went ghost white and hit those stairs like a stone. You need to listen to her."

James dropped his head back into his hands and didn't reply. After a minute or two, he flopped back. "I feel I owe you an apology."

"Me? Why?"

"Everything." James lifted his shoulders then lowered them slowly and purposefully as if knocking all the kinks out or resetting himself. "You're right and you were before too . . . I didn't listen back then . . . to you. I'm sorry. I heaped my own issues on you and that wasn't fair."

Lucy reached for something to say and landed on "Thank you?"

He chuckled at her tone, but only said, "You're welcome."

Chapter 26

Lucy squirmed in her seat. She and James parted ways amicably after the Parsonage, but as the afternoon progressed, she grew fidgety all over again. He was right; they needed to talk. There was more to say. She kept asking herself why it mattered what he thought—logic told her it didn't any longer, but her heart beat a quick retort.

"Here she is." James escorted Helen into the dining room, looking every bit the dashing grandson and hero.

Lucy released a long-held breath and pulled out the empty chair next to her. She kissed Helen's cheek. "You look very well rested."

"Thank you. I feel much better." Helen sat down and James pushed her chair in, then assisted Lucy with hers.

"Grams, are you warm enough?"

Helen tapped her finger on the table. "You need to stop fussing over me."

"And she's back." James threw the comment to Dillon and Lucy.

"I haven't seen you since James arrived." Helen reached over and patted Lucy's hand. "I hope you haven't been avoiding me."

"I didn't want to interrupt your time with him."

Lucy captured Helen's hand within her own. "But I shouldn't have stayed away. I'm sorry."

"As long as you've been well . . . He's been reading to me, but he doesn't do the voices nearly as well as you do." Helen surveyed the table. "Tell me all that I've missed."

Lucy started with the previous afternoon and carried Helen into the morning with their redecorating plans and furniture moving; James and Dillon chimed in and took all the credit. Lucy moved on to the lunch at Wuthering Heights Inn; James raved about the fish and chips, the beer plaques covering the walls, and even Helen's "bedwetters."

Lucy then shared about the Parsonage and James gave her the moment, not interrupting once. She retraced her steps and described every detail, inviting Helen into the rooms and into the emotions. "I've loved the books, and the characters have always felt so real to me, but now the authors feel more that way too. I touched the table where they ate, my shoes clicked on their same floorboards, Charlotte's desk looks just like the one I sit at day in and day out in Sid's shop and polish every Thursday."

She leaned closer to Helen. "That quote from Westminster Abbey fits in a way I hadn't realized either. 'With Courage to Endure.' That's what they gave to their characters, their full experience. And those young women had so much courage. They lived in isolation; they feared living without love; they had responsibility and caretaking for their sick and violent brother; they had to find work . . . Nothing was easy. They all had something to say about their lives, and they said it with strength, through those stories. But I've often gotten so absorbed in the drama, I missed the choices behind them, the very real lives behind them."

Lucy shifted her focus to James and Dillon and found them slightly dazed. "Okay, fine. It was a nice house."

James laughed. "That's exactly what I thought."

"Don't tease her." Helen softened her words with a smile. She turned back to Lucy. "I think I would've felt the same way."

"We could go tomorrow before we head back to London, if you feel well enough," Lucy offered.

"These couple days have made clear the things I must do." Helen reached over and grasped James's hand, which rested on the base of his wineglass. "I know you want me to rest, but I'm ready. Let's go home tomorrow."

"Another day isn't going to hurt, Grams. Do you want to stay, rest by the fire, and see the Parsonage?"

"It's time to go." Helen's tone brooked no opposition.

"Of course." James glanced to Dillon and Lucy. "You two okay with that?"

"Absolutely," Lucy chirped. She caught Dillon's questioning stare as he agreed as well.

The conversation dwindled into light banter as they ate grilled beef medallions with small potatoes and bright fresh peas.

When all the plates sat empty, James cleared his throat and waited for everyone's attention. "I quit my job today," he announced.

"You what?" Lucy's head bounced up.

"I switched departments rather than jobs." James drummed his fingers on the tablecloth. "I sent an e-mail to the partners requesting a full transfer to the pro bono division. I'm fairly certain I heard Hendricks cheering from Hawaii."

"I'm so proud of you," Helen said at the same time Lucy asked, "What made you do it?"

James beamed an acknowledgment to his grandmother and answered Lucy, "I've wanted this for a long time, and the reasons to delay were getting weak, if they ever had any true validity in the first place."

He leaned forward with as much eagerness as Lucy had felt moments before. She recognized it in his eyes as he continued. "This group is doing some amazing work with an NGO in India to secure land rights for women. In one region it simply required a second line on a contract's signature page. There was no cultural deterrent. It took a year of navigating red tape to add it to land deeds, but now that it's there, wives simply sign and, *BAM!* They've got the land if something happens to their husbands. It's changing lives." James sat back. "I want to be part of work like that."

He peeked at Lucy, who instinctively reached across the table to grasp his hand. He stiffened. She realized her mistake and hastily withdrew it.

The kitchen door pushed open, saving Lucyfrom further embarrassment. Bette was approaching with her arms full of dishes. Dillon popped up to help her with the plates, fresh forks, and a domed cake.

"What's this?" Helen asked.

"Sticky toffee pudding in honor of your recovery. Mum made it for you." She set it on the table. "She made it for all of you."

"You'll join us, won't you?" Helen waved her fingers to the empty table beside them. Dillon grabbed one of its empty chairs and swung it over for Bette.

"Pieces for everyone?" Bette asked.

At four nods, she sliced the cake. And with three sets of eyes on Bette, Lucy was able to observe the table more closely. The chatter danced among them as Bette passed out generous slices.

Helen's eyes were light, a peaceful and serene blue. *Summer Sky.* They were as wide as they had been at Sally Clarke's; her mouth was poised in a small, almost secret smile, and her hand rested within James's.

James looked better too. Eyes that had flashed anger at lunch and confusion at the Parsonage seemed quiet now. Although he was probably still suffering from jet lag, the lines around his eyes appeared softened. Lucy smiled as he bit his lip. He did that when he was nervous. She recognized the same gesture in herself and had once thought it serendipitous and special that they shared it.

Lucy's eyes trailed over to Dillon, who helped Bette with an eagerness and tenderness that spoke of more than a passing flirtation. James was wrong—love can start at first sight and it can last. Watching Dillon and Bette, she refused to believe otherwise.

And Bette? Dillon was right. She was sunshine. She burst with openness and energy and, even more so, with love. And she had dimples. Lucy was honest enough to admit she envied those.

Bette caught her staring and winked as she handed Lucy a slice of cake. Lucy accepted it and sat back and smiled as the afternoon's sense of isolation melted away in her first taste of sticky toffee pudding.

After her sleepless *Dracula* night, Lucy stayed with Gaskell and, at the story's end, flipped back through *Wives and Daughters'* good parts. With James in the car back to London, she had determined there'd be no reading aloud. After reading the last sublime scene again, she set the book down and switched off her light. She switched it back on. She picked up her book, put it down again, and decided it was useless. Sleep was nowhere close—so she slipped on a pair of sweatpants and padded down to the Great Room in hopes of finding embers still lit in the fire.

The room was dark except for a single lamp lit in the corner and the glow from the fire. Lucy reached in the bucket, added a log, and nestled into the love seat. She tucked her feet under her and rested her chin in her hand to watch the flames catch.

"Hey."

James. Lucy searched and found him rising from the sofa.

"I didn't see you. What are you doing down here?"

"My room was too quiet, but this isn't much better." James sat across from her in the flowered armchair.

"Jet lag? Or are you waiting for an e-mail?"

He laughed low and short. "Waiting for an e-mail."

"They're in Hawaii. On vacation. And there's a significant time change. It might take a few days. Dawkins might not even look at his until he returns."

"All true, but I can't get my brain to stop. Part of me knows it was right and the other part wonders how badly I've burned my bridges." He leaned back and traced a flower with his finger. "I can't go back after this. If Dawkins can't find a way to make it pay, it's a betrayal, and I'm out. This time I forced his hand . . . I just need to know."

"I know you do," Lucy whispered.

"I must sound so tight and odd to you. You don't always have to know things." James tilted his head. "It's not bad; it's just different and it was one of the things I loved about you. You're so logical, so smart, and your mind is like a steel trap, but it bends around stories and emotions and it has fluidity and color and an expression that I don't understand."

"You sound like you understand me." Lucy couldn't decide if there was an insult or a compliment in his comment so she skipped over it. "If they say no, will you be disappointed you forced the decision?"

"I don't want to be fired, but . . . no." James let out a snort as if his answer had shocked him. "There it is. That's the truth. I won't be."

"Then you have your clarity."

"I do, don't I?" James slowly nodded to himself. "I have my clarity."

Lucy waited a moment while he savored his revelation, then asked, "What made you do it? Did Helen say something more?"

"We didn't talk this afternoon about anything new. I actually beat her in three rounds of gin rummy and read to her. I'm not particularly enjoying *The Tenant of Wildfell Hall*, by the way. The husband's disgusting and I'm a little annoyed she likes your voices better."

"I forgot she wanted to read that." Lucy grinned. "I refused. It was my reading of *The Vicar of Wakefield* that got her. I did the parish vicar, Primrose, with particular aplomb."

Lucy waited and when James said nothing more, she asked again, "So what made you do it?"

"Your comment today stuck with me—that I needed to listen to her. And what you said yesterday—that it was their expectations and not my heart that guided me." He added in a whisper, "That was hard to hear." He shuddered. "But back to the job . . . Once I took myself out of the equation and quit whining that my grandmother was negating my existence, I was left with this sadness. She sounds like she thinks her life was half-lived, don't you think? That she left some elemental part of herself behind in that garage and is only now recapturing it. I don't want to live like that."

James gripped the arm of the chair. "I don't believe it's true, not really, but to some degree, she does." He went back to tracing flowers. "And it got me thinking about what I want in life, what I do for work, how I spend my time—lots of stuff. So I wrote the e-mail and I sent it." He stilled his hand. "There was something easier about sending it from here too. The strings pull tighter at home and I didn't want to lose my courage."

"It's going to turn out well."

"It already has, because as you said, I have my clarity." James sat silently, looking between her and the fire.

After a few moments, he asked, "And you?"

Lucy regarded him and knew that if there was ever to be anything between them, it had to start with honesty. Now. "The postmark from my dad's Birthday Book was from the Lake District."

"England's Lake District? He's here?"

"Due west."

"Ah . . . Grams mentioned yesterday that you had planned to go there. You two really were on an adventure."

"She doesn't know."

"Then how . . . ?" James stared right through her.

"She collected Beatrix Potter figurines as a kid. I . . . I kept telling her that it was a part of her past as much as it was of mine. She finally relented."

"Why lie? Especially after that whole watch thing, it seems like she, more than anyone, would understand."

"I didn't feel I could take that risk. Again . . . it wasn't thought out, not like you seem to think I think . . .'cause I don't think." Lucy blew her bangs back with a huff. "That came out wrong. What I meant to say was that I didn't think it through; I simply told her what I thought she wanted to hear, what was most likely going to persuade her, and what would humiliate me the least. There." She waited.

"And here we are again."

Lucy held out her hand. "We aren't going back there and you aren't going to make me feel guilty. Helen can. That's her right, but not yours." She lowered her hand. "All that said, I am sorry I did it."

James faced the fire and just as Lucy was about to push up from the love seat and go, he asked, "Is he expecting you?"

"We have no communication, you know that. And I'm not sure if it was such a great idea in the first place. I'm relieved it's over. It's time for this trip to end." Lucy pulled at her ponytail. "Did it make you want to laugh? After all I'd told you about my grandfather, his house, my grand-mother's family . . . It was all so refined and perfect, wasn't it?"

"It sounded pretty wonderful."

"To me too." Lucy watched the flames dance. It was easier to talk here in the dim room and the warm firelight. Helen had a point—gothic novels had good fires for a reason. "Most of those details were straight from my dad and I think we can feel certain none of them were true."

"Don't say that. You didn't know. And if you embellished a little, your stories or your father's, that's natural. We all want to believe the best of our families."

"There's a line, James, and we both know I crossed it. Repeatedly. What have we just been talking about?"

They fell into silence. After a few minutes, the silence no longer fell softly; it came in waves and Lucy wanted out. She uncurled from the chair and pushed herself up.

"You have to go." James's declaration cleaved the room.

"I am."

"Sit. Sit." He flapped his arm at the love seat. "You have to go to the Lake District. Call me crazy, but I say we leave it all here. We take none of this home." James sliced his hand through the air, making a cut-off line. "I e-mailed my gauntlet and you're going to the Lake District."

"It's not the same at all."

"I called my father too. I didn't have the nerve to tell Grams that yet. He was coming here, but now that we're heading to London he'll meet us there. Beat us there, actually."

Lucy didn't reply; instead she focused on the fire.

"James?" She sat back and hugged her shoulders tight. "Can I ask you something without you getting mad? Will you listen?"

His eyes flickered and she continued, "Tonight when Helen said she wanted to leave, you asked if she wouldn't rather stay and see the Parsonage. You didn't tell her about your dad coming and you just told me you still haven't the courage."

James's eyes widened slightly, but he said nothing.

She continued, "Why can't you concede that I might struggle with the same issue? That my mistakes are not as calculated as you seem to believe? Now, I am not making excuses for anything I've done. I've asked your forgiveness and tomorrow I'll ask for Helen's, but is it so hard to see how one can follow a thread and miss a truth?"

James wiggled back into the seat and remained silent so long, Lucy expected he wouldn't reply at all. Then, finally, "I . . . You're exactly right. I'm sorry."

Lucy expected to feel relief or vindication, but his admission was enough. She didn't want him to feel more pain or even self-recrimination. She tracked back to the issue. "So why'd you call him? Why not take Helen home to him?"

"I couldn't do it. At home it feels like no one talks honestly, and with what she's facing, we need that. Going home before we have the truth doesn't feel right. If we do, we will act as we always have because we know nothing different, but it doesn't have to be that way. I don't want it to be that way anymore."

James leaned forward with aching earnestness. "In a hotel with history and mess, fictional ghosts, and dust bunnies older than our country, I thought we'd have a chance to dig deep and call out something new. That's what she's trying to do. And you were right, I was more upset about telling my family what you'd done than trying to understand *why* you'd done it or even what it all meant. I went about it all wrong, in my heart and in my head."

"I only wanted understanding. I didn't need to be right."

"You have both. And you're still going to the Lake District. End of story."

"I've never heard you like this. I had no idea you were so dramatic." A chuckle and a sigh slipped out of Lucy together. "I don't have a word for you right now."

"Effusive." He smiled softly. "And a little repentant."

We brought out each other's best. Lucy remembered confessing it to Dillon. She pushed the memory away. "Do I have any say in this? What if I don't want to go?"

"Don't you? I mean, I can't tell you what to do . . . I wouldn't want to. But one summer and look what regret Grams carries. Whether it's all true or not, as you said, she believes it. I don't want that for you and I know you'll have regrets, too, if you walk away now. You're here. You need to see it through."

Lucy whispered, "Thank you," as the last of the flames died into embers.

"You're welcome."

Chapter 27

They talked until the embers cooled and the fire's glow completely faded to black. When the room cooled, they pushed from their chairs, almost bumping in the middle. Lucy led the way up the stairs and they parted silently at the top, James to the left and Lucy straight ahead.

The next morning, Lucy dressed, packed her small suitcase, and headed next door to Helen's room. The door was open so she softly rapped her knuckles against the wood and entered. "Have you got everything packed?"

"Dillon just carried my bags to the car. Do you see anything I've left behind?"

Lucy knelt and peeked under the bed. "All clear."

"Why didn't you tell me?" Lucy felt Helen's hand tap the top of her head.

She sat back on the floor. There was no way to misunderstand the question. Helen sat on the edge of the bed and waited.

"I thought I could get away with it." Lucy held her gaze, willing herself to be as honest as possible—hard as that might be. "If I made it sound like it was for you, then I'd get my way and you'd never know." She stood and dusted her hands against each other. "It didn't feel like that at the time; it flowed out without any thought at all. And that's probably not a good thing, but when I break it down to give you a real answer, that's what happened. Stories sometimes flow out of me and the truth never plays a part at all. I'm trying to focus on that now."

"I understand. I also understand that hope is a hard thing to share."

Lucy scrunched her nose to stop her emotions. "It is, but I should've been honest with you. I didn't know at first, but I knew in plenty of time—you would've understood. And even if you wouldn't have, I should've told you."

"All those 'would'ves' and 'should'ves.' Those are tough words. I have a few of them to face myself. Don't let them build up, my dear. That's one thing I'm learning now, and it'd be nice if I can give you a fifty-five-year head start."

"Helen . . ."

"You have such a road ahead of you." Helen reached out her arms. "'Come further up, come further in,' okay?"

"Our new battle cry?" Lucy stood and hugged Helen's fragile frame.

"That's a wonderful thought and very appropriate. For both of us." Helen squeezed her tight then held her at arm's length. "We'll talk when you get back."

James walked into the room. "All right, Grams. We're checked out and Dillon's pulled the car around." He took in the scene before him and was clearly, and awkwardly, pretending to miss the moment. "Do you need a ride anywhere, Lucy?"

"My bus leaves after lunch. Bette's dad will take me to the stop, but thank you."

James nodded and offered Helen his arm. Lucy followed them out onto the front stoop. On the other side of the car, Bette and Dillon stood in close conversation. He grabbed Bette in a quick kiss then rushed to open the car door. Bette blushed as she caught Lucy's wink.

James seated his grandmother and stepped back to Lucy. "Will you let me know if you find him? We're on a flight out of Heathrow tomorrow."

"I may be right behind you. Who knows?"

James leaned over and laid a kiss on her cheek, lingering there longer than necessary. Lucy felt his lips move against her skin, "Take care."

"You too." She turned into his cheek. "And thank you again."

"Always."

Without another look or word, he dropped into the backseat next to Helen, and Dillon smoothly pulled the car across the gravel drive and onto the road. Lucy stood until she could no longer hear it rolling over the cobblestones.

Bette bumped her shoulder. "Why don't you head out for a walk and then we'll have lunch together at noon. I'll make us a couple sandwiches."

"I'd like that. I never did get to Top Withens."

Bette pointed to a path leading around to the back of the inn. "Follow that up behind the Parsonage and the signage will begin. You can't miss it."

Lucy stopped. There wasn't another path; she couldn't have taken a wrong turn. She groaned, picked up her pace, and crested the next rise. She knew Top Withens was a ruin, and Bette said she couldn't miss it. But it wasn't anywhere! There weren't even any signs. Lucy picked up her pace again, now cantering to the next pasture.

Twenty more minutes and she reached a low stone wall. The ground beyond dipped into a field of amber tipping to green in the morning sun. It rolled in waves until . . . A gray stone blob glinting in the sun caught her eye. *Top Withens.*

Lucy scampered over the wall and ran across the grass to the path. Clearly she'd missed a turn, perhaps several. The sign on the path delineated the entire walking circuit in a single line: Haworth to Ponden Hall, known to be Thrushcross Grange, the Linton home in *Wuthering Heights*, to Top Withens, the Earnshaw-turned-Heathcliff home, and back again. Lucy studied it briefly, certain she'd added a wrong turn within Stanbury Moor, then had doubled back through what appeared to be Haworth Moor. The four miles had spanned to six, possibly seven.

But there it was, directly below her. A glorious ruin with only low stone walls showing where the home used to sit. She grinned and marched down the short slope. She grinned because it needed to be a ruin—just as it was. Even in fiction, nothing could have survived Cathy and Heathcliff. The house needed to die, with the time, with the story, and with their love—as if their deaths had felled everything around them and returned to the windswept and wuthering moor.

There were a few other hikers walking around chatting, but no one broke the general stillness and no one approached her. Lucy stood, ambled, rested on a small wall, then circled the structure and did it all over again, running her hands over the stones.

Her comment to Helen came to her. *If I made it sound like it was for you, then I'd get my way and you'd never know.* She tilted her head. How long had she lived like that? Her mom . . . Teachers . . . Friends . . . Sid . . . If everyone got what they wanted, were pleased with the result and with her for accomplishing it, why should they pay attention to the process? To her? Why, in fact, did the process matter?

She sank onto the wall. *Because it does.* It mattered just as James's regard mattered, Bette's smile mattered, Helen's health mattered, Dillon's good humor mattered. The untouchables that reached into a life and defined it mattered. Every choice mattered. And respecting the best in each and what they called from within her—her best—mattered. And if all of those went away, vanished in the night, she'd be left with the sum of her actions, the life she created, and *that* mattered.

Lucy tried to push away the battering ram of thoughts and enjoy the moment. She was here. Her own pilgrimage to her own sacred spot. She should be able to look across the moor and feel Cathy. Sense Heathcliff. Share with Helen or Agnes. Witness Jane fall down in a faint—emptied—having turned her back on Rochester and his tempting promises of love and travel . . . She'd made a choice . . .

Lucy was right back where she started. She couldn't escape into fiction because that's what the Brontës did best—convey truth within their stories. They pushed characters through choice and change, making them pay the consequences for bad decisions and only giving them that elusive happy ending when they got it right and rose from the crucible cleansed, strong, and whole. They spared nothing. The crucible was hot. It was death for some. Enduring great cruelty for others. Fire for one. Illness for many.

And Lucy found it. A character that made sense; a journey with enough profundity to grasp. *Edward Fairfax Rochester.* She'd pushed away comparisons to James. That wasn't his story—it was hers. Rochester couldn't move—could never move—forward because he hadn't gone back. He hadn't laid down his sin and accepted that there was an absolute right.

But he found it. He ran across the ramparts. He reached for Bertha, accepting all that he was and all he had been, and he paid with his eyes, with his hand, and with his heart. And to show her approval, her seal upon his life and choices, Charlotte had given him the glorious ending.

Lucy reached in her bag and pulled out the book, knowing exactly where to search. *I thank my Maker, that, in the midst of judgment, he has remembered mercy. I humbly entreat my Redeemer to give me strength to lead henceforth a purer life than I have done hitherto.*

There it was. *Mercy. Grace.* And just as she'd told James, fiction conveyed change and truth and was loved and digested again and again because it reflected the worst, the best, and all the moments in between of the human experience.

Lucy pushed herself off the wall and strode down the path, heading straight back to the inn, without faltering to the right or the left, with another of *Jane Eyre*'s words in her mind.

Resurgam . . . I will rise again.

Chapter 28

The bus crested the hill and Lucy sat straight as the village opened beneath her. *Bowness-on-Windermere*. It was tight, quaint, and cute snuggled against the water. It danced in dappled sunshine, let kids run through its streets, and maintained its decorum. It was Wordsworth; it was Potter; it was Austen.

The brakes squealed to a stop right at the water's edge and Lucy felt as if the final step would dump her into the small harbor. There were at least a hundred petite wooden boats docked on piers waiting for tourists to paddle out into the waters in search of swans or adventure. She turned away from the water. *Where to begin?*

Her eye lit upon a large bunny hanging from a window. It wore a robin's-egg-blue coat and sported straight, tall ears. *Peter Rabbit.* She strode toward it and found herself at the bottom of steep stone stairs looking up to The World of Beatrix Potter Attraction. Across the street she found The Old John Peel Inn. She checked in, left her bag with the doorman, and within a quarter of an hour, found herself back at Beatrix Potter, hopping up the steps. She briefly wondered if her search might wait—just for a moment. After all, there were friends to be met and adventures revisited.

But the moment she reached the exhibit's green lattice gate, she discovered only one question emerged. "Do you know an Anthony Alling?"

"Here, love?" The woman waved a finger around the gift shop. "I don't know the name."

Lucy added a few details, received the same reply, and then wove her way back through the shop. Down the stairs she ducked into The Tailor of Gloucester Tea Room and ordered a scone and a cup of tea.

When it arrived, she tried again. "Do you know an Anthony Alling? He lives here and has green eyes and dark, maybe gray hair."

The older woman shook her head, laid down the plate, and walked away.

She returned, once a few customers left, to wipe down a nearby table. "Are you looking for lost family?"

"Not lost," Lucy replied. "He knows exactly where he is."

The woman laughed. "Isn't that the way of it? A boyfriend? A brother?"

"A father." Lucy took a sip of tea.

The woman balled the rag between her hands. "Once you finish your cup, you should head to the Belsfield Hotel on Kendal Road. You'll not miss it. Most people pass through there one way or another, either for accommodations or for work."

"Thank you." Lucy burned her throat as she

threw back the last of her tea, grabbed the rest of her scone, and charged out the door.

On the way up the hill, she stepped into several shops and received the same blank looks and solemn head shakes. Two shopkeepers suggested the Belsfield as well, so she kept on. But between three waiters, two receptionists, and the Belsfield's concierge, she was no closer to finding him.

The sun dipped over the lake as she headed back down the hill. She stopped at a bench near the water and pitched the last crumbs of her scone to the swans. *How tall is he? Do you have a picture? What does he do? When did you last see him?* She closed her eyes. There were so many questions she couldn't answer. And so many she didn't want to. When one receptionist had asked precisely about his height, she'd replied, "When I was eight, he was this much taller than me." She had held her hand about a foot over her head before realizing how ridiculous it looked.

When the swans devoured the last nibble and waddled after a Dutch family, she pulled out her phone.

"Good morning. Hmm . . . It's evening your time. Are you back in London?"

"I'm in Bowness-on-Windermere, Mom."

"Your e-mail said you were going back to London. Isn't that a little hard on Helen?" Lucy had to give her mom credit. She was working hard to keep her tone light—only the slight flattening of the vowels gave her tension—and disapproval—away.

"James arrived and took her back to London. He sent me on."

"James. Is. There." She said it slowly, chewing through the implications.

"He took Helen to London this morning. But yes, he was in Haworth with us and I told him everything—even that I had successfully manipulated his old, sweet, sick grandmother into coming to the Lake District. It's not like he could think less of me."

"Don't say that. It's not true."

"He could think less of me?"

"Lucy." Her mother moaned as if their age-old game was too tiring. Perhaps it was.

"I'll stop. He was decent about it, Mom. I don't know what he thinks, but that doesn't matter so much. I'm beginning to think it's more important that I told him for *me*. I can't control what he does next."

"I agree with that."

Her mom fell silent again and Lucy knew she was waiting. She was a master at waiting, drawing people out by being still, being quiet, and truly listening.

"I can't find him. I've wandered all over this town and it's tiny, by the way, asking people all these stupid questions, and I can't find him."

"He may not be there. What if he was passing through?"

"He wasn't. It's Rio, Mom. He'd stay." Lucy crumpled the scone bag in her fist.

"I don't know what that means."

"It's from Ransome's *Swallows and Amazons*, one of his—our—favorite books. The town is called Rio in the story, but it's Bowness. I think if he mailed the package from here, it's because he's here. He wouldn't pick some other random lakeside village. He's either here or all Europe opens up, the whole world opens up, and I need to give up now."

"How long will you look?"

"Today was pretty frustrating and it's only been a few hours. You should've heard me. It was basically"—Lucy raised her voice to a baby-doll pitch—"'Have you seen my daddy? He's got green eyes, but that's all I know 'cause he left me when I was eight and he's never written a letter, but I got a book, with a postmark . . .' It was pathetic."

Her mom chortled softly. "I'm so sorry. That does sound horrible. Do I tell you to quit?"

Lucy skipped the question to ask her own. "What if he knows? What if he's heard me asking or heard about me asking and doesn't want to see me?"

"Lucy." Her mom's tone signaled a lecture. "I need you to hear me. I've let you romanticize your father for a long time now, maybe too long, because I thought it was important. Every girl needs a dad, even if he's terribly flawed. And there were the books. He reached out every year and I thought that was good, but it's not healthy."

She drew a long breath; the exhale blew across the ocean. "You are the one searching for him. He hasn't come back *ever* for you. Remember that. It's harsh, but it's true. And if by some miracle, you're right and you find him, then you must accept him for who he is and not who you want him to be—and not as someone who can have any power over you. You don't need his approval. Do you understand that?"

"Yes," Lucy whispered.

"And if you don't find him, are you willing to let it go, come back, and live your life?"

Lucy closed her eyes and saw James. *Call me crazy, but I say we leave it all here. We take none of this home.* "Yes."

"That lacked conviction."

"I'm borrowing some, but it's enough." Lucy rushed on, not willing to explain. "If there aren't any leads by tomorrow, I'll catch an afternoon train to Heathrow."

"I wish I could help you."

"You always help, Mom." Lucy gazed out across the water. "I feel like if I could see him, I could put all this behind me and stop making the same mistakes. I'd get unstuck and I want that, Mom. I need that now."

"He won't be able to give that to you even if he's cleaned up his act. And what if he hasn't? Lucy . . . Have you thought this through?"

"Sort of." Lucy wiped under her eyes with the palm of her hand then flipped it over to wipe her nose. She knew her mom heard the snuffle when an "Oh, sweetheart" danced lightly to her ear.

Unable to stop more tears, Lucy pressed her thumb and finger into the inside corners of her eyes. "I have to go, Mom. I'll call you later."

She tapped off her phone and shoved it into her bag. She then strolled back up Crag Brow and bought a ticket for The World of Beatrix Potter, wanting nothing more than to push through the green lattice gate and get lost for an hour.

Lucy wandered through the displays, delighted with the life-size replicas of Peter Rabbit, Benjamin Bunny, and all her childhood favorites displayed in diorama fashion. She patted Mrs. Tiggy-Winkle on the head, walked the lane toward Mr. McGregor's garden, and caught a glimpse of Squirrel Nutkin scurrying away without his tail. The exhibit ended at the statue of young Beatrix Potter releasing Jemima Puddleduck to the sky, looking happy and free. Lucy patted that too. *You did good, Bea.*

"Lucy?"

She froze, instinctively understanding the

moment's significance. Twenty years in the making and she couldn't turn to face him too quickly. She felt her heart pound in her ears. If he'd said something more, she missed it within the roar inside her head.

She slowly spun and there he stood—only inches taller than herself and slighter than she'd remembered. He was delicate, like a distance runner, and smaller boned than even herself. His dark hair was cut short on the sides with gray dusting above the ears. She studied his mouth. He had the same mobile thin lips that she remembered always moving, smiling, curling around a new accent, or pursing in concentration.

"It's been a long time," he said. His voice too— she recognized it with such clarity that he might have called her name yesterday and every day for the past twenty years.

She glanced up to his eyes and startled herself with the reflection of her own. Her mother had never said anything—and yet she had to have seen. Each and every time she looked at Lucy, she must have seen him. The similarity went beyond color. Identical arched brows—the right forming a V rather than a U at its apex—framed their deep-set green eyes.

He nodded at her. "I'd recognize you anywhere."

"And me you." She bit her lip, slowly letting it

drag through her teeth. "How did you find me? Who told you I was here?"

"Joyce, at the tea shop, said someone was looking for me. She said, 'your daughter.' It could only be you." He tilted his head back to the exhibit. "And this was a fair place to start."

"She said she didn't know you."

"She wasn't sure. I go by Montrose now. It was my mum's maiden name." He stared a few seconds more. "Where are you staying?"

Lucy pointed across the street. "I got a room at The Old John Peel Inn. I liked the name. I had reservations at the Belsfield, but . . . Plans changed and their rooms were too expensive for just me . . . I'm babbling."

"The John Peel is clean, but the food . . . I'd rather take you somewhere more comfortable. You . . . You will have dinner with me, won't you?"

"You're the reason I'm here."

"I'm glad." He spread his arm before him. "Come on then. We have some catching up to do."

She fell into step beside him, saying nothing, simply glancing at him every few moments to convince herself he was real, and that he was handsome and trustworthy looking. She noted the incongruity of linking those but found she didn't care. He could be all three, but she only required the first and the last.

He walked down the hill to Ash Street and

turned right. "It's a little touristy, but Don's a good man. He saves me a table when he can."

Lucy followed him under the black awnings of Hyltons to a table in a side alcove. She thought back to Domestique in Chicago, with the one alcove and its incongruent 1950s wooden table amidst the sleek postmodern decor. That alcove matched this entire restaurant. The whole place held the same warm and worn aesthetic. Servers moved in between tight tables while at least three different languages mingled in Lucy's ears. "This really is a tourist town."

"Plenty of visitors, tours, tearooms, and treats. You name it, we've got it." Her father raised his brows as he walked around the table and took the chair in the corner, looking out into the restaurant. Lucy sat across from him.

"You've grown so much. Look at you, you're an adult." He leaned forward and rubbed his fingers across the tabletop. "I knew you were, of course, but in my mind, you're still eight. Each and every year on your birthday, you are eight."

"The books did get a little more sophisticated."

He laughed low and deep, naturally, like he did it often. "They did. When I arrived here last year, I wanted so badly to send you more Ransome, but you're grown up now. So I chose the Ruskin."

"Your first nonfiction." Lucy silently chided herself. *That's your first comment?*

"It was and I selected it for a reason. But first,

tell me about you. I've got twenty years to hear about."

Lucy's eyes flickered. "I . . . How do I begin that?"

"Start at college and take me from there."

Lucy recited what felt like part résumé, part life story. She told of studying art history in college because she loved it, business because she needed it, then not distinguishing herself in either because the library had a marvelous nook in a forgotten window, which was perfect for reading and which, in all four years, not another person discovered. So that was college. Good friends and hundreds of books.

She told about the computer programming class that led her to an internship at Sid's and how building him a database led to a job and now, she hoped, a career. She talked about girlfriends who stuck and a few boyfriends who'd drifted in and out of her life as quietly and gently as turning a page. She finally mentioned James. And there she stalled, unwilling to turn the page, afraid to find herself at the end of the book.

"So he's here?"

"In London with his grandmother. They'll head back to Chicago tomorrow morning."

"I'll need to thank him for sending you on. This is nice, Lucy. I'm sorry it's taken so long."

"About that . . ." Lucy took a bite of the pasta her father had ordered for them both and used the moment to formulate her question. "You sent me a book every year, but no note, nothing. Why *did* this take so long?"

Her father leaned back in his chair and wiped his mouth with his napkin, holding it there. He slowly lowered it. "I'm sorry for that. I . . . I'm not sure if your mom told you, but I spent some time in prison a while back."

"Statesville in Joliet. I Googled the postmark and figured it out."

"I should've expected that . . . That experience was unfortunate. A dear friend left me a significant gift from her estate and her children contested it. They claimed I defrauded her."

"Did you?"

"She changed her will on her own and was in her right mind when she did it, but the judge didn't see it that way." He waved his hands. "That's neither here nor there. I'm telling you as a way of saying that I didn't want you to know about that then, and after, well, I had things to do. Time slipped away. But all that's in the past. Here you are."

"Yes. I suppose it is." Lucy dropped her eyes and mumbled, "Things to do." She chewed on the phrase, wondering if it tasted sour, and soon found it had no taste at all. She looked back to her father, "What do you do? And how'd you get here?"

Her father's lips curved up on both sides.

"You'll love it. I've got a good job going here."
He spread his arms wide on the table, gripping the
edges. "And I've wanted to come back for years.
When Mum died, Dad couldn't get out of England
fast enough, but it was my home. I never forgot."
He surveyed the restaurant with a proprietary air.

"A couple years ago, I needed a break from the
States so I came home. I understand this country
and its pace and flavor. It's not so rigid. There is
a flow of life, of understanding, in England and
Europe that is at odds with American thought. But
I'm glad you caught me now because next fall I'm
heading down to the south of France for a few
years to try out life in a warmer climate. It'll be
time to move on." He acknowledged a few
patrons he knew before returning his attention to
her.

"Willa and I picked out the village. You've got to
explore while you're young, right? You hear me?"

"I hear you . . ." Lucy tried to smile. "Willa?"

"You'll like Willa. I met her last summer, but . . ."
He narrowed his eyes. "She doesn't know I have
a daughter—and certainly not one your age. She
thinks I'm forty. I never told her that, mind you;
she got it fixed in her head somehow and it's
pointless to tell her differently now. She's closer
to your age. Thirty-three." He bobbed his head as
if making the introductions. "How long are you
staying?"

"If I hadn't found you, I was going to leave

tomorrow. I didn't think past that, but I'd like to stick around a few days, at least." Lucy hiked a shoulder and let it drop. "Get to know each other?"

"Grand. I'll tell Willa about you tonight. Don't worry. I had you young. Happens all the time . . . Perhaps let's not mention your age, if you don't mind?" He let his voice lift as if the decision was her own.

Lucy nodded. And not until she felt a sting in her mouth did she realize she was biting the side of her cheek. She laid down her fork. "I don't need to stay."

Her father reached his hand across the table and grabbed hers. "I want you to. This is our time." He dropped his hand to motion for the check, and once he'd paid, he ushered Lucy from the restaurant with a small but firm pressure in the center of her back.

Chapter 29

The next morning Lucy climbed out of bed early and went for a walk. The town wasn't awake yet, but Pasty Presto down the hill was open and serving coffee. She grabbed a cappuccino and a small bun and ambled to her bench along the water.

The swans, probably fully aware of when the tourists brought their crumbs, hadn't arrived yet.

She sat as the waves of Bowness Bay lapped the shore—tiny when compared to Lake Michigan, miniscule when compared to an ocean.

What she'd thought was a tsunami, twenty years pulling back from the shore, was hitting more like a ripple—changing nothing and unable to sweep the sands smooth.

Each tiny wave brought a discordant memory from the night before. Puzzle pieces that didn't fit. Or worse, puzzle pieces that did. She couldn't deny a picture was forming, one in confirmation of her mom's expectations rather than her own hopes. She kicked at the pebbles in front of her, skidding them into the water.

She tapped her phone. Nine o'clock. It was time. She tossed her paper cup into a bin and followed her father's directions to The Ship Inn. A little farther down the shoreline, the restaurant was already bustling with patrons and mature smells of grease, eggs, and fish when she arrived. She peered around and finally found her father and a young woman with brown cropped hair huddled in the corner. He was leaning over, talking close to her ear and smoothing her hair as if soothing a child. It was mussed, as if she'd worked to achieve the bed-tousled look, or had, in fact, just climbed from bed. Lucy glanced away.

"Lucy!" He half stood and waved, reaching around the woman to hug Lucy as she neared. "I'm glad you're here. Come meet Willa."

Lucy stretched out her hand as she sat.

Willa grabbed it with well-moisturized, thick fingers. She gripped hard, rolling Lucy's knuckles across one another, and let go before Lucy could react. "Anthony told me you were here. In the year we've been together, I've never met any of his family. Never even knew about a daughter." She threw Lucy's father a quick look before affectionately kissing his cheek. Lucy noticed a tiny diamond in her nose that caught the light as she swung her head back.

"Yes." Lucy was at a loss for more words.

"The family resemblance is uncanny. What eyes you two have!"

Lucy couldn't help herself and softly mumbled, "All the better to eat you with, my dear."

Her father heard her and shot her a look as Willa continued unaware, "But that hair! That must come from your mother." She reached over and rubbed together the ends of Lucy's ponytail.

Lucy resisted the urge to pull away.

"Are you on break?"

"Break?" Lucy flicked her neck, sending her ponytail over her shoulder, as she caught her father's fixed look. She took a moment to absorb the unspoken currents: Willa was questioning her age, checking up on Anthony, calculating the length of her stay—taking her measure. And her dad? He required backup. What had he said?Lucy couldn't remember. She could only hear another childhood command, returning after a long sleep. *Never give more information than necessary.*

Lucy determined her own course. "I came for work." She pressed her lips shut, refusing to elaborate.

Willa's eyes flashed confusion then resignation.

The conversation flowed formally while the server took their orders and delivered teas and another coffee for Lucy. They waited for their meals in relative silence.

As soon as breakfast arrived, Willa picked up her fork and approached Lucy from a different angle. "Your father says you're a reader. You read a lot in college? You must come this afternoon." At Lucy's blank expression, Willa gently pinched his arm. "You didn't invite her? She could be our guest and see what you do."

Willa leaned toward Lucy. "I'm sure your father told you about our tours. They're not your run-of-the-mill walks to see this and that. They're literary tours. They were Anthony's idea and they're wildly popular. Walking tours, mostly, for now." Willa nudged Lucy's father, who opened his mouth, but she spun back to Lucy before he said anything.

"Anthony tells about the area and the sites, but he also reads to them some of the poetry and fiction that came from here. He's got readings from *Pride and Prejudice*, Beatrix Potter, some book about swallows—"

"*Swallows and Amazons*. It's an adventure story," he interjected.

"I didn't mean it was about birds," Willa retorted, her short hair appearing to stand on end. "But that'd be right too," she whined before turning back to Lucy. "He talks about some of the animals around here, especially at the Beatrix Potter bits, and there's Wordsworth and Coleridge and that other guy . . . The critic. You know . . ."

"Ruskin?" Lucy added with understanding.

"Ruskin! Tourists eat it up. It's like they've been transported in time." She snuggled into Lucy's father's side and cooed. "He is so talented."

Lucy smiled genuinely for the first time. "I can imagine you'd be really good at that, Dad."

"I love it." He smiled back. "That's why I sent you the Ruskin book." He leaned forward, gently dislodging himself from Willa's grasp. "He was a philanthropist, thinker, and the Victorian era's most famous art critic. Bringing him into the tours provides a personal opening into the art and social movements of the time—that's the Golden Age around here and he embodies that vital link between fact and fiction."

As they ate, Lucy's father gave his part-life-story, part-résumé, and a description of their tours. Willa interjected every time he paused.

As he talked on, however, Lucy noted a side conversation—unspoken but equally informative, perhaps even more so. Every time Willa strayed into details from his time before Bowness or to their future plans for France or Italy, Lucy's father steered the conversation back on track with a quick "Where's the jam?" or a soft "May I try your eggs?" Then a cough and a subsequent search for cough drops, or a "Where is that girl? We need more tea." And each time, Willa lost her trail and bounced back onto the approved topic. Lucy made note of each digression.

As the plates were cleared, Willa leaned forward and snaked a hand out, dark blue nails flashing, to grasp Lucy's as she held her third "just a touch to warm it" cup of coffee. "Isn't he brilliant? Oh, and I keep forgetting that next—"

Anthony sneezed and bumped her, sloshing Lucy's coffee over the rim.

"Do you have a Kleenex? My allergies are acting up."

"In here somewhere . . ." As Willa pulled back and dug into her brown bag, Lucy watched her dad. His steady green eyes stayed trained on Willa's search. "Here you go." She waved a crumpled tissue at him.

He folded it into his hand. "We need to finish a few details for this afternoon. I must gather my notes and get a few supplies. I try to tailor the tours and today we have an American couple and an Australian family. All are good walkers, they say, so I want to take them up Brantfell Road. There's a rocky outcrop up there and my *Pride and Prejudice* quotes really take flight. Wordsworth too. I sometimes have to read them in Fallbarrow Park when patrons can't take the hills, but it's not the same. So if you can shift for yourself a couple hours, we can meet up and you can come along for today."

"I'd like that."

"Good." Anthony stood and scooted Willa's chair back for her.

"We're leaving?" She pouted. "I could stay and chat."

"There's a lot to do." He reached down and squeezed Lucy's shoulder. "We'll meet you at one o'clock in the square outside Windermere Lake Cruises, right on the water."

"I sat near there this morning. I know where it is."

"It's a small town." Her father slid Willa's chair out farther.

Willa bobbed her head toward Lucy. "We'll have such fun. If you're like your father, you'll be such a help today."

Lucy's father gently pulled Willa away. Lucy picked up her mug and mopped the spill with her napkin.

Lucy wandered up the smaller side streets and bought a few gifts and souvenirs, including another snow globe and two key chains for her new collection. One was a replica of the local church and the other a tiny figurine of Peter

Rabbit. She found a few more odds and ends, a bottle of gardenia perfume for her mom, and a couple more silver thimbles for Sid. Waving a small thimble on her finger, she played with the idea of keeping them for herself but suspected Sid would know just the client who would adore them. The thought made her smile.

Shopping finished, Lucy stood at the edge of the lake as several small wooden boats pushed off the shore with kids and adults swaying back and forth searching for their balance and jostling the oars. She turned back onto the sidewalk and tapped her phone, missing only one person.

It rang five times before Helen answered. "I couldn't find it in my bag. We're about to leave for the airport. Have you found your father?"

"I have."

"And?"

"It's good. He runs literary walking tours."

"That sounds just up your alley. Why don't you sound happy? What's wrong?"

Lucy stopped walking and stepped into a small open park. She leaned against a tree and faced the lake again in time to see one of the boats tip and two kids splash into the water. "I expected to feel like you did when you gave the watch back. It was like you were floating. In an instant, you were free. Remember at the Bloomsbury Coffee House when we declared each other 'safe' and we could share and talk . . . You didn't need me after Peel Street, but I've found him and I . . . I'm still calling you."

"Tell me what's going on."

"I don't feel different. Missing him, finding him, that's been twenty years in the making and it's done, and yet, I'm not lighter. I've laid nothing down. I feel the same." Lucy clamped her eyes shut, trying to work out the words. "Nothing is what I expected."

"Few things ever are. Giving that watch back was the starting point for me. It wasn't the end and yes, I felt good that evening, but emotions fluctuate. You know that. They never stay. It's what we do with the facts that counts." She fell silent and Lucy suspected she was searching for a chair.

She continued, "Did you know Charlie was here when we arrived yesterday? We talked all yesterday afternoon and then through dinner, and it wasn't good at all. He's very angry . . . And yet, remember how I said my eyes felt wider?"

Lucy nodded, before recognizing that Helen wouldn't catch the gesture.

Helen continued, "His are today too. They've lost that tight look that he's given me for years. So I think, despite the difficulty, we are on the right road. You stay on it too."

Lucy nodded again. "I will."

"You aren't any more responsible for your father's choices than Charlie was for mine. I learned that yesterday; he felt such pressure to live up to what he thought I was and wanted him to be. I suspect James has suffered under that same weight. Don't you make that mistake. And as for what you said in the tea shop? Emily Brontë was wrong if she ever meant that our ancestors fix us and determine our lives and choices. People can be redeemed."

"Maybe I was projecting." Lucy heard a rustle as if people entered Helen's room to collect bags. "Have a safe flight."

"James is here. Do you want to talk to him?"

"Not right now."

"Okay." Helen's voice dipped low and sincere. "Enjoy your visit."

Lucy thanked Helen and slipped her phone back into her bag. *Enjoy your visit.* It seemed so simple, almost too simple, for all she hoped to accomplish here. But perhaps Helen hadn't said the words blithely. Perhaps that was the proper perspective. This was merely "a visit" and she need only enjoy it. *No more, but no less.*

As she watched the lake, another boat came alongside the capsized kids and an older man dragged them aboard. A young woman then jumped into the water, righted the capsized dinghy, and alone rowed it to shore.

At one o'clock Lucy stood at the back of the small group wanting to watch her father at work more than participate. Willa's short hair was sleek, styled, and tucked behind her ears; her outfit, sophisticated and refined; and her voice . . . Lucy almost didn't recognize her as the same woman. She spoke slowly, with more intonation and definition.

Lucy stared as Willa passed around tea in paper to-go cups to the adults and bottles of ginger beer to the kids. She sprinkled little comments among the group and soon everyone was talking and laughing—even the two new families who'd joined the tour since breakfast.

Willa glided between the women. "I love your shoes . . . Such the right choice for today . . . And you were wise to bring dark glasses. It's a gorgeous spring this year . . . Have your kids tasted ginger beer? Such a treat . . ."

Lucy had to give her credit. Each woman and child stood taller and swelled with pride at their importance, dress, and general preparedness by the time Willa stopped talking and shot Lucy's father a *We're ready* glance.

The motion sent Lucy's eyes toward her dad as well. He'd clearly been working the same magic with the men. It brought to mind Sid's advice one day as they had sat debating a sketch. *Enchant the wives and stay within budget to please the husbands. They may not care about the rooms, but they want to keep their wives happy and feel smart doing it.* Her father clearly followed the same dictum—but played it with a different hand here.

Catching Willa's look, Lucy's father raised his voice and addressed the entire group. "We are so delighted to have you join us on our little adventure today. We will start with a short walk through Bowness-on-Windermere, this lovely town with foundations dating back to 1415, as you'll see when we visit St. Martin's church. And, since you all are such strong walkers, I'm going to treat you to some special stops more abroad than the usual fare. This will allow you to more fully appreciate the romance and unique history of the area."

He started through the town, calling above the din created by cars, tourists, and general commotion. Within minutes they were on a small outcropping nestled into the lake. He pointed to the sky. "'I wandered lonely as a cloud; That floats on high o'er vales and hills, when all at once I saw a crowd, a host, of golden daffodils; Beside the lake, beneath the trees, fluttering and dancing in the breeze . . .'" He continued in a strong, melodic voice, weaving a spell around his walkers.

Even the children quieted and listened. And just when the first child twitched, he drew himself upright and laughed. "Wordsworth is a genius and probably the most noted poet from the area. Those were just a few choice lines from 'I

Wandered Lonely as a Cloud,' composed here"—he spread his arms to encompass the lake, the town, the listeners—"in 1804."

Without another word, he walked farther down the walk and up a scanty path into the trees, talking Wordsworth and poetry as they followed. At a bend, he shifted topics. "Now, ladies, this lovely path is for you. Visiting manor homes, such as Darcy's Pemberley, is out of the scope of our walk today, but you will find 'a noble fall of ground, or a finer reach of the woods' and 'spots where the opening of the trees gave the eye power to wander and charming views of the valley.' And here, note the . . ."

With dips and rises in intonation, Lucy's father made it clear when he was quoting from *Pride and Prejudice*, again imbuing the walk with an almost magical aura. Lucy began to believe that she herself was following in Elizabeth Bennet's footsteps and holding her gown high, so as not to stumble over branches along the path.

As they emerged onto a one-lane road overlooking the lake, her father's tone changed again. "Here you see some of the spectacular views that inspired, not only the great poetry you've heard, but some exquisite landscapes and even portraiture. This was a thriving art scene and John Ruskin, the leading art critic from the Victorian era, embodied that sensibility right here in Bowness. He was an avid watercolorist, social thinker, essayist, and philanthropist. Here are some of his favorite views . . ."

Lucy turned toward the lake, letting his words wash over her as she wondered where the line spanned between fact and fiction on this tour. She had read the Ruskin book, and while most of her father's facts were true—even those he tinged with a softer glow—he did create links and made inferences never stated. She began to note how often he used words such as "surmised" or "tacitly understood" or, her personal favorite, "privately known."

". . . And today I have the special treat of my daughter's presence. An art expert and specialist in the field of silver and antiques, she can answer any of your questions about the art, lives, and interests of this area and its Golden Age."

Lucy blinked, catching the last words as every head pivoted to her. She gave a small wave as her father walked on. Only one woman dropped back, the American with the *right choice* shoes. "How do I know I'm getting a good deal if I buy something here? How do I know it's a real antique? What does that even mean?"

Lucy fielded the question with honesty. "There's no way for you, as the customer, to truly know unless you have some experience and a feel for what was made within different eras. The term 'antique' classically means older than one hundred years. I *can* say I spent the morning in and out of every shop in Bowness and nothing caught my eye that wasn't appropriate. There was one shop, Finley's Fine Treasures, that— Ouch!"

With a crash, Willa tripped and plowed into Lucy and clutched at her to keep from falling. "I didn't even see that. Thank you for catching me. I almost fell." She held her hand to her throat and glared at the ground as if it had bitten her. "I've been on this walk so many . . ."

Lucy quit listening as the woman tourist touched her arm, mumbled a quick thanks, and returned to her husband. Lucy turned and whispered to Willa, "I gather I misspoke?"

"Not at all. You're wonderful." Willa took a few steps in silence. "Finley overprices a touch, I know, but she's a dear friend and sends lots of business our way."

Lucy nodded, casting a quick glance to her father. He was absorbed at the front of the group. "You both are good on these tours. I can see why they're popular."

Willa beamed. "I don't have all the schooling Anthony does, but I take care of the details. He's forgetful about those, but what a wonder with the talking! He tells such a good story, makes you *feel* the facts rather than just hear them. That's a gift, you know."

Willa cast her eyes to the front of the group with such adoration that Lucy trailed Willa's gaze. Her father gave Willa a quick wink before addressing a tall man's question. "You can see why everyone loves him." Willa gripped her elbow.

"I can, which makes it surprising that the tours aren't selling well. My dad mentioned that you're moving to France," Lucy whispered.

"Oh no." Willa tucked closer. "They're selling like mad. We've pre-booked more extensive, driving ones with overnight stays, all through next summer. Multiday packages and real 'Sensory Experiences,' as he calls them. They're so popular, clients smack down a 90 percent deposit just to get on the books, but we—"

Willa twisted toward the front again and jumped. "Oh, he needs me . . ." She darted up to assist one of the kids who drooped beside his mother and instantly her voice regained its slow, cultured tones. "Is this walk too long for you, dear? Well, I may find a treat right here . . ."

Lucy lost the rest of Willa's wooing as her father's lilting accent recaptured her attention. "Beatrix Potter, as a young girl, lived . . ."

The tour landed back in the town square, where the men all shook hands and pressed bills into their tour guide's hands. "Couldn't have been better," "Jolly good afternoon," and other compliments hung in the air around them.

Lucy heard her father gently chide one man, "It's a commitment, but we're filling fast. I strongly recommend registering soon for the three-day package we discussed. I don't want you to miss out. It's a much finer experience because we have the time and ability to introduce you to the food and wine and some of the finest accommodations in the area. And"—he addressed the man's fawning wife—"if you're committed to seeing Bath, we can offer the same experience there. I've studied Austen's Bath years intimately."

"That's the trip I want to take." She beamed.

Lucy's father nodded in agreement and stepped away, allowing the couple to talk. Within moments, the man returned to him and said, "We'd like that trip."

As Willa gathered their information in a ledger book, Lucy left the group and retreated to the water's edge. Within moments, she heard the pebbles crunch behind her.

"You were marvelous today." Her father moved closer.

"I was a participant. Only one woman asked a question." Lucy glanced over her shoulder to find everyone had gone. "They all loved every minute, even the kids."

"It's a good tour."

Lucy twisted again, realizing *everyone* had gone. "Where's Willa?"

"She went to run errands. I told her I wanted to spend some time with you alone."

Lucy stumbled back. "You don't need to do that, Dad. I came to get to know you, and Willa's a part of that."

"I appreciate that, but I want to give my daughter my undivided attention. Let's grab an early dinner. All that walking has worked up my appetite."

Chapter 30

Lucy laid down her fork. "Willa said the tours are popular, and I heard you mention Bath to that couple. You've found the perfect job, haven't you? You seem happy here."

"It's taken years to figure how to make my passions pay, but I've finally done it." Anthony leaned back and rubbed his chin. Lucy could hear the scrape of stubble on his palm. "People pay lots for tours and sightseeing, but at the end of the day, all they get are cold facts and old monuments. You give them a story and it all comes alive. It becomes an emotional experience, one that resonates with their souls and their desires. That's what I offer and why I can charge more."

"I helped the owners at the inn in Haworth redecorate some rooms and name them to create an 'emotional experience,' and you're right, it's important. Sid and I—"

"I'd hate that work. Jerry runs the Stags Head on Church Street and it's too hard a life." Anthony rested his fingers under his chin.

Lucy leaned back. "I . . . Bette loves it."

Anthony waved, dismissing the subject. "But the tours! We're all wired to crave and worship something and I tap into that, Lucy, the emotional need." He slapped his hand on the table in his excitement. "It's not in movies, which hit the box office and disappear, and it's not even in the bestsellers. Those are almost as disposable and shallow. To capture that moment of stillness and transcendent completeness, you must go to the classics or poetry. It's still alive in poetry, even the modern stuff. The soul soars with those words."

He waggled a finger at her. "And all those Austen and Brontë films? They've blown the market wide open. The market craves those stories, pays for them, and now travels to see where the drama occurred. They've given place and a visual touch-point to the emotions."

Lucy tilted her head and sifted through his speech, and once she got beyond feeling affronted on Bette's behalf, she realized she agreed with some of what he said. Hadn't she helped Bette capitalize on these emotions as they named the rooms?

He continued, "So yes, the tours work, but I'd like to move them somewhere warmer now. The damp cold seeps into my bones. There've been a few BBC movies lately that take place in France . . . Not the stature of a *Downton Abbey* or *Poldark*; that's really put England back on the map. But the movies and a few books have opened France for tours like mine."

He leaned over his empty plate. "You can be a part of it, Lucy. Remember all the books I sentyou that take place there? *The Three Musketeers*, *The Count of Monte Cristo*, *The Scarlet Pimpernel*, even some of Dickens . . . You could come back at Christmas and lead tours with us. With your help, we could add more. Willa can't lead them, but we two could and she could handle logistics."

Lucy weighed her next words. "I don't get a lot of time off work, Dad. Maybe I could squeeze in a few weeks next summer. You'll be back here?"

Anthony's eyes drifted to the ceiling as he became lost in thought. "Willa wants to head to Italy after France, but that'll take a couple years. You can't rush it. It takes time to curate contacts and a proper clientele, and I'm too old to rush." He took a sip of wine and swallowed and sighed as if restored by a good vintage and better plots. "That's another reason I'm glad you found me. As you get older, Lucy, you learn that family matters. It's good you're here."

"Dad, I need a little clarity. Are you asking me to join you here or in France? Because I thought you had tours booked here in England. Isn't that what you set up today? A tour to Bath for next summer?"

"Well, I wouldn't say . . ." Her dad held out his palm—the embodiment of openness and clarity.

Lucy resisted the urge to grab it and roll his knuckles as Willa had hers that morning. Instead, she forced her voice into a melodic and conversational tone. "Or should I plan on finding you in France?"

"We do plan to leave here . . ." He shifted his gaze from one table to another. "We don't need to talk about this now. All the details will sort themselves soon. We can talk more at breakfast tomorrow."

Lucy scooted her chair back a few inches. She leaned back as well, as if distance would allow the pinpoints of the picture to blur together and create a cohesive whole.

Her dad surveyed the room and she realized she had only one question. "I need your advice, Dad." She waited until his eyes, so like her own, drifted from the tables, tours, plans and scams, France and Italy, and sharpened in their focus on her. "If you decided that France wasn't for you and that you wanted to stay here and grow roots, what would you do? In other words, what would you do if you found *home* and never wanted to move again?"

Lucy had to give her father credit. In that moment, he didn't look left, he didn't look right, and he didn't prevaricate. He stared her straight in the eye and whispered, "You never violate home. If you want to stay, you must do everything on the up-and-up and always keep it that way."

Lucy nodded, grasping the many layers of meaning. He was subtle. His answer reached back twenty years, thirty years, maybe even two generations, and it was clear. She quirked a small smile. Helen had been right after all—on all counts: every gothic story needed a good fire to warm the shadows and cast light on the secrets; she could enjoy this trip because that's what it was now, only a trip with nothing more required from it; Emily Brontë *was* wrong; and, finally, there was most definitely a bend in her road.

Lucy sighed, feeling restored herself, as the strings that had pulled for so long cut free. "So, Dad, tell me how you and Willa met."

Off he went in one direction, allowing Lucy's thoughts to travel an entirely different path.

Chapter 31

Lucy ran her hands across the wooden desk. It was a lovely little piece. Early twentieth century, beaten, but well repaired and lovingly polished. The wood felt like velvet. She'd miss this—bumping into history at every turn. Sid's gallery held it, but its essence was more refined, polished, and erudite. There was something earthy and elemental about living with and knocking into objects every day that were one hundred, two hundred, even three hundred years old. She thought of that sweater she'd shrunk, and she committed to salvaging it in some way, even if it became a square in a new creation.

She laid down her pen and reread the letter.

Dear Dad,

I'm so glad I found you. Twenty years is a long time to wait, a long time to wonder. There is so much of myself I see in you and I don't know that I'll ever look in the mirror again and not remember your right eyebrow, matching my own, your green eyes, or the way both our left eyes crinkle shut when we smile. I've noticed that about myself in pictures and now I know I've inherited the "disappearing eye" from you.

There are other things, perhaps, I get from you too: an insatiable love for story and history and an ability to become so absorbed that I miss appointments, schedules, and sometimes, reality. Those last issues may be mine alone, but your Birthday Books certainly fostered such distraction with so many wonderfully rich tales. Thank you for that connection and for encouraging a love for reading and learning. I hope, after this letter, you will not stop sending me a book each year.

I need to go now. And while perhaps I should give you the respect of speaking to you directly, I also feel I need to protect myself and you from hasty words or judgments. I heard you last night and understand your path and plans. And I thank you for your clarity in answering my question. I will be forever grateful for that moment, perhaps our only moment, of pure honesty. I agree, home must always be protected. Unlike you, I have found my home. But contrary to your advice, I've made mistakes. Everything has not been on the "up-and-up."

Now I must return and make things right, protect the people I love, and redeem my mistakes. I want to be more than I am right now. In my imagination, I linked our stories, our lives, and our salvation. If you were thriving and doing well, then so could I. But my journey is my own and I'm responsible for the consequences. I can't use you as a scapegoat or a savior.

I may not search for you again, Dad. In many ways, I feel I caused you more concern than joy. Be safe and be well. And if ever you don't feel that the stories truly speak to your soul and provide the "transcendent" experience you crave—

or if you get to the place where you don't need them "to pay"—come find me. I'm beginning to suspect true wholeness lies somewhere else entirely.

All my love,
Lucy

Lucy reached for the envelope the hotel's receptionist had given her. She folded the letter into thirds, slid it inside the envelope, and licked the seal. She carefully wrote "Anthony Montrose" on the outside and slid it into the outside pocket of her handbag. She grabbed her suitcase, gave the room a last good-bye, and pulled the door shut behind her.

Upon reaching the cramped alcove, which served as the inn's lobby, she handed the letter to a man pushing a vacuum. "An Anthony Montrose is planning to meet me here for breakfast. He's about fifty with short black hair, graying on the sides, about my height, and he's got green eyes. He may be here already, waiting in your pub." She gestured across the room. "Could you find him and give him this? Or give it to him when he arrives?"

He widened his eyes as she handed the letter to him, but made no comment. Instead he headed to the pub's door. Lucy reached out. "No. Wait. Please give me ten minutes before you look."

"All right." He said the words smoothly and

evenly, as if such requests were made every day.

Lucy stepped out the front door. She took a deep breath, capturing the crisp morning, the soft breeze, and the hint of sun. Raindrops from the night before had left everything shiny and new as if fireflies made of light, air, and hope danced off leaves, car windshields, signs, and store windows. She felt her face crack in bright and genuine delight as she turned right and loped down the hill toward the bus stop.

Lucy hopped on the bus and replayed the last few days. *Was it that long?* She raised her hand and counted it off in hours. *Only forty.* She rested her head against the window's cool glass as the scenery flashed by—gates, moss-covered walls, shops, and cars, whizzing by so closely that she felt as if she could reach out and touch each.

It's not genetic. Crazy, but not genetic. She stopped her line of thought. Her father wasn't crazy; he simply played by his own rules. Bette might call it Moral Relativism. Lucy's mom would call it "Me. Me. Me," as she had chimed all through Lucy's childhood when she felt her daughter had done something selfish, wrong, or unkind.

Lucy reached into her bag and pulled out her copy of *Jane Eyre*, the one her dad had sent for her thirteenth birthday. That had been his gift to her. The stories. If she could carry anything away from these forty hours and call it her own, it could be that. Nothing more, but nothing less either. She rolled the small paperback in her hands, feeling its material weight—paper, ink, and a worn and torn slick cover.

As the bus pulled onto the highway and accelerated along the straight, smooth road, Lucy let herself trail through her favorite scenes. Jane Eyre running into the passage, into the garden, calling, *Where are you?* knowing Rochester was out there and needed her. Then sitting with Rochester and asking, *Have you a pocket comb about you, sir?* She loved that line—true love defined by a pocket comb.

It really was that simple, that tangible, and found in day-to-day acts. Her mind drifted to *Wives and Daughters* and the moment when Roger realizes he loves true-and-loyal Molly. It took him time, he made mistakes, but he found his way. And in *Wuthering Heights* when Nelly declares, *I believe the dead are at peace . . . At peace.*

She envisioned *North and South*—at the end, when John takes Margaret into his arms and pulls her hands from her face. What had she said? About his mother? Oh . . . *That woman.* She was certain Mrs. Thornton would exclaim that disapprovingly upon hearing of their impending marriage. *That woman . . .* The words stuck in Lucy's mind. She played them over and over, knowing they pointed elsewhere, but she couldn't place it. *That woman . . .*

"What a woman!" Lucy barked aloud then ducked down into her seat. That was it. James had said that about Jane Eyre when they first met. He'd admired Jane's courage, her moral fiber, and her strength at the end of the story. She was the conqueror . . . She wrestled loose her happy ending. *What does it take to claim that?*

An hour later and still pondering the question, Lucy found an empty seat on the train to London. In fact, she found a nearly empty car. Only an old man and a couple of teenagers, making out in the back, shared her company. She dropped into the seat farthest from her companions and tapped her phone.

"Hello, *meu pequenino*, are you on your way home?"

"Maybe." She skipped over Sid's Portuguese, knowing it would be an endearment because that was Sid. She closed her eyes and recited her new battle cry. *Come further up, come further in.* "Sid? I need to talk to you."

"What about?"

"The MacMillan vases and the books." Lucy laid the whole truth before him, starting with her first book sale, when she found herself telling a story . . . to sell the story. She concluded with the call from MacMillan's assistant, Aidan, and how she'd agreed to pay him a fee, a bribe, to move up the list and procure Sid's three vases immediately rather than wait over another year.

"He asked for money? For him personally?"

"In exchange for 'a favor' as he called it. He asked for five hundred pounds to guarantee immediate delivery. I paid it and entered it in the books as a purchase for *The Purloined Letter*."

"That's not remotely funny." Sid remained silent for a few heartbeats. "What do you expect me to do?"

The question wasn't rhetorical or sarcastic. Lucy could tell that Sid genuinely wanted to know; he was out of his depth. She heard his breath catch over the line.

"I can't process this," he added.

"I should've waited until I got back. Some things are better in person, but I didn't want to wait and I knew you'd need time." Lucy willed her heart to calm. "For now, you need to know that I'll make things right. As right as I can in each and every case."

"The books?"

"All of them. I'll figure it out."

"The MacMillans? I almost sold one. Me." He was quiet a moment. "That's my name on the door."

"I know, Sid, and I'm sorry." She imagined him standing in the gallery by the George III desk looking out the window, his name painted on the glass in crisp Helvetica font in glossy black.

"Could you please set out all three vases? I'll call Jones and Jones to come crate them and ship them back."

"Yes . . . I need to hang up. This is too much, Lucy."

"Wait. Please," she cried out. The teenagers broke apart and searched for the sound. She shifted low in her seat.

"I'm still here."

"While you're thinking, digesting, cursing me . . . Please know I'll never do anything like this again. Any of it. I won't cross that line. I'll make everything right. I want to stay at your gallery in whatever capacity you'll allow me. You don't owe it to me, I know, but I'm begging for a second chance."

"Why should I give you one?"

"No reason at all."

"And that's supposed to sway me?" His voice arched high as if *he* was now begging.

"You asked why you should give me one; that's the answer. If you asked why I want a second chance, that's something else entirely."

"Then answer that question."

"Because I need a mentor. All my life I have been seeking ways to define myself and I've been following all the wrong cues. I understand that each and every decision is my own and that I'm accountable, but I also need a guide, Sid. I'm not guaranteed a happy ending just because I make it to the last page—every choice along the way matters and they have real consequences. I want to learn from you. There is no one I admire or respect more."

She'd launched it in one breath. She took another and pressed on. "You seek to truly understand your clients, to bless them, not so they can bless you, but because you want to bring them joy. You *get* the proper place of things in a life and you treat what you do with a light and respectful heart, knowing that deeper truths exist and more important aspects of life hold greater value. I spent a lot of time hauling down curtains and moving furniture with Bette in Haworth and I never felt so alive. I was helping her, Sid, and it was creative and colorful, and I felt creative and colorful and I think Bette's still on cloud nine. I'm rambling . . . But will you think on all of that, please?"

"Yes," he whispered. She heard a soft clicking sound and knew he was tapping his toe against the floor. "I hear you. Now I need to go."

"Okay." She closed her eyes. "Thank you, Sid."

Lucy clicked off her phone and tilted her head to the window. *Come further up, come further in.* She felt if she kept repeating it, she could stay closer to the truth and have the courage to endure it. She tried to smile but couldn't. She only managed a tiny wavery thing she caught in the window's reflection. "What have you done?" she whispered to it.

Lucy closed her eyes and let the cadence of the train provide a tempo for her thoughts. She thought about her apartment with its few furnishings and knew she'd do it differently if she could. The space would be filled with "gems" like Sid often found during his travels and at garage sales. She, too, could restore them by hand and make them unique by adding color or a stain or simply scrubbing them with steel wool to change their texture.

She would cover the walls. Load them with pictures of her friends, moments of laughter and love. She could enlarge that beautiful black-and-white photo of her mom and her at the beach when she was sixteen and hang it in her living room as the centerpiece. Her dad would be there too. She'd find a good picture, hang it, and let him be himself. No better, no worse. The smiling face of a man she did believe, in his own way, loved her.

The drapery panels. She'd finally hang them too. There were no patches left to fill. Waiting was arrogant and cowardly at the same time. It said she couldn't be satisfied, was always holding out, and was never content. Also cowardly because she was leaving an escape open, never letting anything tie her too closely to a home. And the result? Beauty wasted and lying on a cold wood floor and books with no shelves of her own to hold them.

Lucy tapped her phone again.

Her mother answered with a soft "Did you find him?"

"I did and he's everything, I suspect, you thought he'd be—living with a woman about my age who thinks he's forty, asking me to lie so she wouldn't do the math, working a touring scam and running away with the deposits, using all the stories I believed were sacred and defined him, me, and our relationship—It was eye-opening."

"Your tone makes me want to laugh, but I don't think it's a laughing matter." Despite her words, her mom's tone held no laughter.

"It is." Lucy wiped at her eyes, unsure if she was on the brink of tears or laughter herself. "Why didn't you ever tell me? Sit me down and make me listen to what he was? Deep inside."

"What good would it have done? Some things you needed to learn on your own. And you *are* so like him . . . I know you don't like it when I say that sometimes, but there is good there too. You loved the stories, the playacting, and had—still have—an amazing imagination. Look at your creativity now. That's a gift from God. He gave it to you both, and your father helped cultivate it in you." Her mother paused then asked quietly, "Are you okay?"

"I am. Mom . . . I've been such a fool. I was so

certain that if he was okay, then I could be too. You've been telling me for years he couldn't do that. And I wanted him to; it made it easier for me . . . I called Sid and told him everything." Lucy laid her head on the cool window.

"I don't know what 'everything' means, but this time your tone tells me it isn't a laughing matter."

"It's not. I've made a real mess of things, but I'm coming home to set them right. I've got a stop in London, then there are a couple flights with open seats out tonight."

"How can I help? Do you want me to drive into the city? I have appointments tomorrow afternoon, but I can be there by seven o'clock."

Lucy rubbed her eyes again. "There's nothing you can do to help, Mom, but I'd love the company."

Lucy disembarked at Paddington Station and crossed to the Bakerloo Line. She rushed back up at Wembley Station, dragging her rollerboard behind her. She headed west to a small shop with two words beautifully scrolled across the red doorframe. *Duncan MacMillan.*

The setting sun sent a vivid color palette of pinks and blues across the sky. A glow of rose highlighted the single, exquisite vase resting in the window. It was easily three times the size of those she'd acquired for Sid, with the same gold cascading over the top into a puddle of midnight.

The gold morphed in texture and radiance, burning even brighter, as it threaded along an edge to pool near the bottom of the blues, as if finally finding peace. Lucy felt a surge of courage and pushed open the door.

A woman with emerald cat-eye glasses and a severe bob glanced from her computer screen then returned her focus.

Lucy walked to her desk. "My name is Lucy Alling and I purchased three vases for a gallery in the States, but I need to speak with the manager about them."

"Was there a problem?" The woman sat straighter and glared over the rim of her glasses. She picked up a pen and rapped it against her desk. She appeared confident, efficient, even bored, but Lucy read tension in her eyes.

"No problem with the vases, just with how I acquired them." Lucy sensed that her next question would shake the woman's equilibrium. "Is Aidan here?"

The woman stood. "Aidan no longer works here. Why don't you tell me what this is about?"

"I think you must know."

Without a word, she took her seat and stabbed a red-nailed finger to the chair across from the desk.

Lucy sat. "Aidan contacted me and offered to move up my gallery's order for a fee. I paid it."

"Which are you?" She pulled a paper from her

drawer. "Sid McKenna, Weis Haus, Holmann, or Fine Arts? I assume from your accent McKenna or Fine Arts."

"Technically, McKenna, but my boss knew nothing about it. He didn't ask me to pay the bribe and was horrified when I told him about it an hour ago."

"Really?" The sarcasm struck Lucy.

"Yes."

"We've fired Aidan. Why are you here?"

"I came to apologize and I've arranged for the vases' return. As soon as I get the tracking numbers, I'll pass them along to you."

The woman sat perfectly still, leaving Lucy to take another step.

She pulled a card out of her bag. "Here's my card and here"—Lucy dug for a pen and wrote her cell number on the back—"is my phone number. I don't know what comes next. Do you want me to stay in London until you get the vases?" She slid the card across the desk then clenched her hands in her lap. "I'm trying to make this right."

The woman removed her glasses. Lucy noted her eyes were hazel, with distinct threads of green and gold—not unlike a cat's. She swirled the glasses in her hand. "Duncan is firm that he doesn't want any press. We aren't demanding the return of the vases. Later this week, I was planning to notify each of the four galleries that paid Aidan. A shot over their bows is the least they deserve. But the customers? None of them are to blame. Have you promised or sold the vases?"

"We can return all three without breaking any commitments to our customers."

The woman set down her glasses and fingered Lucy's business card. "Well, Lucy Alling, I appreciate you coming here. I'll let you know if I need anything more from you."

"Thank you." Lucy stood and turned to the door, only to spin back. "So you don't need me to stay here, in the country or anything?"

The woman leaned back in her chair, bouncing slightly, and laughed. "That you came here today speaks volumes. I have your number. I suspect this will be my easiest conversation regarding the matter. I doubt San Francisco, Berlin, or Vienna will be so contrite."

"I suppose not . . . Thank you." Lucy rolled her suitcase out into the evening glow and hailed a cab. She rewound the day in her head as the cabbie whisked her to Heathrow. *My name on the door.* Then the woman saying, *We aren't demanding . . .*

She pulled out her phone and tapped James's number. She didn't wait for a hello when he answered but rushed ahead. "Did you all get home safe?"

"Yes, Grams is fine and I—"

"I'm sorry to interrupt, James, but I need to ask you a question. A legal question. I told Sid about

355

what I'd done with the books, but I realized that as I undo all that, he's at risk. His name is on the door."

"Yes, he is."

"That's not going to work. He can't pay for any of this. How do I make it so he's not liable?"

"You're his employee and it's his business, Lucy. How did you think that worked?"

"Clearly, I didn't," Lucy snapped then bit her lip. "Sorry. Please, James, how do I separate myself from him and him from this?"

"That's what you've got to do. Separate him from the book business. Buy it and take it out from under his gallery, rename it, whatever. If you pay him rent, you can then sell out of his space and it can legally remain independent. Or move it if you want. That's the best you can do at this point."

"How on earth am I going to do that? Even with all my savings, I don't have that kind of money." Lucy deflated.

"You asked what you should do, not how you're going to do it." She heard James's breath shudder over the line. "I wish I had something better to tell you, but there aren't many options here."

"Okay then. Thank you."

Lucy mentally drained her savings and was adding up everything she owned when James called out, "Wait. Don't hang up." He dropped his voice. "You asked me a question a couple days ago, at the inn, during lunch, and I didn't answer it honestly, about true lo—"

"That's okay, James. Don't worry about it. Oh . . . We're at Heathrow. I have to go." She hung up.

Chapter 32

Two weeks later, Lucy looked up from her account files to find hands pressed against the window. She blew back her bangs as she ran to the door, unlocked it, and threw it open.

"I called you. Did you get my messages?" Lucy hugged Helen, noting that she felt thinner, more petite, if that was possible in such a short period of time.

"I did, but I didn't want to call you back. I wanted to come see you. Then one day became two, then three, and over a week, but I'm here." Helen took in the gallery. "And so are you, I see."

"In a fashion. I bought the book business from Sid and am renting this corner of his store." Lucy crossed back to her desk. Helen started to follow then stopped and gaped at the mahogany bookcase.

"A lot of the books are gone. I sent the ones I tarnished to a shop in New York. They'll sell them with full disclosure and make good money too . . . And slowly, step by step, I'm making everything right. Some things I can't, but for the most part, people have been very gracious and allowed me to do something."

Helen continued to the desk and sat in the offered chair. "Oh, Lucy. This must be so hard." Helen's soft tone conveyed a complete understanding of Lucy's situation.

"Some parts are very hard, but, oddly and rightly, the books are the least difficult. They are stories. They needed nothing from me then and nothing from me now."

"And Sid?"

"If anything could make me cry, it's him." Lucy pulled out her desk chair and sat. "I forced him to fire me. I truly believe he wouldn't have. He would've stuck by me, but James said if anything happened later, about the books, that difference could be material so I couldn't just quit. I needed to be fired."

Lucy surveyed the store. "He's letting me rent space for almost nothing in exchange for watching the gallery for him. As hurt and betrayed as he feels, he still puts me first. And he is hurt, Helen. I can see it in his eyes."

"I suspect it's also hard for him to see you struggle. He loves you very much."

"A wayward daughter?" Lucy quipped.

"Prodigal daughter, perhaps."

"No more about me. How are you? Have you

made any decisions or has Charlie made them all on your behalf?" Lucy lightened her tone.

"Charlie . . . He has taken the helm as I anticipated, but it's good. He needs to be involved." Helen held on to the upright handles of her handbag as if they provided support.

"He's met with my doctors and, though it was hard to hear, he agrees that there are no more avenues." She held her hand up as Lucy's lips gaped open. "I'm at peace with this, Lucy. And I'll tell you, I'm enjoying a rare time with my family. Charlie and I talk, really talk. And Leslie? I've adored that woman for years and now there's no chasm between us. Was it the watch? Was it recognizing my own mortality? Perhaps. Or maybe it was something so easy as accepting who I truly was the entire time. I can't say anymore."

Helen glanced up to the ceiling. "And my granddaughters? How they love my stories. Molly drove up from college last weekend and stayed with me. We had such fun. She's coming back in another couple weeks and even called me yesterday to tell me she's not moving in with her boyfriend." She grinned. "Leslie's laying the credit for that at my door; she says Molly's not as rebellious lately."

"That's cute, but I'll cry if I start to laugh."

Helen shook her head. "Don't start crying now, Lucy."

"What about James? This must be tough for

him." Lucy leaned forward, resting her elbows on her desk.

"James has had the last couple weeks off. That was another reason I couldn't drop by earlier." Helen shifted her bag. "We've had some wonderful times and good long talks. I didn't realize in Haworth that I'd hurt his feelings."

"He told you that?"

"Once I started looking, I could tell." Helen rested a finger on her temple. "The eyes don't hide much, do they?"

"They don't."

They talked a few more minutes about Lucy's apartment and her decorating plans, and how Sid's work schedule was only now lessening as spring drifted into summer.

Helen talked about how Charlie was setting up the guest room at his home for her to come for an extended visit. Helen didn't need to tell her that, while she was touched by Charlie's offer, it scared her. Lucy knew.

And Lucy didn't need to tell Helen that in the past weeks, as she'd become increasingly aware of when she wanted to embellish a story, or add a flourish of fiction to a tale, or a shade of color to a truth, she worked hard, each and every time, to shut it down and stick close to the facts. Helen understood.

"I'm so sorry, dear, but I need to go." Helen rose and draped her bag over her arm. "I'm meeting

Leslie for coffee then on to another doctor's appointment, but I'll be in next week. Do you still enjoy Book Day?" She turned back to the bookshelves. "Or is that gone too?"

"That's gone too." Lucy nodded. "And I don't miss it. In fact, I'm enjoying reading books and the business more now that it's not all wrapped up in my head together. They've unwound, if that makes sense."

"It does."

Lucy walked with Helen to the door. As she opened it, she said, "If you talk to James, will you tell him thank you for me? He gave me good advice about all this." She raised her hand. "Don't. You're still under the 'no-meddling' edict and I've already thanked him."

"He's out of town until next week, so this time I'll keep my word." Helen smiled and lifted her cheek for a kiss. Lucy obliged.

After shutting the door, Lucy leaned against it, looking back into the now bright gallery. Only eight o'clock and the sun had already lit the room, and while it was still two hours until she would unlock the door again, the day had begun.

Sid was late. Lucy noted the time again in his red leather appointment calendar and paced back to the front of the gallery. She knew Sid no longer kept her fully informed of his schedule. The easy communion they had shared over the years was fractured. There were no jokes, no foreign language endearments, and no sandwiches left on the corner of her desk when she became so engrossed in her work that she forgot to eat. There was formality and quiet. If it was possible for antiques and books to become any more quiet in their inanimate natures, those at Sid's gallery accomplished it.

Lucy shook off the regret and focused on the tasks before her. Even though she no longer worked for Sid, she listened when he made appointments and scheduled meetings so she could help him stay on task; she laid out sample books she heard him mention; she kept the gallery spotless, organized his desk while he was out, checked his billing and inventory for mistakes, and did everything she could behind the scenes to make sure he was on time and tracking everything correctly. They weren't her responsibilities, but they weren't Sid's strengths and helping him mattered.

"I have a surprise for you."

Lucy found him standing at the doorjamb to the workroom. "You're late for a meeting with the Bewigs."

"They canceled. I have a surprise for you." He tilted his head back into the workroom.

Lucy smoothed her dress and followed him.

He stood at his worktable with his hand resting on a small wooden crate. "Open it."

"I've never been good with these." Lucy picked up the drill and popped off one screw, two screws . . .

"Hand that thing back," Sid huffed. "We'll be here all day." He popped off at least fifteen screws in less time than it had taken her to do two.

Lucy pulled off the top. "What is it?"

"Find out." Sid pulled off a layer of packing straw.

Lucy moved aside a last layer of stuffing and pulled out a brown-wrapped package, immediately recognizing the shape and the weight. "This can't be . . ." She pushed the crate aside to rest the package on the worktable and slowly unwrapped it. The gold cascading over the vase's rim was the first feature exposed; it opened further to reveal the blues, the greens . . . All of it. "How is this possible? I e-mailed them three times. They never replied."

"I called them."

"Why?" Lucy crossed her arms, not in frustration but in protection. "I told them you weren't involved, that you knew nothing. They believed me."

"I know they did. Jemima said that immediately. But I needed to check on you, Lucy, even protect you if I could." He propped himself against his drafting table and mirrored Lucy's crossed-arm pose. "And yes, I was involved. It's my name on the door and, in the end, I'm accountable. I feel in some ways my expectations set you up, that I wasn't a good role model."

"That's not true. I made my own choices, Sid." She ran a finger over the vase's rim. "How'd you get this?"

"Jemima and Duncan were very impressed that you came in. She offered to let us keep all three vases, but I refused." He chuckled. "I gather the other galleries were more than eager to do so, but . . ."

"It didn't feel right."

"It didn't. But she did insist I keep one, and I knew which one." Sid pointed to the crate lid. "I had to call Jones and Jones after they collected them and have them bring that one back. I was glad I labeled all three."

Lucy reached for the crate's lid. In small letters in the corner, she read *Hope.*

"Isn't that what you named it?"

"I did." Lucy blinked. "I'm so sorry, Sid."

Sid stepped toward her and held her by the shoulders. "No more of that."

"What do I do with it? I'm in the book business now."

He retreated a couple steps. "I've been thinking about that and I propose that someday, after your book business is established and in the clear to your satisfaction, I could hire you on a free-lance basis."

"Really?" Lucy heard the wonder in her voice

and sputtered out a laugh. "Can you tell I'd like that?"

"So would I." He cradled the vase and carried it into the gallery. Lucy followed. "And until that day, or a time when we decide together there is a client worthy of this gem, we will enjoy it." With that, he rested the vase back on the George III chest.

Lucy reached over and spun it carefully to display her favorite side. "Thank you, Sid."

Chapter 33

L ucy threw her sandwich wrapper in the trash can next to the bench and closed her book, dropping it into her lap. She sighed and recounted the story thus far. It was not what she expected, but she had to admit, it was beautiful. She also had to admit that her original assessment was correct: the Russians left her vaguely uncomfortable. She huffed, but it caught in her throat and ended up a snort.

"That's attractive."

Recognizing the voice, Lucy slapped her hand over her eyes. "Of course you had to hear that," she called to James who was still a few steps away.

He stopped in front of her. "What are you reading? Some great Victorian romance?"

"You'd think, but no." She held up the book. "Your grandmother has inspired an expansion within my literary diet."

"It's certainly gotten verbose."

"That's Dostoevsky's fault."

"*Crime and Punishment?*" James took the book and fanned its pages. Lucy caught the motion, but knew he'd find no fore-edge painting there. It was the library's copy. "That's rough going."

"It's not the slog I thought it'd be at all. I'm kinda enjoying it so far." Lucy laughed. She had meant the laughter as a gesture of camaraderie, an icebreaker of sorts, but it escaped as a nervous twitter that emphasized the moment's awkwardness. She straightened. "Were you looking for me?"

"Not really." James looked back across the park. At her soft "Oh . . ." he added, "I knew exactly where you'd be."

"How's that?"

"Remember that time you lost your phone?" He dropped onto the bench next to her.

"You did not!"

"Yes, it was very bad and I've never done it before, but your number and password were still logged into my account."

"Hand it over." Lucy held out her palm and James slapped his phone into it. She flipped it over and tapped in his password.

"How is that any better?" He leaned over her.

"It's not my fault you haven't changed your password. And you're sitting right here. There's no comparison."

Lucy tapped on the *Find My iPhone* app and deleted her information. "James Carmichael, what's become of you?" she teased and handed him back the phone.

A soft expression settled in his face as he reached for it, his fingers brushing hers. Rather than reply, he leaned back on the bench and tilted his head back. He appeared to be watching the clouds drift by.

Lucy did the same for a few minutes before asking, "So what has become of you? Helen mentioned you had a couple weeks off work and tripped the light fantastic with her."

"Nah, and I think those days are behind her."

"She mentioned that too. I'm sorry," Lucy said. "She said she'd be in again this week, but I haven't seen her."

"She's slowing down." She caught James glance at her in her periphery. "I think when Dad and the rest of us learned there were no viable treatment options, she quit putting on the brave front and deflated. I'm not saying that she isn't living well right now—she is; she's just living more quietly."

"I can understand that. And I'm not upset she hasn't been by. She has her priorities; that's you all." Lucy didn't turn to him. "Will you do me a favor, though? Next time you see her, give her a kiss from me. Don't tell her. Don't say anything because I really do understand. Just give her a kiss."

"I will, and I promise, I'll say nothing."

"Thank you." Lucy ran out of words.

There were none left between them, and she suspected, there was no happy ending. Simply an ending.

As if agreeing with her assessment, James stood and stepped away. He turned back. "Were you heading back to work when I came up?"

"I was." Lucy drew herself straight and collected the mess around her: her book, her water bottle, and various papers that had fallen from her handbag. "Sid's got a two o'clock. I have to get back and man the store."

"I was surprised when Grams told me you still worked for him."

"I don't. I bought the book business, just like you suggested, and he lets me watch the store for a cut off the rent. I have to tell you, it's been a lifesaver. The books don't make a whole lot and I want to stay near Sid. Someday, he said we could work together again."

James started walking. Lucy stepped beside him. "That's great, Lucy. What do you call this new business?"

"Lucy Alling Books." She dropped her hands. "I didn't want to make anything up, even a name. So there you have it."

"I like it."

"What else did Helen tell you?"

"That you're decorating your apartment; you've purchased bookshelves; and you're a collector—no, a hoarder—of every tchotchke that falls your way."

Lucy's laugh was loud and genuine this time. "That's so not true. Not entirely. I have been adding pieces to my apartment and I've got the most wonderful coffee table. There was a mistake at the fabricator's and the birds resting on the cross-legs look more like ducks. The client didn't want it, so I got it for the cost of hauling it away. I named the table 'Jemima' and it looks wonderful. Other than that, there's a woven cotton rug that a client of Sid's was throwing out, with every color under the sun in it, and there are three bookshelves, low ones, I found at Goodwill for thirty-nine bucks. But as for tchotchkes, there is only one collection, my British key chains, hanging from a corkboard in my kitchen."

"And your drapery panels? Are they up?"

"No." Lucy studied the path in front of them. "I sold those."

James stopped and grabbed her arm. "You what?"

"I needed money for the book business. I brought them to Sid's finisher and he went nuts. He had three designers in a bidding war over them and I got almost enough to cover the book business. I needed a little from my savings, but not much."

"I had no idea." James dropped his hand.

"Why should you?" Lucy walked on. "About that, James . . . I have your chair and your bookcases. I don't use them and they're sitting there. I didn't have the courage to call and then Helen said you were away, but you're back now and I want to send them over. I can hire a moving company so you don't need to be there, but . . ."

Lucy caught James's grin. "What?"

"When you're nervous, everything becomes one long sentence. I think we've had a two-sentence conversation."

"Probably." Lucy felt her face redden. "When can I return them?"

"How about Saturday? I'll bring a van by and we can load them together."

Lucy dug her heel into the path. Even though she feared her face still matched her hair, she needed clarity. "What's going on here, James? Because I don't think I can do this." She waved her hand between them.

When he made no reply, she laid it out plainly. "I don't want to move furniture with you. I can't be your friend."

"I don't need any more friends." James stopped as well, but he continued to stare straight ahead.

"Then what?"

James slowly turned. "Would you have dinner with me sometime?"

It took Lucy a heartbeat to remember the question. Said in the same tone, the same manner, and with the same inflection. And just as on that first day, it took only another heartbeat to reply.

"Yes."

"Okay then." He beamed. "Tonight?"

Lucy walked into the restaurant. She'd decided to meet James rather than accept his offer to pick her up. She thought if she simply headed there straight from work that it'd be easier, that she'd put less hope into the evening, that she'd hold fewer expectations, and that she'd be less disappointed if it all headed south and ended. None of that was true.

And it hadn't helped that when Sid returned from his meeting and found her bright red and fretting, he'd sent her home to change clothes and prepare for her "date," declaring her nervous banter and pacing to be a distraction.

Once home and alone, she fared no better and tried on eight outfits before choosing one and heading to the restaurant. She searched the bar and realized arriving alone at a crowded restaurant didn't accomplish anything she hoped—the chaos and noise grated, she couldn't find James, and she felt panicked. Her gaze finally landed on him— calm and dressed just as he was that afternoon.

He wove his way to her and gave her a quick kiss on the cheek. "You look beautiful."

"I had time to go home after all." She smoothed her white organdy skirt with embroidered flowers along the hem.

James slipped his hand into hers and led her past the hostess to a table. He glanced back once, twice . . . "I don't remember your hair being so curly."

"I often straighten it. It was in a bun this afternoon, but it's always this curly. You saw it on the moors that day."

James's eyes lit and Lucy felt her face redden. "You're right. I did." He pulled out her chair.

Their server introduced himself and then left them with menus and silence. James spoke first. "What shall we eat?"

Lucy tucked her lips in, not wanting to hope. "I'm thinking the sea bass, and if I know you, you're eyeing the filet."

James didn't lift his eyes from the menu. "That sounds good, but I was actually considering the scallops."

The word *Liar!* was on the tip of Lucy's tongue, but she couldn't say it. She couldn't make fun of such a delicious olive-branch offering. Scallops were Lucy's favorite, never James's.

She peeked at him again, but he was studying the menu as if it was the most interesting read. She wanted to break through this dance, whatever it was, and find clarity. Find definition. This seesaw uncertainty was going to break her and had been threatening to since he asked her to dinner.

She opened her mouth to ask. She closed it. She opened it again and watched as his eyes trailed down the menu. He smiled at something he read. *Pulled pork?* His eyes trailed farther and pinched at something else. *Beets?* He reached the bottom and raised his brows. *Crème brûlée? Chocolate cake?*

And then it struck her—he was calm. The man who always sought clarity and rubbed his nose raw when he didn't have it, was at peace. And that meant one of two things—either he'd fundamentally changed, as she seemed to be doing daily, or there was clarity right here and now.

He looked up. "Have you decided yet?"

She felt herself calm. "I have. I know what I want." He waited. "I'll order the scallops. You?"

"The filet." James laid down his menu. "Tell me about the book business."

Lucy told him about buying the business and forcing Sid to fire her, making confessional phone calls, returning books, selling books, offering replacements for other books—and, above all, being so thankful that no one had ever mentioned Sid's name or questioned his integrity.

"And what about you? Are you enjoying the India work?"

"India? I wasn't in India. I was in Myanmar doing advance work for a water filtration project. Didn't Grams tell you?"

"She said you were out of town. I assumed it was the India project."

"Now she decides to zip it?" James pulled his fingers across his lips. "No, the firm I'm with has a project in Myanmar and another in Liberia right now."

"Wait? What? The firm you're with? Aren't you with the same firm?"

James laid down his menu. "Dawkins fired me, Lucy. I got the e-mail while we were in London. I can't believe you didn't know." At Lucy's head shake, he continued. "It's okay, though. A couple other partners were furious with him and made some calls on my behalf. Within a few days, I got an offer at McDermott, Will and Emery. Last week I was getting up to speed in Myanmar."

"I'm completely stunned."

James told her more and Lucy felt herself relaxing—and no longer worrying about clarity at all. Whatever this was and whatever it would become was enough.

"Lucy?" When she glanced up from her dessert, she found James leaning forward, his face pinched. "I need to say something. In Haworth, you asked me a question and I gave you an incomplete answer, and when I tried to tell you when you called from London, you were worried about Sid and arriving at the airport and . . . What?"

Lucy was smiling. "You sound like me. Go on. I'm wondering how long you'll make this sentence."

It worked. James's face relaxed in an animated smile. "Very funny." He leaned back. "You asked if I believed in love at first sight and I said no."

Lucy's heart dropped and the whole evening became confused. "I remember."

"It wasn't a full answer and I've been thinking about it . . . While I don't believe in love at first sight, because I think it takes more work than that, I do believe that one soul can speak to another and find an inexplicably deep connection over a short period of time, unimaginably short, and know that it will never forget that soul, that moment, or the light it emits forever. *That* I believe in. I didn't tell you that . . . And I wanted you to know."

Lucy felt her mouth go dry. She pursed her lips, afraid to speak, and her images from that day returned. Cathy called out at the window and Heathcliff reached for her. Jane stepped back to the tree as Rochester clasped her close and kissed her. Dillon made his way back to Haworth and grew old at Bette's side.

And James? Lucy desperately wanted to know. She licked her lips, willing her voice to come out sure and smooth. "What do you do when that happens?"

"That's a little more complicated, isn't it? I mean, just because one soul will love another forever, doesn't mean it should. It doesn't always work out. But then, as you say, and I've come to agree, people change. And when two people figure out how to do that together, then yes, *that* can last forever."

"Oh . . ." Lucy's heart melted.

"One more thing . . ." He paused and Lucy felt as though she might leap from her seat. "I have tickets to a play next month. They were getting passed around at the office yesterday and I snagged them. Do you want to go?"

"What's with lawyers and superfluous play tickets?" Lucy laughed. "*Pippin* again?"

"*Sense and Sensibility*. The Musical. What do you say?"

Lucy leaned forward. Within a heartbeat, without wavering or blinking, she replied, "I'm all in."

Acknowledgments

My first three books sit closely on a shelf. They don't form a series, but common threads are so readily apparent. Women seeking voices, places to stand, true life, love, joy, and family—and all with a healthy (sometimes saturating) dose of classic literature. They've been such fun! But there's a deeper thread and—while I'm beyond thankful for the incredible words penned and emotional journeys conveyed by Jane Austen, the Brontë sisters, Charles Dickens, Jean Webster, Alexandre Dumas, and too many others to name—I need to give a shout-out to probably the most pervading influence in my thinking and writing. Thank you, C. S. Lewis.

I also offer my deepest gratitude to Daisy Hutton, extraordinary editor, publisher, and friend. Thank you for believing this story could be so much more than I first envisioned. I'm thankful for your faith and your trust—and thrilled we'll get to do this all over again . . . And again.

And to the incredible team at Thomas Nelson—Katie Bond, Elizabeth Hudson, Jodi Hughes, Kristen Ingebretson, Becky Monds, and the amazing sales team. Many thanks for all your hard work to bring these stories to the world, wearing so many hats—and with such incredible style!

To my Grove-y sisters and dear friends, Thank you. Sarah Ladd, Kristy Cambron, Beth Vogt, Katie Ganshert, Cara Putman, Melissa Tagg, and Courtney Walsh . . . I cherish our friendship, prayer-chain e-mails, understanding, and our blog. I feel so blessed to be counted within this group. And a special thanks to Rachel McMillian and Hilary Manton Lodge for answering my desperate Facebook plea, for your friendship . . . And for the title! To Elizabeth Lane—Thanks for dreaming up the "events" with me, first readings, last readings, and always answering the phone. And to Claudia Cross—I'm so delighted to be on this road with you; our fun together is only beginning. Kindred spirits all!

And speaking of kindred spirits—Thank you to my family, Team Reay, for the everyday gritty camaraderie and to four generations of unfailing love and support. There wouldn't be a glimmer of an idea, any ideas, without you.

Last, but not least—Thank *you*. So many of you have joined me on this bookish journey— readers, reviewers, bloggers. There is such joy out there! Thank you for reading and sharing with me! I hope you enjoyed Lucy and Helen.

Discussion Questions

1. The Lewis quote at the front of the book describes an aspect of Lucy at the beginning of this story. Why do you think she'd lost the power to enjoy books? Is there something in our lives that we can fail to see clearly and lose enjoyment for?

2. Sid is one of the author's favorites. What character trait do you think she found so attractive? She doesn't tell you a lot about his background—any thoughts as to his story?

3. Was James justified in feeling so hurt when he found the forged inscriptions? How did he perceive Lucy's struggle? Was it a betrayal, like he claimed?

4. Why did Helen hold on to the watch? What was she really afraid to let go? What did it cost her along the way?

5. In London both women begin to change. Why? Do you think James is right that "strings pull tighter at home"?

6. Lucy talks about "boiling a frog." What does she mean?

7. What changed in Lucy at Haworth, even before her wandering to Top Withens? And at Top Withens, why did Edward Rochester's journey make such sense to her?

8. Do you agree with Lucy that each person has his or her own worldview? How did hers change? How did James's? Helen's?

9. How do you think Helen's journey will affect her final days with her family?

10. Lucy's meeting with her father was not what she expected or hoped. What do you think of her letter? Her reasons for leaving without a personal good-bye? What did walking away mean for her? And what do you think she meant when she said "wholeness lies somewhere else entirely"? Do you think her father will understand?

11. In the end Lucy works hard to change—even her reading choices change. Do you think she'll succeed or, as James once contended, do you think "people don't change"?

12. Will Lucy and James make it as a couple? Why or why not? Do they see each other more or less clearly now?

13. This story is one of choices. How do you see them playing out with each character? In your own life? Are the choices not made as powerful as the ones we consciously make? Is there a difference between them?

About the Author

Katherine Reay has enjoyed a lifelong affair with the works of Jane Austen and her contemporaries. After earning degrees in history and marketing from Northwestern University, she worked in not-for-profit development before returning to school to pursue her MTS. Katherine lives with her husband and three children in Chicago, Illinois.

Visit her at:
Website: www.katherinereay.com
Twitter: @Katherine_Reay
Facebook: katherinereaybooks

Center Point Large Print
600 Brooks Road / PO Box 1
Thorndike, ME 04986-0001 USA

(207) 568-3717

US & Canada:
1 800 929-9108
www.centerpointlargeprint.com